Copyright 2020

Laurence E Dahners

ISBN: 9798650825289

This book is licensed for your personal enjoyment only

The Thunder of Engines

A Stasis Story #2

Laurence E Dahners

Other Books and Series

by Laurence E Dahners

Series

The Ell Donsaii series
The Vaz series
The Bonesetter series
The Blindspot series
The Proton Field series
The Hyllis family series

Single books (not in series)

The Transmuter's Daughter
Six Bits
Shy Kids Can Make Friends Too

For the most up to date information
go to
Laury.Dahners.com/stories.html

Author's Note

This is the second book of the Stasis Stories
Though this book can "stand alone" it'll be much easier to understand if read as part of the series beginning with "A Pause in Space-Time (A Stasis Story #1)." I've minimized the repetition of explanations that would be redundant to the first book in order to provide a better reading experience for those who are reading the series.

Table of Contents

Prologue 9
Chapter One 19
Chapter Two 45
Chapter Three 88
Chapter Four 121
Chapter Five 159
Chapter Six 199
Chapter Seven 235
Chapter Eight 262
Chapter Nine 283
Epilogue 309
Author's Afterword 322
Acknowledgments 323
Other Books and Series 324

Prologue

Kaem Seba in grade school

When Rob thought Texas was the largest state in the US, Ms. Bowman asked Kaem whether that was correct.

Kaem had been daydreaming. Without thinking, he said, "No. Alaska's the biggest." Though it was brief, Kaem didn't miss Rob's glare.

Later, on the playground during recess, Kaem was talking to his friend Curt. Curt wasn't a good friend; it was just that there weren't many African-Americans in Valen. Curt was the only other one in Kaem's grade so they sometimes hung out together. However, since Curt liked sports and Kaem couldn't play them because of his sickle-thalassemia, their friendship was quite limited.

A sudden shove knocked Kaem to the dirt. He righted himself, sat up, and turned.

It was Rob. Quite a bit bigger than Kaem, Rob was a bully. He said, "Hey, show-off, next time keep your mouth shut!"

As Kaem climbed back to his feet, he made the mistake of trying to be helpful, "Um, you can look at the globe in the classroom. Alaska's—" The rest of Kaem's response was cut off when Rob tackled him, bearing him back down to the ground.

Scrambling astride Kaem's stomach, Rob started flailing at his face.

Kaem heaved up, trying to throw the bigger boy off, but failed. He settled for covering his face as best he could.

Fortunately, none of the teachers saw the commotion.

~~~

When Kaem got home, his mother took one look at the scratches and abrasions on his face and immediately knew, "You've been in a fight!"

Kaem shook his head dolefully. Knowing it was hopeless, he said, "No, I fell into the bushes at the edge of the playground."

That story had satisfied his teacher, but *far* from satisfied his mother, Sophia. "I'm going to talk to your teacher. They have rules against bullying and those rules should apply double to a sick kid like you.

"Mom! I don't want you telling everyone I'm sick!"

"Oh, come on. Look at you! It's not like they don't know already."

The worst thing about that day wasn't getting beaten up by Rob. It was realizing everyone could tell he was sick by the way he looked.

~~~

When Kaem's dad got home, his mother told him his son had been beaten and how she planned to go to the school and complain.

To Kaem's great relief, his dad vetoed the plan. "Absolutely not. Maybe we'll need to do that if it keeps happening. But if you do it the first time something like this happens, the other kids'll hate him."

"He didn't tell," Kaem's mother said indignantly, "but he should've. Those injuries didn't come from a fall into the bushes."

"Yes, yes, Sophia, I can see for myself." his dad said placatingly. "But for boys, it's much better if they can stand up for themselves."

The Thunder of Engines

Her eyes widened, "Emmanuel, Kaem can't stand up for himself! He's sick!"

"Sophia, this is a man's thing. Let me talk to him about how he might defend—"

"No!" she interrupted, shaking her head. "Kaem can't be fighting! I won't hear of it!"

"Okay," Kaem's dad said, lifting his palms in surrender. "No talk of fighting. But, also, please don't run to his teacher for every problem." He turned his attention to Kaem, "Do you want us to talk to your teacher?"

Heartened by his dad's support, Kaem shook his head, "No. *Please* don't."

"You'll tell us if this boy hurts you again?"

Kaem nodded. He didn't like getting beaten up, but hoped the problem would fade away. If his mother got involved at the school... It didn't bear thinking about.

***

The next day was Saturday. Kaem's mother worked weekends, servicing the laundromats, but his dad had the day off. After they ate their breakfast, Kaem wanted to watch TV, but his dad said, "Let's talk about how you might be able to defend yourself from that boy."

Kaem felt startled. He agreed with his mother about fighting. He couldn't have pounded on Rob the way he'd been beaten himself. That much hard exercise would immediately exhaust him because of his anemia. It could even make him have a sickle crisis. "Um, Dad, I don't think—"

"I know, I know," his dad interrupted. "You can't fight. A struggle would wear you out and might make you sick. But, most fights are won or lost in seconds.

They virtually never go on and on like the ones in the movies."

Kaem tilted his head curiously. "Really?"

His dad nodded. "Watch some real fights on YouTube, most of them are over in a few moments. All I want to show you is how you might get in *one* punch. If you do it right, one strike might *end* the fight."

"Um, I'm not real strong. I don't get much exercise."

"I know son. This might not work. But don't you think you'd like to know how to at least *try* to win a fight? Someday, if you *do* want to know how, it'll be far too late to learn then."

Kaem shrugged, "Okay. I guess I should learn, but I'm planning to avoid fights."

His dad put a big hand on his shoulder. "That's a great idea. But, here, let's move the dining room table." They quickly cleared an area in their crowded little apartment. Kaem's dad picked up what looked like a football wrapped and tied into a couple of layers of sweatshirt. "Okay—"

His dad was interrupted when Bana came out of the bedroom. She looked around, "What're you guys doing?"

Kaem's dad stared at Bana for a moment, then said, "One of the other kids beat up Kaem."

To Kaem's surprise, Bana's eyes widened in surprise, then narrowed in anger, "Who?! Who was it? Doesn't he know you're sick!?"

"No! Or, at least I hope not. I don't think it's anyone's business that I'm sick."

"Well, *who* was it? I'll…" she paused, evidently thinking better of uttering whatever she'd been about to say in front of her father. In a more subdued tone, she said, "I'll teach them not to touch you."

The Thunder of Engines

Horrified, Kaem said, "Bana, you're a girl!"

With a self-satisfied smirk, she said, "I know."

"You can't fight with a boy!"

Bana's eyes flicked to her father, then she mouthed, "I already have," at Kaem. "And, I won."

Their dad understood Bana's mouthed words just as well as Kaem had. In an appalled tone, he said, "You've been fighting boys?!"

She nodded, "Uh-huh. And kicking their…" she thought better of what she'd been about to say, rephrasing to, "kicking their bottoms too."

"But Rob's not just a boy," Kaem said, "he's a year or two older than you."

"Rob Sanders? I should've known," Bana said indignantly.

Kaem looked at his father. Emmanuel looked as bewildered as Kaem felt.

"So, why're you moving all the furniture?" Bana asked, moving on to another topic.

"I was…" Their father paused a moment, nonplussed, then said, "I was going to teach Kaem how to throw a punch. He can't get in a real fight because of his illness, but sometimes a good punch can finish a fight before it begins."

"Oh, great!" Bana said. "I want to learn too."

"Girls shouldn't fight, Bana," their dad said.

"Mom says women need to be able to defend themselves," Bana said indignantly. "She says she's going to get me a little Mace sprayer when she has the money." Her eyes flashed at her dad, "I think I should learn to throw a punch too."

Their dad rolled his eyes. "Okay," he said resignedly. He started with Kaem. "Stand with your left side toward your opponent," he said, maneuvering Kaem into the position he wanted him in, then holding up the sweatshirt covered ball representing Kaem's opponent, positioning it a little higher than Kaem's head. "Look at him out of the corner of your eyes, so you're less confrontational. Talk him down if you can. Slowly bend your knees. It'll make you less threatening and also lets you throw a harder punch.

"Now, if you decide you're going to have to throw your punch, try not to give any signal that you're about to do it. Just suddenly throw your fist from down low there by your side, up around and right *through* his nose. Throw it like you're trying to punch your fist *in* one side of his head and *out* the other."

"His nose? I thought I was supposed to hit his jaw?"

Kaem's dad said, "Hitting the jaw doesn't do that much damage. You'd rather not hit his mouth because his teeth could injure your hand. Getting hit on the nose *really* hurts, so it's a good target. If you miss a little and hit an eye, that'll stop him too."

"I don't want to blind him!"

"You're not *aiming* for his eye, it's just what you might hit if you miss his nose. Your fist shouldn't fit into the eye socket and blind him anyway. The jaw's not good. The teeth are dangerous to your hand. The forehead's solid bone. You might knock him out but you'll probably hurt your hand hitting his forehead. So, aim at the nose."

"What if he's too tall?"

"Aim for the front of the neck... but that could kill, so don't do that... unless you have to. Or try to kick him in the..." Their dad broke off, eyeing Bana.

"Kick him in the nuts?" Bana asked, a mischievous look on her face.

The Thunder of Engines

He sighed, "Yes." He paused as if wondering whether he should explain what happened if you kicked a man in the "nuts." Apparently, he decided that, as a boy, Kaem should know. Bana seemed to have already learned from someone else. Instead, he focused his gaze on Kaem. "Okay. Look straight ahead, then turn only your eyes to your left to see his head." Emmanuel shook the sweatshirt covered ball. Slowly bend your knees a little, then suddenly... PUNCH! Right *through* his head."

Kaem slowly bent his knees, watching the ball at the very periphery of his vision, then he pivoted, throwing his fist across his body, shoving off with his right foot, extending his knees and firing his fist out and through the ball.

To his astonishment, the sweatshirt and ball flew out of his father's hands, glancing off the wall and bouncing into the kitchen. There it knocked over a container of dried beans, spraying beans everywhere. "Oh-no!" he exclaimed, clapping his hand over his mouth.

Kaem glanced at his father. The man looked astonished. He lifted his eyebrows and observed, "You may not have much endurance, but you're fast. Also, I don't think your disease makes you weak." He stepped into the kitchen and swept his eyes over the beans scattered across the floor. "Come on, we'd better clean this up. If your mother finds a single lost bean, she'll start asking questions."

"Wait!" Bana exclaimed. "What about my turn?"

Emmanuel rolled his eyes, "We don't have enough trouble from the mess Kaem made?"

"*Kaem* didn't do it. You're the one that let the head slip out of your grip. Hold on better this time."

Their dad sighed, picked up the sweatshirt wrapped ball, and walked back over to where he'd been. When

Bana took her position, he adjusted it a tiny bit, but Kaem thought it'd been fine. His dad had adjusted her so she'd feel like he'd taught her something. When Bana struck, the ball didn't fly away, but Kaem thought that was only because their dad was expecting it this time. She'd certainly hit it at least as hard as Kaem had.

Their dad complimented them both, then set them to work cleaning up the beans, exhorting them with the threat of the questions their mother would ask if she moved the toaster and found a cluster of beans.

When everything had been cleaned up, Kaem asked, "What do I do if this punch doesn't work?"

His dad ruffled his hair, then sadly said, "Then you turtle. You curl up in a ball, arms around your shins, face between your knees. All you'll be able to do is wait until he's bruised his toes on your ribs and goes home."

Kaem stared at him disappointedly.

"Sorry son. I wish I had something better to offer you in that situation."

***

Kaem resolved to avoid embarrassing Rob, thinking it the best solution to being bullied. If he'd understood a bully's psychology, Kaem would've known that strategy was doomed to fail.

Monday of the next week, Kaem was on the playground, talking to Luanne, a girl he'd found friendly. A sudden shove knocked him almost to the ground. Catching himself with only one hand and a knee all the way down on the ground, he scrambled around and rose. It was Rob again.

Rob said, "You shouldn't be talkin' to her!"

The Thunder of Engines

Before Kaem could ask why, Luanne interjected, "Why shouldn't he?"

"Because… you know…"

Kaem thought, *Even Rob knows he'd better not say it's because I'm black.*

Having gathered his wits, Rob said, "'Cause, you're nice. And, he's… *not*."

Thinking of his father's lesson, Kaem moved back over near Luanne, switching to her other side so he could face her while keeping his left side toward Rob.

"Seba! Are you trying to ignore me?"

Kaem watched Rob out of the corner of his eye, resuming his conversation with Luanne. "Sorry your brother's sick—"

Kaem bent his knees a little as Rob stepped closer, interrupting, "I told you to stay away from her. You need to be taught another—"

Kaem executed the punch his father had taught him, pivoting, spinning and sending his fist as hard as he could toward Rob's nose—and as if trying to punch all the way through his head and out the other side. He hit the boy's nose off-center to the right, his fist skidding off and slamming into the kid's eye socket.

Rob flailed backward, staggering, then landing on his buttocks.

Kaem cringed back, thinking, He's gonna kill me!

But Rob reached up and put his hands over his nose. As the bigger boy started crying, blood flooded through his fingers.

Did I just kill *him?* Kaem wondered in horror.

Rob's eyes crossed. Seeing the blood, his sobs turned into full-on screaming.

I guess he isn't gonna die, Kaem thought. He looked around and saw the teacher that monitored the playground coming their way. *This probably isn't good.*

Bana's voice came excitedly from behind him. "Way to go brother!"

Then the teacher was there, asking what'd happened. Luanne stuck up for Kaem, saying that Rob had been threatening Kaem.

But, of course, while the monitor was cajoling Rob into letting her see his face, she said, "If Kaem was being threatened, he should've reported it to me. That's what the monitor's for. Children aren't to take such things into their own hands." She sighed, "It looks like it's just a bloody nose. Come on young Sanders," she said to Rob, "let's get you to the nurse." She looked at Kaem, "And *you've* got to talk to the principal. Come along."

No! Kaem thought.

Chapter One

Kaem Seba's junior year at UVA

UVA physics professor Giles Turnberry looked out over his quantum mechanics class, wondering how many were understanding what he said. He noticed the black kid, Seba, wasn't even looking at the equations Turnberry'd written out. *He doesn't pay attention and he asks the most bizarre questions,* Turnberry thought. *Yet, suspiciously, he didn't miss a single question on the first exam... is he cheating?*

Turnberry cleared his throat and called on the kid, "Mr. Seba. In what situation will this solve the equation?"

Without even looking up at the equations Turnberry had on the display, Seba said, "When $k'(x)$ equals zero." Then as if anticipating Turnberry's next question, he said, "It's a good approximation anytime k' is very small or whenever k' is much smaller than k^2."

"It's good to see you read the book," Turnberry said, not sure whether he felt admiration or irritation.

"Yes, sir," the kid said.

"You want to come up here and take us through the WKB approximation?"

That got the kid's attention. His surprised eyes suddenly turned and focused on Turnberry. The professor fully expected the kid to beg off. Instead, Seba stood uncertainly. "Yes, sir," he said, shuffling along the row of seats and making his forward way to Turnberry's electronic whiteboard.

The kid stood a moment, then turned, looking lost. Turnberry thought, *Not such a wiseass now are you?*

Seba cleared his throat nervously, then said, "Um, how do you clear the board?"

Turnberry blinked. He'd expected a declaration of surrender, not a confession of incompetence with the e-board of all things. He told Seba how to do it.

Board cleared, Seba picked up the electronic marker and started writing equations, succinctly explaining what the different symbols and letters represented and how to derive the next equation from the one he was on.

For a minute or two, Turnberry found the clarity of Seba's explanation staggering, then suddenly suspected that he only found it so because he understood the principles already. He looked around the classroom. Most of the students seemed to be following Seba, but one had his hand up. He said, "Mr. Seba, you have a question back here."

Seba turned, looking surprised, though Turnberry wasn't sure whether he was surprised that someone couldn't follow his explanation, or so deep into the details that he was surprised to realize that there was still a class behind him. "Um, yes?"

The student who'd had his hand up posed a question. Seba went back two equations and unerringly clarified. Getting a nod from the confused student, Seba resumed where he'd left off.

Turnberry studied what Seba'd written. *He isn't just parroting what's in the book!* Turnberry thought. *What Seba's putting up is different. And it's more... clear-cut! This kid may not look like he's paying attention, but he knows this stuff backward and forward.* A moment later Turnberry realized, *He wouldn't have to cheat to get the best scores on our tests. He could write the damned textbooks! Where the hell'd he come from?*

Turnberry resolved to talk to the other faculty. *We should be trying to get this kid into our graduate program! He could make some real contributions to the world of physics.* A sudden worry cropped up. *What if he doesn't have the kinds of original ideas we'd need in a professor?* Turnberry shrugged, *If so, he could sure as hell teach physics at a non-research University.*

***

Ricard Caron stared at Elgin Munger, CTO of Martin Aerospace. "What do you mean, 'it doesn't work'?"

Munger looked irritated. "We built your 'stazer' from the diagrams you showed me, plugged it in, and flipped the switch. *Nothing* happens."

"You have to hook it up to some kind of cavity, right?"

Munger nodded. "The cavity's not well specified, but we did shine either the laser, or the microwave emitter, or both, into several cavities. Nothing happened." He paused and stared at Ricard. "Or, maybe it did. Since I have *no* idea what's *supposed* to happen, it's pretty hard to be sure it didn't."

Ricard frowned, "What kinds of cavities?"

"Metal, ceramic, sintered carbon..."

"No, I mean, what size and shape?"

"Six-centimeter cubes."

Ricard sighed, thinking, *I'm going to have to show him the test sample of stade we got from those idiots at Staze.* He'd wanted his own people to make a completely different setup without seeing Seba's sample. That way if they ever went to court, his science team would honestly be able to say they'd never seen stade before they made it themselves. Munger was the only one who'd seen the files that'd been hacked out of Seba's computer and Munger was only told to build something that worked the same way, but designed differently. Ricard didn't want it to look like a copy of Seba's stuff so he'd insisted Munger take handwritten notes from Seba's files while they were displayed on Ricard's computer.

Ricard turned to Abe Goldman, "You've got the patent app submitted?"

Abe rolled his eyes, "Yes. But I don't like patenting something I don't understand." He glanced at Munger, then back at Ricard. "Now I think I'm hearing that I'm trying to patent something *you* don't understand either? Something that doesn't even work?"

"It's *going* to work," Ricard growled. "We know it's possible. Yes, you'll have to submit a correction of some quote-unquote 'errors' before the final patent's granted, but we've established priority, right?"

"Right," Goldman said with a frown. "*How* do you know it's possible if you can't get it to work?"

"Just trust me. I do," Ricard said to Goldman, waving him off. "You can get back to work. I need to talk to Munger some more.

An uncomfortable silence stretched as Goldman got up, gathered his notes, and left the room. Ricard thought, *I'm going to have to fire that SOB.*

Once Goldman was gone Ricard turned to Wang Chen. "Can you get us any better information?"

The always inscrutable Chen spoke in a near monotone. "Very difficul', jus' breaking into Seba's computer one time. Then need two day' time on Martin Aero' supercomputer wit' access to quantum processor to break encryption. Make many people angry who mus' wait to use computer. Got everything on device while we were there." Chen shook his head, "Not recommend we try to do again."

"Goddammit Chen," Ricard said, pounding a fist on the table, "you must've missed *something*! Munger can't get it to *work*!"

Chen's expression didn't change. "Sugges' either mistake on plan, or Munger follow diagram wrong."

Sounding unhappy, Munger said, "Where *did* you get these plans?"

Ricard didn't answer that but posed a question of his own. "Did you read the description? Did you try to understand the principles involved so you could figure out whether the guy made a mistake drawing up his diagram?"

"Whether *who* made a mistake?" Munger asked. "And, why aren't we asking *him* how to build this damned thing?"

Ricard stayed on the offensive. "You *didn't* read the description, did you?"

"*Yes*, I read the damned description! It *doesn't* make sense. Keeps using equations that can't be found with google searches. Then there are these constants I've never heard of. The description makes bizarre statements based on them. Are you *sure* this does whatever it's supposed to do? *I* think it's someone's delusional fantasy."

Feeling incredibly frustrated, Ricard pulled out the envelope containing the sample of stade they'd received. He slid it to Munger, "*This* is what you should be able to make."

Looking puzzled, Munger took the envelope and opened the flap. He peered in, said, "A mirror?" He slid his index and long fingers into the envelope to pull it out.

Ricard snickered when Munger's fingers came back out without the sample. He said, "Coefficient of friction's zero."

Munger looked up at Ricard with a startled expression, then reached in again.

After Munger's third try, Ricard snatched the envelope out of his hands and, grasping the end opposite the opening, jerked on it. This left the stade tumbling weightlessly in the air.

Munger's eyebrows went up.

Ricard said, "Same density as air."

Munger tried to grab it, but it got away from him.

Ricard trapped it, then held it out, caught by opposing corners.

Munger took it by the other two corners. "What's it good for?"

Ricard said, "It's stronger and more heat tolerant than *any* known material... Make a good rocket engine, eh?"

Munger gave Ricard an uneasy look. "Better than our new tungsten alloys?"

"*Way* better. So much better we don't even have equipment that can measure it."

Munger's eyes went back to the sample. "Shit..."

"Yeah. There go the bonuses you were gonna get for your role in developing the alloys." Ricard leaned across the table and, speaking with great intensity, said, "I want you to drop everything else and *make this work!*" He glanced at Chen, "*All* our jobs depend on it."

Munger looked at Ricard, "Why aren't you licensing it from whoever developed it? *That's* what the company

The Thunder of Engines

needs. I could chase my tail for years trying to figure this out and never get it."

"Munger, any tech guy who could find his own *balls* should be able to figure this out. We've given you the files on it straight outta the guy's computer. *Now* you've got a sample. As to 'why not license it,' the son of a bitch wants two million dollars per engine."

"Dammit Ricard, if this stuff's as good as you say, that's cheap!"

"Two million dollars is *not* cheap," Ricard said dangerously. "Besides the dumb bastard hasn't even applied for a patent." Ricard smiled disturbingly. "We're going to beat him to his own invention."

Munger stared at him a moment. "I think you're gonna regret this."

Ricard narrowed his eyes. "Does that mean you're not gonna play ball?"

"I'll do what I'm told, but I don't like it."

Ricard waved him away, "Go. Figure it out. Save us all."

Munger looked back and forth from Ricard to Chen and back to Ricard. He got up and made his way out of the room.

Ricard turned back to Chen. "We need Seba's device… or whatever it is. The working model he made the samples with."

Chen gave him a basilisk stare, "If you have paten' application made, send him letter saying he mus' cease and desis' making stade. Say you want his devices to be sure he not using them."

"We only have a patent application. We can't *forbid* him making and using until the patent's granted."

"So? He dumb college studen'. You tell him cease and desis', he do it."

"I'd rather not generate anything in writing that could come back and bite us on the ass. *You* could call him and tell him to send it to you."

Chen blinked. "Okay."

"But, if he doesn't give it to you, I want you to figure out how to get the device some other way."

"You mean steal?"

"If you have to, yeah."

"If I do that, I steal computer too. Then we search hard drive whenever we want."

Ricard nodded, "Good idea."

***

Arya listened to Vinay, the young man across the table from her. There didn't seem to be any danger he might want to hear anything she had to say, so she was saved from carrying any of the conversational burden.

He and his parents had come to meet her and her parents at her parents' house. Her parents were quite excited about him. He was twenty-five, handsome, well dressed, and had started his own business. His parents seemed successful, drove a nice car, and lived in southern Pennsylvania, not too far from her parents' home in Hagerstown, Maryland.

At least he isn't constantly making stupid jokes the way Kaem does, she thought. Then she started thinking about how Kaem sent all the money he could to his family in West Virginia. *Kaem may make stupid jokes, but he's kind. And he damn well isn't* boring, *like Vinay here.*

That brought her thoughts back to Vinay. He was still talking about the business he was so proud of. "So, I

The Thunder of Engines

told her that we had a business to run and that our customers couldn't be distracted by her daughter."

Arya broke into his stream of consciousness, "But hadn't you told her she *had* to come in to work because another employee was sick?"

"Yes, that employee's also proble—"

Arya interrupted, "Surely you didn't want the first employee coming to work sick and giving her illness to your customers, did you?"

"Well, no but—"

"And you practically forced your second employee to come to work in place of the sick one. What was she supposed to do with her daughter?"

He frowned as if it were obvious, "Leave her with her mother!"

"And if her mother has a life?"

"Has a life?" he said, a puzzled expression on his face.

"Yes. If her mother's got something else she has to do besides babysit, then what?"

"Well," he said dismissively, "some other relative then. American Testing's policy—"

"American Testing?"

"Yes, I'm their franchisee and—"

"So, you didn't *start* this business, you bought a franchise?"

"Well, yes it's a franchise, but I found the space and built my own franchise."

"Ah," Arya said. She thought, *And a franchise is a business. Not everyone wants to build something new when someone else has already figured out something that works.*

But, even if Vinay hadn't been a conceited bore, she wouldn't have wanted to marry someone who didn't want to build his *own* business, rather than co-opting someone else's plan. And she *wouldn't* marry someone who fired an employee for bringing her daughter to work when she'd been pulled in on her day off.

She settled back to pretend to be interested in what Vinay had to say. *It'll be good to get back to school and Staze,* she thought. *Kaem might have an annoying sense of humor, but he's decent. He wouldn't have fired that woman.*

And, he's a genius, so there's that too.

***

Ron Metz was sitting in a campus coffee shop, pissed about the paper he'd been assigned. An Asian guy sat down across from him. The guy said, "You Ron Metz, right?"

"Who the hell are you?" Ron asked.

"I man want offer you good money for small job."

Ron's eyes narrowed, "What?"

"You roommate to Kaem Seba, right?"

Ron nodded slowly, wondering where the guy got his info. *And why's he interested in a loser like Seba?*

"You friend of Seba?"

Metz snorted, "Seba's an asshole."

"That mean you no like him?"

"Correct. I no like Seba. He's a loser. In his junior year and still living in the dorms. It's my serious misfortune to have him as my roommate." In a sing-song voice, Metz imitated Kaem, "'Turn down your music, Ron. I can't study with you dancing around, Ron.'" Ron grumbled, "The guy's got no life."

"We no like him either. He steal secret from my company."

That seems unlikely, Ron thought. *Doesn't sound like the straight-arrow Seba I know.* He lifted his chin interrogatively, "Who are you and who do you work for?"

"Call me Kim. Company rather I not say its name. Embarrassed that simple college student cause them much trouble. Even worse now you tell me student a loser."

"Ah," Ron said thoughtfully, I don't like Seba anyway. I'll bet there's something in this mess for me. He asked, "What do you want?"

"Wonder if you could get secrets and equipment back from Seba. Save company going to police. Better for everyone: We have our secrets. Seba not go jail. Ron Metz get paid good money."

"How good?"

"How good what?"

"The money you're going to pay me," Ron asked with exaggerated patience. "How good is that money going to be?"

"Ah," Kim said. "Two thousand dollars."

"And what exactly are you wanting me to do?"

"Seba have some electric devices in room?"

Thinking of the drawer under Seba's bed that contained a bunch of electronic modules, Ron slowly nodded. Seba didn't seem to use the modules much anymore. The guy had some newer electronics mounted in a rack. He'd gotten that stuff recently. "How long ago did your stuff go missing?"

"One, maybe two months."

That'd be the stuff in the drawer. "I'm pretty sure I know what you're talking about. There's some stuff he got about four to six weeks ago. He keeps it in an under-bed drawer."

"Ah. Good. He also steal digital plans. He have computer?"

Ron nodded, "He's got a laptop, but he's always got that with him. He's also got a desktop he uses for his fancy physics projects."

"Desktop big?"

"It's got a huge monitor, but the CPU's case is small."

"We only need CPU case so we can get hard drive. You get these items for us?"

"Not for two thousand."

"How much?"

"Four thousand," Ron said, expecting to be negotiated down.

Instead, Kim immediately said "Okay"—making Ron wish he'd driven a harder bargain. *How can I...?* he wondered.

Slowly Ron said, "There's a problem."

"What?"

"When Seba's stuff goes missing he's gonna call the cops. They're gonna wonder why someone broke into *our* room but only stole *his* stuff."

"That okay. We be far away by then."

"No, that's *not* okay. They might suspect *me*. But they won't suspect me if some of my stuff gets stolen too."

"Oh..." Kim said thoughtfully.

"So, if my laptop and sound system gets stolen too, that'll keep me safe. Understand?"

Kim shrugged dismissively, "Okay."

"So, I need four thousand more to buy a new laptop and speakers."

Ron expected pushback since his laptop and sound system only cost about fifteen hundred. Kim just said "Okay" again.

The Thunder of Engines

Should've asked for even more money! Ron thought irritatedly.

He and Kim spent time working out a plan, Ron trying to think of ways to charge more. But by the time they broke to go their separate ways, he'd only managed to up the price another thousand.

***

Jerome Stitt looked up. April Lee was standing in front of his engineering station. "What?" he asked impatiently.

"You've been assigned to my project."

"What?!"

"I'm heading up a new high priority project. Mr. Prakant told me to requisition whoever and whatever I want. I told them I wanted you."

"But…" he shook his head abruptly as if to clear it, "Why, April? You hate me."

She nodded calmly. "That's right. I hate you because you're an asshole. But I need the best people I can get and you're a really good engineer." She leaned a bit closer, "Also, I don't *like* being called April. Call me Lee."

"You're gonna have to get someone else. Sanderson's riding my ass on this project. He'll never let me go."

"Already approved. Goran talked to Sanderson."

Stitt blinked, then looked around the room for whoever was setting him up. No one was even watching. "Will Goran doesn't even know who I am!"

"No, but he knows who I am and what kind of priority Mr. Prakant gave my project."

He sighed, "What're we doing?"

"*I'm* flying to Virginia. *Your* job is as a part of a team that's going to figure out how to make a glass mold that we can use to cast a small rocket engine's combustion chamber and nozzle. The prototyping shop's already thinking about how to do it, but, once you're up to speed on what they're doing, you need to figure out whether they're doing it the best way or whether there's somebody we should contract it out to instead."

"A glass mold? You mean one made out of glass? Or are you talking about some kind of glass process I've never heard of?"

"A mold made out of glass."

"Oh, come on!" Stitt said, glancing around the room again. A few people had looked toward them at his exclamation, but curiously. Not as if they thought something funny was happening. He looked back at Lee, "A *glass* mold for a rocket engine?! That's just ridiculous. You can't cast high-temp alloys in a glass mold, it'd melt. Someone's pulling your leg!"

She said, "Come with me," and started across the room toward one of the little conference rooms. When he didn't start after her, she turned and preemptively beckoned him after her. She stopped at the desks of Teri Nunsen and Evan Ulrich, telling them, "Come with us."

Teri got up, looking puzzled. Ulrich turned around, also looking for whoever was pranking him. He saw Stitt. He said, "You know what this is about?"

Lee turned around and came back a few steps. She darted narrowed eyes over the three of them. "Mr. Prakant has given me a project that he's assigned the highest priority in the *entire* company. I can requisition *anyone* I want. I'm requisitioning the three of you because I've seen your work and know you're not only good, but that you're capable of thinking for yourselves. Now, do I have to call Mr. Goran and tell him you're giving me trouble, or are you going to *get off your asses* and come with me?"

"I'm all for it," Teri said. "But what do I do about the work I'm currently assigned to?"

"Don't worry about it." She turned toward the conference room again, "Just come with me and stop being a pain in the ass."

The three young engineers glanced at one another. Teri said, "All three of us are working on the new booster engine. If you take all of us from the same project it's going to fall way behind."

Lee got a small smile and said, "Good thinking. Don't worry about it. Let's go."

They followed as ordered. Jerome Stitt admired his view of Lee as she walked in front of him. She was good looking, spunky, and extremely bright. *Why do I give her so much shit?* he wondered. If he'd met her away from work, he'd have bought her a coffee and tried to move on from there.

When they were all in the room, Lee closed the door and turned to study them without inviting them to sit down. She looked at Stitt and said, "I should thank you for sending Mr. Prakant's assistant to me when she came down with those material samples." She narrowed her eyes, "I know you *only* did it to crap on me, but it turned out to be the most amazing opportunity of my life." She turned to the rest of them, pulling on a string dangling out of her pocket. A mirror slid out of the pocket and she grabbed it by the corner where the string was tied through a hole. "This is the sample she had."

They all stared. It, after all, just looked like a mirror. About three by six inches with little holes around its edges, one of which had the bit of string tied through it. Stitt leaned a little closer, noticing that it didn't have a layer of glass like a normal mirror. It seemed very thin, though it was hard to judge its thickness because it was so reflective that he was seeing nothing but a bunch of reflected images from around the room. Teri asked, "Is it some kind of silvered plate?"

Stitt thought, *Hmm, maybe?* A thin layer of silver on glass was the best way to make a mirror because silver had the highest reflectance. Silver's cost and tendency to tarnish resulted in most mirrors being coated with aluminum though.

Then Lee let go of the little mirror.

It floated in the air.

The corner with the string attached slowly started sinking.

An aerogel! Stitt thought. Aerogels were polymer foams that had so much air in them they weighed virtually nothing. They were amazing insulators, which Stitt could imagine being useful for keeping cryogenic liquids cold. But they weren't strong enough for the rigors of rocketry. He'd gotten through this thought process when he realized the damn thing wasn't falling. Aerogels weren't *that* light. *Unless it's filled with a lighter than air gas. Partially helium maybe?*

Teri reached out and took the mirror, or tried to. When she grabbed it, it slipped away, kind of squirting toward Stitt.

Thinking disparagingly of Teri's clumsiness, Stitt caught it. Or tried to. Thumb on one side and fingers on the other side, he got what seemed a good grip. But the damned thing just slid right out from between his digits.

The Thunder of Engines

Lee said, "It's called stade. Its coefficient of friction's zero."

"Bullshit," Stitt said. "Nothing has a coefficient..." His brain caught up with his mouth. It'd just slipped out of his fingers and he hadn't felt *any* resistance to that motion. If its coefficient of friction wasn't zero, it was damned close. "Sorry. Its coefficient is obviously very low. But I doubt it's really zero."

Lee had captured the mirror in a basket of her fingers. "Okay," she said. "You might be right. Let's just say its coefficient of friction's so low we can't measure it."

Evan Ulrich muttered, "I'll bet I could measure it."

Lee studied him a moment. "You can try. When you're not doing any of the more important stuff for this project."

Jerome said, "Okay, so it's some kind of silvered aerogel with lighter than air gas substituting for the air. I imagine it's a great insulator and might help keep cryogenic fluids cold, but there's no way it's going to tolerate the stresses of a launch."

Lee turned her gaze back on Stitt, "It's not an aerogel but you're right about it helping with cryogenic fluids. Its thermal resistance is infinite. Before you also say *that's* not possible either, I'll grant that it might be that its thermal resistance is so close to infinite that we can't measure any heat transmission. As to your thought that it won't tolerate the stress of launch, that's not a problem either." She held out the mirror, still surrounded by her fingers, "Here, break it."

Stitt reached for it, then drew back frowning, feeling like he was being condescended to. "What's going to happen?" he asked suspiciously, thinking it'd be something embarrassing.

She regarded him steadily, "You won't be able to break it."

Giving her a chary look, he said, "And if I *can* break it, it's going to hurt me?"

Lee shook her head and spoke exasperatedly, "Stitt, for God's sake! I'm not trying to jack you around the way you've been doing me for the past year. I promise you; you won't be able to break it. Its flexural strength is at least 360,000 megapascals! Why do I say 'at least?' Because *this* specimen, the one in my hands, broke Space-Gen's biggest testing machine when the machine hit fourteen metric tons-load. At that load, this very specimen hadn't even *started* to bend. Hell, it hasn't even been scratched!"

Stitt stepped forward and—while she continued to restrain it—gingerly put his fingers under both ends of the little mirror with his thumbs pressing down in the middle. He slowly applied more and more pressure, trying to keep his fingers from skidding around on its surfaces. Then, without bending an iota, it suddenly shifted to one side and his fingers slipped off. It jumped out of Lee's hands too, squirting off toward Evan Ulrich.

Ulrich snared it in a basket of fingers the way Lee had, then turned to the table and placed the middle of the mirror on the edge. He leaned on it hard. For a moment Stitt thought it wasn't going to slip on him, then as Ulrich got most of his weight on it, it shot out away from him along the edge of the table. Caught by surprise, he fell almost to the floor. In the process of catching himself, Ulrich let go of the stade specimen, which, after a few twists and turns slowed to a stop in midair as if taunting him. He started to go after it but Teri got there and snagged it before he took his second step.

The Thunder of Engines

Lee spoke as if nothing remarkable had happened. "So, one of the reasons I picked the threeback and pulled of you, rather than some of the *other* really smart engineers…" she glanced at Stitt, "some of whom *aren't* assholes… is specifically because you're all working on the new launch engine." She glanced from one to the other of them, "Which has just become obsolete."

Teri and Evan got surprised looks on their faces. Stitt tried to keep from looking surprised but thought he failed. *Of course it has,* he thought.

Lee said, "We've been assigned to design and get built, molds for the casting of test cryotanks and rocket engines made out of stade. The company that's going to cast them, Staze, is going to charge Space-Gen by pricing the finished samples as if they're made of gold by volume. That's going to make them *very* expensive, so we want our test engine and tanks to be small. Our objective is to be sure they can, in fact, cast shapes as complex as a rocket engine out of stade. Then to fire up that engine and make sure that, despite the astonishing properties of the material itself, it doesn't fail for some other reason."

Teri looked up from the specimen she'd been fiddling with. "They make this stuff by casting?"

"No. But they said we could think of it that way. This is in terms of the fact that we need to make molds *as if* they were casting the material." Lee looked around at the others. "Here are the parameters I understand so far. I don't understand the process well enough yet. That's why I'm flying out to Virginia in a day or so. So I can get a better feel for what we're doing. We do *not* want to make molds that won't work."

"The company making this stuff's in Virginia?"
Lee nodded, "Charlottesville."

"What's the company's name again?"

"Staze." She spelled it for them but then gave them a distasteful look. "It's privately held, so don't waste time trying to figure out how you can invest."

Lee stepped over to the whiteboard and drew a cross-section of a generic rocket engine with a spherical combustion chamber and a bell-shaped nozzle. It had pipes entering the chamber to deliver fuel and oxidizer. "So, this is what we know so far. They can't cast features smaller than one millimeter. This is important because if we want to use threads to attach the fuel and oxidizer feeds, they'll have to be coarse. Also, realize that, because stade's extremely rigid and completely frictionless, anything that's screwed together will readily unscrew itself. If we go that way, we'll need to design a mechanism that'll *keep* it screwed and some kind of gasket to get a seal despite an imperfect fit of impossibly rigid components. The one-millimeter limit's also important because it'll let us build our mold in two parts and clamp them together. We won't have to worry about stade leaking into cracks between the two segments."

"Wait?" Teri said, looking puzzled. "Why that limitation on the size of features? Is the stuff they cast it out of thick and pasty or something?"

Lee snorted, "The guy said we could think of it as casting, but that it wasn't actually casting at all."

"The guy?!" Stitt exclaimed. "The guy? Is that like 'the guy' that fixed your sink?"

Lee nodded and gave a little laugh, "It kinda feels that way. Whenever I call with engineering questions, I wind up talking to a guy named Kaem Seba. If I call with business questions, I talk to Arya Vaii, a woman."

The Thunder of Engines

Stitt drew back, "Should Space-Gen even be dealing with a penny-ante place like that?"

Lee took the piece of stade from Teri and waved it at Stitt, "If the people who made this stuff were deaf, dumb, blind, meth-addicted, psychotic orangutans from the depths of the jungle, we'd *still* want to buy it from them. It's going to change the world and they're the *only* ones who know how to make it. It isn't just going to change the world of rocketry; it's going to upend the entire world of engineering. If you want to be in on this from the start, you'd better *shine* over the next few days." She looked at the three of them in turn, as if to be sure they'd gotten the message, then said, "Remember, I'm gonna leave tomorrow or the next day, whenever I can work it out. Your mission's to find and adapt a design for a small engine and work out how to make molds for it. Also, molds for a cryotank. They may only be bench tested and never fly, but size them so they *could* be components of a flyable rocket in case our bosses decide they want to do it. The glass the castings are made out of will need to be silvered, so don't use some glass formula that won't take silver. Don't decide you can save money by making the walls of the chamber or bell really thin. Yes, this stuff is strong enough, but it can't be cast less than a millimeter thick. If you come up with a design, send it to me to approve before you have someone start building it. I might've learned something your design'll need to take into account."

Lee turned to Teri but pointed at Stitt, "*He's* an asshole, but a really smart one who has more experience than we do. If smarts and experience were *all* it took to run this, he'd be in charge while I'm gone. But we need an actual *team,* so, *you're* in charge. Make assignments. Make things happen." She glanced around the group, "Staze says they don't want to cast any test components bigger than one-meter in their greatest dimension. Space-Gen doesn't want to *pay* for any big components when they're paying for them as if they're made out of gold. So, think *small*. But not tiny. Chamber and nozzle in the ten- to fifteen-centimeter range so we'll have something we can fire up. Something that'll burn hot and hard and put out significant thrust. We want to stress the stade as much as we can. Made out of stade, it shouldn't need tubing for cryocooling, so follow the KISS principle."

Lee turned to Teri again, "If Stitt gives you *one iota* of trouble, call me and we'll dump him. I've already picked out someone to replace him."

She turned to Stitt. "By 'trouble' I mean any of your asinine practical jokes, general disrespect, *or* trying to boss Teri around instead of letting her succeed as your leader, got it?"

Stitt nodded, feeling a little dazed by the change in the woman.

She turned and strode to the door, opened it, and then turned back. "Space-Gen's paying a million dollars a week until we get this test done, so we need to get it done as, soon, as, possible!" She left without saying goodbye.

When did she turn into such a hardass? Stitt wondered, about to say something snide to the other two. No. I'd better not. I'm not going to buck Apr…Lee, 'cause I badly want to be part of this project. Bad enough I'll gladly put up with her crap.

***

The Thunder of Engines

While they waited for the faculty meeting to start, Giles Turnberry turned to one of his friends, Arthur Mandel. "Have you ever had a kid named Seba in one of your classes?"

Mandel nodded. "Yeah. Odd kid. African-American. Does *great* on tests. Scores so well I thought he might be cheating. Is that what's got you worried?"

Turnberry chewed his lip, "I've worried about that, yeah. Um, do you have any evidence of it?"

"Other than never missing a question?" Mandel chuckled. "No. I watched him like a hawk during a couple of tests. If he's cheating, I can't see how he's doing it. I don't let them have their phones or earbuds during the tests. If he's got the answers written somewhere, I can't see him looking at them. In fact, he never looks away from the screen his test's displayed on. Doesn't make notes. Doesn't write formulas. Doesn't use a calculator function. Unless, somehow, he's got the University system subverted so it displays the answers for him..." Mandel shook his head, "I just can't see how he could've been cheating. Did you figure it out?"

Turnberry shook his head, then snorted a little laugh, "I'm thinking he might actually *be* that smart."

"No!" Mandel said, with overly wide eyes as if confronted by an impossibility. "What would make you express such revolutionary ideas?!"

Turnberry laughed at his friend's performance. Then leaned closer and confided quietly, "I did the unthinkable."

41 | Page

"What's that?!" Mandel said, wide-eyed again.

Turnberry lifted an eyebrow, "I caught him not paying attention in class so I *called* on him."

Obviously, having been listening, John Stavros, turned from the seat in front of them, "Bet he knew the answer, didn't he?"

"You've had the same experience?" Turnberry asked Stavros.

"Yeah," Stavros laughed. "Thought it was just a fluke the first two times. It's not. He *always* knows the answers. And asks questions that make me wonder if I truly understand physics."

"Oh, come now Joe," Mandel said. "*Never* admit to having a student who can ask questions you can't answer!"

Thinking back to that day, Turnberry said, "He answered my question so well, I thought he'd just happened to read the chapter and had that one fact on the tip of his tongue. So, I called him up to the front and challenged him to take the class through the WKB approximation."

Mandel said, "Oh, that was a *low* blow."

Turnberry shook his head. "Not for him. Not at all. He had a moment's trouble with the e-whiteboard, then explained WKB better than I ever had. I... um," Turnberry found he didn't want to admit to it, but then plunged ahead, "I saved the record so I could teach it that way in the future."

This time when Mandel's eyes widened it wasn't playacting. "So, you're thinking...?"

The Thunder of Engines

"I'm thinking this kid's special. That we should be trying to recruit him into the graduate program."

"You think he'd be interested?"

Turnberry shrugged. "I don't know. But I think some students don't try for advanced degrees simply for lack of encouragement."

"What kind of career do you think he'd use a Ph.D. for? Industry? Academics?" Mandel asked, "Do you think he has original ideas he could found a research career on, or just regurgitates existing knowledge particularly well?" Mandel had several grants and tended to consider research by far the most important part of an academic career.

Turnberry said, "From my one experience, I think he could be an amazing teacher."

"What if he isn't an original thinker? Encouraging him toward academics won't be a kindness if he decides he wants to teach at a major university then can't get any grants."

Thoughtfully, Turnberry said, "He does ask weird questions. Maybe he's *full* of original ideas."

Mandel scoffed, "Weird questions are *not* the same as original thought!"

Stavros turned around again, "They might be in Seba's case."

"*What* original thoughts?!"

"Maybe we think they're weird because they're so original we can't follow what Seba's thinking."

Mandel scoffed again. "I think he's good at parroting what we teach him but doesn't really understand it. *That's* why his questions are so odd."

Turnberry said, "Well, I'm gonna ask him if he's interested in academics."

"Good for you," Stavros said.

"I think you're wasting your time," Mandel rejoined.

Chapter Two

Kaem's phone chimed with an incoming call. When he looked at it, he saw it was April Lee, the young woman from Space-Gen who'd been pestering him with questions. He told the phone to answer, "Hello?"

"I've arrived. Where should I meet you?"

"Arrived where?"

"At the airport."

"You're *here,* in Charlottesville?" Kaem asked, startled.

"Yes. Of course. I told you I was coming. Space-Gen's paying you a million dollars a week for God's sake. They want me to move as fast as I can."

"Well, yes, but I thought you were coming in a few days. Um, what is it you want to do?"

Impatient sounding, she said, "See your factory. Learn how you cast stade. I need to better understand the parameters for how we should build the molds for our motors. We can't afford to waste time building unsatisfactory shapes that won't work."

"Um..." Kaem paused, thinking furiously. "We don't exactly have a factory. We've, um, leased some space, but we haven't moved in yet."

There was what Kaem thought was a stunned silence, then she slowly said, "You guys are just a startup? *That's* why you don't even have a website?"

Kaem wanted to deny it, but it was, after all, true. He thought of saying something pompous about the value of their intellectual property. Anything to keep Lee from thinking they were fly-by-night. He settled for honesty, saying only, "Yes."

After another silence, she asked, "Have you made stade for other companies?"

"No."

After another silence, Lee said, "Besides the samples you sent us, what else have you made?"

"Lots of those samples. Also, some fifteen- by fifteen- by fifteen-centimeter cubes."

"So, you don't even *know* if you can make complex shapes? *Or* make something as big as a rocket engine?"

"We *can* make them. We just haven't done it yet."

Lee said, "I sure hope you're right. I need a sit down to talk to you about whether you think our plan for casting the test engine's viable. And I've got to see your setup with my own eyes so I can get a grip on how it all works."

Slowly, Kaem said, "I don't know if I can make that happen today."

"We're paying you a million dollars a *week*. And, the contract you signed said you'd assist and cooperate. You'd damned well *better* make it happen!"

It won't hurt me to miss a class, Kaem thought. He could watch the recording later, though he liked to ask his own questions of the professors in person—which the recording wouldn't allow. He said, "It's nearly lunchtime. I'll meet you at the Cavalier Buffalo for lunch and to answer your questions. Meanwhile, I'll talk to some of our people about setting up a demonstration, okay?"

"Okay," Lee said, sounding reluctant. "I'll take an Uber to this Cavalier Buffalo."

"Sure, I'll... I'll get there as soon as I can."

~~~

The Thunder of Engines

As soon as he hung up, Kaem turned toward the Buffalo. As he walked, he called Arya Vaii. "Hey, that April Lee from Space-Gen's here to look at our setup and get a demo. Any chance they'll let us into the building we're leasing ahead of time?"

"What?! Why didn't you tell me she was coming?"

"I didn't know. I mean, I knew she was going to come, just not that she'd get here today." He sighed, "I could listen to her messages to see if she did tell me it'd be today, but that won't solve the problem we have. I-I don't want to take her to Gunnar's shop. It looks... it doesn't look very professional."

To Kaem's relief, Arya didn't waste time protesting. "I'll talk to the owners of the space. You call Gunnar and see if he can move his stuff."

Of course he can, Kaem thought, *it's only the two mirrored boxes.* He didn't say it though. "Will do. I'll have to pick up the electronics from my dorm before I meet you there."

Without hesitation, Arya said, "I'll meet you for lunch. Then I can take her to wherever we do the demonstration while you try to get there with your stuff before she does. Where are we meeting?"

"The Cavalier Buffalo."

"Jeez, Kaem, couldn't you have suggested somewhere a little more upscale?"

"I don't *know* anyplace more upscale."

"Ah, yes, sorry. If they'll let us use the space I'll probably be late getting to the Buffalo because I'll want to go look at the place and make sure it isn't a mess."

"Okay." Kaem hung up with Arya and had his phone call Gunnar Schmidt. "Gunnar, someone's here from Space-Gen to look at our setup—"

"What the hell, Kaem? A little warning would've been nice!"

"Sorry, Gunnar, I didn't think she was coming for a few more days, but she called me a little bit ago to say she's already here."

"I suppose you want me to straighten up my shop," Gunnar said grumpily.

"Well, Arya's trying to get us early admission to the place we're leasing... but yes. In case we can't get into the rental it'd be nice if your shop looked... as professional as possible. If we do get into the rental, we're hoping you can meet us there with the molds?"

"Molds?"

"Yeah. The mirrored cavities we've been forming the stade in. We've been calling them 'molds' when we're talking to the people at Space-Gen. It's just easier to get the idea across to other people. They understand casting stuff in molds. It's much harder explaining mirrored cavities with microwaves in the central space and laser light in the surrounding one."

"Okay," Gunnar said, sounding unconvinced. "I'll start cleaning up. How will I know if I'm meeting you at the rental space?"

"Arya or I'll call." Kaem signed off and looked ahead. It was a few more blocks to the Buffalo. Uphill, so he'd have to walk slowly or he'd get exhausted. He hoped he wouldn't be too late.

~~~

The Uber dropped Lee off at the Cavalier Buffalo. *This looks more like a college dive bar than somewhere you might have a corporate meet!* she thought. My kind of place, but...

She walked inside and her opinion didn't change. She wondered if she should feel disrespected, then

The Thunder of Engines

thought, *How they treat me's immaterial. They've got stade and nothing else matters.* We've *got to have it for our rockets.*

No greeter or hostess met her. She looked around the room, wondering how she was supposed to find Kaem Seba. She didn't know what he looked like. *I should have used a video chat one of the times I talked to him.* She asked her phone if it could find a picture of Kaem Seba from Staze.

It replied, "No Kaem Seba associated with a company named Staze."

They not only don't have a website, she thought, *they don't have anything out there yet.*

She had it search for just Kaem Seba in Virginia. That brought up a picture of a UVA physics student. *He's still a student?!*

There were other Kaem Sebas, but they weren't in Virginia. To a quick survey, it looked like they were all in Africa. She studied the picture a moment, then looked around the room. *What about that guy over there with his back to me?* She walked over but it wasn't the Kaem from the picture.

Deciding to get a booth for when he did show up, Lee slowly turned, looking for the best location. When her eyes crossed the entrance, she saw Seba standing there, surveying the room. He looked peaked.

She walked his way, giving him a little wave and thinking, *He doesn't look very healthy. If he drops over dead, I hope someone else knows the secret of making stade.* Arriving in front of him, she said, "Hello Mr. Seba."

"Ms. April Lee?"

She nodded, extended her hand, and said, "Call me Lee. I don't like my first name."

"Call me Kaem," he said, shaking her hand. "I was just about to call you because I'd realized I didn't know what you looked like. Where would you like to sit?"

Lee pointed out the booth she'd had her eye on and they headed that way. She said, "So, you haven't graduated yet?"

"Um, yeah. Is that a problem?"

"No," she laughed, "I only graduated a year ago. I'm really lucky to be running this project. Through a stroke of serendipity, I was assigned to evaluate the sample of stade you sent us. Our CTO said I could run with it until I screwed up. Hope I don't screw up too soon." She glanced at him, "UVA's got you listed as a physics student. I was thinking you'd be a materials engineer or maybe a chemist."

Seba looked surprised, then understanding seemed to dawn. He said, "I guess that'd make sense if stade was a material."

What the hell?! Lee thought. She opened her mouth to ask what he meant but a waiter chose that moment to arrive.

"Welcome to the Cavalier Buffalo," he said. "Do you already know what you want?"

Seba looked at Lee, saw the confused expression on her face, and turned back to the waiter, "I think we'll need menus."

As the waiter walked over to get menus, Lee said, "Not one of your regular haunts?"

"Um, no," he said. Then to her surprise, he followed with, "I'm really poor so I only eat at places on the university meal plan." He looked around. "Sorry, I should have suggested someplace nicer than this for our meeting, but even this place is more expensive than my budget can tolerate. I've only been in here once

The Thunder of Engines

before and that was … for a celebration." He shrugged, "It was nighttime and dark and I was excited, I didn't realize how shabby it is."

Suddenly taking a liking to him, Lee snorted, "The corporate people would probably be offended, but I'm just out of college and I like dive bars. We're okay." She looked around, "I'm surprised your Ms. Vaii didn't suggest someplace more upscale though. When I talked to her I got the impression she's into that."

"Um, maybe." He gave her a sly grin and lowered his voice, "She was pissed when I told her I said we'd meet here."

The waiter had returned to take their orders. Seba quickly selected the cheapest hamburger, so Lee did the same. She'd resolved to put the tab on Space-Gen, but wanted to keep the cost low in case Seba paid for it out of some sense of obligation. Then she had a sudden thought, *Wait a minute. If he's got the rights to stade, he's gonna be rich as Midas!*

But he's not now. Doing him a good turn won't be any skin off me and... he's going to be someone I'd like to be able to call a friend.

Deciding she'd better get back to doing her job, Lee said, "What'd you mean earlier when you said, 'if stade was a material'? Are you saying it's just a process for binding other materials together?" Struck by a thought, she asked, "Is that why the first set of material properties you sent us declared a density typical of water, then the actual specimens turned out to be the density of air?"

Seba looked uncomfortable, "I can't tell you that."

"Why not? We're under an NDA. Your information's safe."

"Yeah…" he frowned, "but our attorney said we shouldn't tell anyone how this works until we have patent protection—which we haven't been able to afford yet. So, we can make samples for you and commit to making engines for you if you decide that's what you want, but we don't want you to know how it's done. We especially don't want to explain the principles behind it."

A very pretty Indian looking girl walked up and slid into the booth next to Seba. She frowned at him, "Move over Kaem. There's plenty of room."

Apologizing, Seba scooted over, then said, "April Lee, this is Arya Vaii."

Vaii leaned forward and scrutinized Lee's eyes, "Wow! Yellow-green! Your eyes are striking." She leaned back and studied Lee's face, "How'd it come about? Asian dad and Caucasian mother?"

Lee felt stunned, getting hit with such a bald question. "Umm…"

Vaii waved dismissively, "Sorry, I'm nosy. Too nosy. Ignore that question. What've you guys been discussing?"

Lee snorted, "Kaem was trying not to tell me what stade is. I'm trying to remember if there're any clauses in the contract you signed that compel you to explain it to us."

"There aren't," Seba said.

Vaii said, "Even if there were, Space-Gen hasn't deposited the money in our account yet. As I read the contract, I don't think you've got an enforceable contract until you do."

Shit! Lee thought. *I told the people down in finance this was a rush priority!*

The Thunder of Engines

Lee opened her mouth to speak, but Vaii had already turned to Seba, "On my way over here I got a call from Orbital Systems. They want to buy stade too."

"How much are they offering?" Seba asked.

Vaii laughed a single "Hah," then rolled her eyes. "They wanted *all* rights for ten million. I told them they couldn't have *any* rights. They could only bid on having us build them rocket engines and cryogen tanks and that they'd have to bid a *lot* more than that." She turned to look at Lee, "Then I realized I didn't know if we'd received Space-Gen's money yet, so I checked. We haven't. We signed that agreement three days ago."

Lee consciously relaxed her jaw. "I'm sorry. I didn't know. I *told* them to rush the payment."

Seba said, "The way I read the contract, it isn't enforceable until we receive our first payment. Also, they don't owe us another payment until seven days after the first one. They may be trying to save money by extending the start date."

Lee frowned at him, "Do you have a photographic memory or something?"

"For things that matter to me." He lifted an eyebrow but produced a small smile, "Like that contract." He sighed and turned back to Vaii. "How'd you leave it with Orbital Systems?"

"I told them that I didn't think Space-Gen had an enforceable right of first offer yet. The person that called me is getting back with his people."

The waiter was arriving with the hamburgers, but Lee got up, saying, "Let me make a call."

Seba nodded. Vaii was ordering a fish sandwich.

Lee asked her phone to connect her to Prakant. She thought she'd need the CTO to light a fire under the

CFO. Something she didn't think she, as a junior engineer could do.

The call was answered by Mary Willis, Prakant's assistant. "Hello, Ms. Lee. Mr. Prakant's busy. Can I take a message?"

Lee's first impulse was to demand her call be put through to Prakant. Instead, she explained what was happening.

At the end of the tale, Willis said, "Ah, he'll want to hear this. Let me interrupt him."

Mary's a good person to have on my side, Lee thought.

After a few minutes, Willis came back on the line. For a moment Lee was disappointed, but Willis set her mind at ease, saying, "He said to tell you he appreciated getting word and he was going to light a *bomb* under the CFO."

"Thanks. I'm going to get back to my meeting. I hope they deposit it in time to hold our rights."

~~~

When Lee was leaving the table, Arya was placing her lunch order with the waiter. That done, she glanced after Lee and then turned to Kaem. "I got a key code to get into the facility so you can do a demo for Lee if you like. I texted the code to Gunnar and he said he was on the way over. I'm assuming you still want to keep all the rights to Stade? We'd only contract with Space-Gen to do things like build rocket engines and cryo-tanks, right?"

Kaem was chewing, so he held up a hand. Swallowing that bite, he gave a little laugh, "Yeah, though, since we're having them manufacture the molds and then all we have to do is staze them, I kind of feel like *they're* building them." He grinned, "But we should *definitely* say *we're* building them when we're talking to companies."

"So," Arya said thoughtfully, "Space-Gen won't have a contract for anything deliverable will it? All they'll have is a promise we won't sell rocket engines to anyone else without letting them know first so they can prepare a counteroffer?"

"Mm," Kaem said, thinking, "I think what they'll want is an *exclusive* right to buy engines and tankage from us. Space-Gen wants to be the *only* company that has stade engines. If they had to, they'd settle for being *one* of the companies that have stade engines. What they *don't* want is for Orbital Systems to have an exclusive contract for engines so Space-Gen can't have any. They wouldn't be able to compete then."

"And what do *you* want?"

Kaem looked thoughtful, "I'd like there to be competition out in space, so I don't want anyone to have a monopoly on engines in the long run. But *we* need start-up capital to fund our other projects, right? So, I'd go for giving them an exclusive contract to buy engines and containers for, say, three to five years. That big chunk of money would let us get started with other projects and we could still let other companies back into the industry later. The limit on the length of their exclusive deal would make sure Space-Gen started buying engines from us right away since they'd need to make hay while the sun was shining."

"Why *wouldn't* they buy engines right away?"

Kaem shrugged, "If their contract's not time-limited, then there's no reason for them to hurry. Our downside is that we don't get enough orders to maximize the growth of our company. The world's downside is that it doesn't get into space as fast as it wants to."

Arya drew back and gave him an appraising look, "That's... devious. I like it. You're more of a businessperson than I gave you credit for."

Kaem shook his head, "I think of it as aligning people's motivations with what's best for everyone."

Lee returned. Sitting down, she said, "I've gotten word to our Chief Technology Officer and he's promised to get you your money ASAP."

The waiter brought Arya her fish sandwich. Kaem spoke to Lee, "Are you still wanting to see our setup?"

Lee had just taken a bite and started chewing, but she nodded eagerly.

"I'm going to head on over there now then. Gunnar and I'll get a demonstration set up for you. We should be able to make a few test samples like the ones we sent you, okay?"

Lee swallowed, "Sure. I'd love to see it. Any chance you could cast something with a more complex shape?"

Kaem frowned, "We... don't have any molds for anything with a complex shape... But, I've had an idea we could try. Maybe it'd give you confidence that we *could* cast something shaped like the bell of an engine nozzle."

"That'd be great!"

Kaem nodded, "Arya'll bring you over when you guys are done eating."

Arya turned to Lee, speaking as if in confidence, "This is the way it is, working with Kaem. He's always running out before the check comes, sticking someone else with the bill."

Kaem dug in his pocket, saying, "Oh! Sorry."

Lee waved him off, "Oh, don't worry about the bill, Space-Gen's covering lunch."

The Thunder of Engines

"Ooh," Arya said, rubbing her hands together. "An expense account? We *really* should've gone someplace expensive!"

~~~

Kaem had his phone order an Uber before he even got out the door of the Cavalier Buffalo but still had a few minutes to wait on the sidewalk. He spent them thinking furiously.

When the Uber got there, he told it to take him to the Dollar Store first. There, telling the Uber's AI to wait, he went in and got a small glass drink tumbler and some aluminum foil. On his way out he passed a Mylar balloon display. Having a sudden thought, he turned around, went back, and grabbed a shiny metalized one.

Next, he had the Uber take him to the dorm where he picked up the electronics for creating stade.

Back in the Uber, he gave it the address of their new rental property.

Pulling up to the building, he took in its industrial metal exterior, suddenly thinking of how it would look to others. *It's functional,* Kaem thought, *which is what I wanted, but now I can see why Arya was less than thrilled.*

When he got to the door, it was unlocked. He walked through the anteroom to find Gunnar in the main workroom, setting up a couple of the folding tables the building came with. He'd also put out a set of six chairs. Gunnar looked at Kaem and growled, "This is FUBAR."

"What's that mean?" Kaem asked, pulling up the rolling suitcase that contained his rack of electronic gear.

"You don't wanna know," Gunnar grumbled. "How much time do we have?"

"I don't know. Arya's bringing her when they've finished lunch."

"They're getting *lunch*?! *We're* gettin' the short end of the stick."

Rather than admit he'd already had lunch *and* gotten it on Space-Gen's dime, Kaem said, "I made a couple of stops on the way here, so they might get here pretty soon." He turned to the door. "I've got to go back out to the Uber and get another load."

As he walked away, Gunnar asked, "You want me to set up the mold for the six-inch cubes, or just the one for the test samples?"

Kaem glanced around the big room and said, "The more the better. We're looking pretty bare here."

When Kaem got back, Gunnar had both of their "molds" set up on the table. Kaem tried setting the tumbler in the cube and was relieved to see it fit. He said, "Gunnar, I've had an idea."

"Oh no," Gunnar said, as if something terrible had happened.

"What's the matter?" Kaem asked.

"You've had an idea."

Kaem laughed, "Come on. They aren't *all* bad."

"Well, no," Gunnar said, "I'll admit you did have one good one. But the rest of them always mean more work for me."

"You and Arya are such pessimists it's astonishing I ever get a chance to smile." Kaem waved as if dismissing Gunnar's concerns. "Ms. Lee, the Space-Gen engineer that's here, asked if we could make any more complex shapes. I think their concern is that we might only be able to make simple polyhedrons, *not* rocket engines."

The Thunder of Engines

Gunnar looked contemplative. "I guess she might be right, but I'll bet she isn't."

"Well, me too," Kaem said, tearing off a sheet of aluminum foil. He started stuffing it into the mouth of the tumbler, saying, "But I'd like to be able to prove her wrong. It occurred to me that if we put a glass in the cube, covered inside and out with aluminum foil, that it might make a recess somewhat like a rocket nozzle in one of the faces of the cube." He started wrapping the outside of the tumbler in foil. Finishing, he set the foil-covered tumbler in the cube upside down, with the mouth of the tumbler resting on the bottom mirror inside the cube.

Gunnar studied it a moment, then said, "I see what you're going for, but the laser light in the mirrors surrounding the cube's cavity isn't going to get past the mirror's silvering and into the walls of that drinking glass."

"Yeah, I was thinking we'd have to scrape the silver off the mirror where it's in contact with the glass."

Gunnar rolled his eyes. "Then you'll want me to silver it again?"

"Not if this proves aluminum foil makes a 'good-enough' mirror."

Arya opened the door. Gunnar leaned close and said, "If we could've been using aluminum foil the whole time, instead of me having to silver these damned things, *I'm* gonna be pissed!"

"I'll be apologetic," Kaem said with a grin before turning toward the door. "Hi, Ms. Lee." He indicated Gunnar, "This is Mr. Gunnar Schmidt. He's our expert fabricator."

Lee distractedly shook hands with Schmidt, but her eyes were mostly on the forms for the cube and the testing samples. Stepping closer, she said, "So, silvered glass like you said? Can I take pictures?"

"Uh-huh," Kaem said, turning the rack of electronics so he was looking at the back. He opened the door and started jacking wires into the backs of the components.

Lee started around the table, saying, "What do you have there?"

Kaem turned the rack so she wouldn't be able to see what was wired to what. "Sorry, this part's confidential. No pictures over here."

"But... we've got that NDA," Lee said, longingly.

"Hmm," Kaem said, "I don't believe we actually have a contract yet, do we?" he glanced at Arya.

Arya said, "I'll check," and started mumbling into her phone. A moment later she shook her head and said, "No. Should we even be doing a demonstration?"

Gunnar said, "What do you mean we don't have a contract?!"

Arya said, "It's signed, but it doesn't go into force until they've paid us that million-dollar retainer. They haven't deposited it yet."

Gunnar drew back, "Hell no we shouldn't be giving demonstrations!"

Mildly, Kaem said, "The contract only says we can't agree to a deal with anyone else without talking to Space-Gen. I've realized I'm not even sure why they'd want to pay us for a contract to that effect. They can pretty much count on us to ask them for a better bid if someone makes us an offer. We'd be foolish not to."

Arya and Gunnar looked at one another. Kaem could almost hear them thinking, *But we need that money! And, why in the hell is Kaem letting Lee know he's having such thoughts?!*

Arya looked down at her phone. "I've got a call from Martin Aerospace." She turned and strode to the door, stepping out into the anteroom as she said, "Hello?"

Kaem looked at Lee. Her jaw looked tense. She said, "Is Staze just the three of you so far?"

Kaem nodded affably. "You want us to make a piece of stade for you?"

Eager now, Lee said, "Yes, please."

Sounding on-edge, Gunnar said, "I'm not sure this's a good idea."

Kaem spoke placatingly, "We're only going to show her how our part would work if Space-Gen sends us a mold." He stretched out a hand holding the cables, both the electrical cable to the radar emitter and the fiberoptic laser light-guide cables.

After rolling his eyes, Gunnar took them. He asked reluctantly, "Which... form... do you want to hook up first?"

Kaem closed up the back of the rack and turned it around. "Let's make her a cube first," he said. He opened the front door of the rack so he could start setting the controls on the electronic modules.

"You, um," Gunnar started, then after a moment's thought, went on, "You want me to take the aluminum foil out of it for this run?"

"Uh-huh," Kaem responded, continuing to set switches and turn dials to the proper settings. "Have you got enough of the base liquid for it?" This was in the way of a reminder. He and Gunnar had talked about making a stade containing water because just closing it up with nothing in it—except air—would suggest that they weren't doing something to a "material" and provide a hint that they were doing something to space-time itself. Kaem didn't think it was a hint that would let anyone replicate the stazer, but it wouldn't hurt to play it safe.

Gunnar opened the door of the cube form so it kept Lee from seeing as he took out Kaem's foil-wrapped glass. Then he turned the form onto its back. He bent and came up with a couple of unlabeled liter bottles from a box on the floor. Kaem knew they were water but hoped Lee might think they were something else. Gunnar started pouring them in.

Kaem did the math. *A fifteen-centimeter cube holds... 3.375 liters. He'd been thinking it would be considerably less. I hope Gunnar's got two more of those bottles.*

This proved to be the case and Gunnar soon had the cube filled with water. He leveled it a little with a folded bit of paper, then added a tiny bit more water until it bulged up a little from surface tension. Gunnar looked up at Kaem and Kaem gave him a nod.

Gunnar slowly closed the door and latched it, squeezing out a few drops of water.

Kaem put on a look of intense concentration as he flipped a series of switches and adjusted a dial. He sat back and pulled out his phone, setting a timer on it.

Gunnar said, "The capacitor—"

"Got to let it catalyze, remember?" Kaem said, wanting the process to look much more complicated than it was. He hoped Gunnar would understand and play along.

Gunnar looked flummoxed for a moment, then the corner of his mouth turned up the tiniest bit just before turning serious again. "Oh yeah. Sorry."

After a minute, the phone's timer went off. Kaem looked up and made another series of adjustments to the electronics. Once again, he sat back to watch the numbers count down on the phone's timer. This time when it went off, he flipped a large switch on his gear, one that made a loud snap. He looked up at Gunnar and said, "Check it please?"

Gunnar gave him a questioning look, probably because—not having heard the capacitor charge and discharge—he knew no stade had been formed. Nonetheless, he carefully turned the latch and slightly opened the door. Looking up at Kaem, he shook his head.

Kaem said, "It's stizzled though, right?"

Gunnar nodded, looking worried. Kaem thought Gunnar was concerned that Kaem was carrying the masquerade too far, not that Kaem couldn't get it to work.

"Okay, close it up again. We'll get it this time."

Kaem made more adjustments, this time setting it up correctly. When Gunnar heard the capacitor charging, he looked relieved. When it snapped, Gunnar started reaching for the latch before Kaem finished saying, "That should've done it. Let's have a look."

As Gunnar slowly opened the door to reveal the reflecting surface of the stade's perfect mirror, Kaem surreptitiously flipped random switches and twisted knobs just in case Lee somehow got a look at the settings. If she did, she wouldn't learn anything.

Gunnar turned the box over, but the stade wouldn't fall out. Setting it back on its side, he got out his knife and worked it in between the stade and the sides of the box to break the seal on the vacuum holding the stade inside. This time when he tipped it, the stade readily slid out, thumped onto the table, slid across, and fell to the floor, skidding across the room. Kaem got up and moved that direction, but when Lee went after it, he let her.

Showing her experience with stade, she corralled it rather than trying to grab it. "This is a lot heavier than the test specimens you sent us," she said, obviously puzzled as to how she was going to lift it when she couldn't get a grip on it.

Kaem said, "One hand stops it down low, the other hand tips it up, then slides under. Then you can get both hands under and around the lower corner."

Lee did so and walked back toward them, staring down at the block of stade as if mesmerized. "How do you control the mass? The test specimens had such low density they essentially floated in the air."

Kaem said, "We can make them even lower density than that. And, we can make high-density stade as well."

"Lower density than air? So, they'd float up like a helium balloon?"

Worried that saying "yes" might twig her to the fact that it depended on what you filled the mold with, Kaem said, "Even lower density than that."

She looked a little suspicious, "Like the density of hydrogen?"

"Even lower than that," Kaem said, thinking, *Vacuum.*

"Oh," Lee said, looking puzzled, which was just what Kaem wanted. After a moment, she asked, "What would you use higher density stade for?"

Has she simply been too focused on uses in rocketry, or is she wondering whether we've considered the possibilities for using stade outside the aerospace industry? Kaem wondered. He thought of a way to answer without answering and said, "If you wanted a

The Thunder of Engines

blast shield under your rocket's launch site, it'd be nice if it weighed enough that it wouldn't blow away wouldn't it."

She nodded thoughtfully as if she'd found his answer enlightening but not giving any insight into the motivation of her question.

Kaem stepped over to speak quietly to Gunnar. "You think you could trim the foil and try scraping away the silver under where the glass would sit? I'd like to try my idea."

"Yeah," Gunnar said, unsurprisingly sounding exasperated.

Kaem turned back to Lee. "You want me to make you a test sample?"

She brightened, "Yes, please. Um, can I look at the sample mold first?"

Kaem thought for a second, decided she couldn't learn anything important—other than things she really did need to know if she was in charge of making rocket engine molds at Space-Gen—and said, "Sure." He started disconnecting the cords and fiberoptic cables from the cube-shaped stade form, then waited for her to finish studying the form for the test samples so he could attach the leads to it.

Lee had picked up the test-sample form and started examining it from all angles. Saying, "Confusing to look at with all the reflections, but seems simple enough," she set it back down and took a couple of pictures.

Kaem connected the cables to it, then picked up Gunnar's partially empty water bottle and, behind the cover of the opened lid, made as if he was pouring a dollop of water into that form the way Gunnar had into the cube-shaped one.

Lee stepped his way as if to look at the water in the form, but Kaem managed to close and latch the form before she could see it was empty. He went through his routine of several sets of adjustments of the switches and dials, glad to see Gunnar hard at work scraping inside the cube.

When the capacitor finally snapped, Kaem stepped over and popped out the sample. Cradling his fingers around it he held it out to Lee, saying, "Here's one that's air density."

The door opened and Arya came in looking… shattered. She walked over to Kaem.

"What happened?" Kaem asked, concerned.

"Martin Aero…" her eyes went to Lee. "Um… I think we should talk privately." She started toward the door and waved Kaem and Gunnar after her.

Kaem caught her elbow, "I think we need to ask *Lee* to wait outside." He turned to Lee with an apologetic shrug, "Sorry, but we can't leave you in here with our setup."

She said, "I understand," gave the equipment a wistful look and started for the door.

Kaem looked at Arya, "What'd they say?"

Arya gave Kaem a searching look. "They say *we're* infringing *their* patent for a method to form stade."

"What?!" Kaem asked, not believing his ears.

Voice trembling, Arya asked, "Is stade *really* your invention, Kaem?"

Feeling like he'd been punched in the gut, Kaem said, "Yes," but the word barely qualified as a croak. *How?!* He would've sworn no one else could've come up with his idea. It was just too bizarre. When he'd first had it, he hadn't expected the numbers to work.

The Thunder of Engines

When the numbers turned out to fit… He hadn't believed that either. Even when Arya had agreed to help pay to get it built, he'd been full of doubt. Fear that he was wasting everyone's time and Arya's money.

Right up till the moment it'd worked.

Even then it hadn't worked the way he'd expected. He'd expected his watch to disappear, then suddenly reappear at the date and time in the future he'd sent it to. Later he'd realized that having something reappear in a new place/time, co-inhabiting the same space as molecules already present in that place/time—even if those molecules were only air—would've resulted in an explosion. When the mirrored surface of that first stade became evident, he hadn't had any idea what'd happened. Then he'd suddenly realized that the piece of space-time in the box *was* moving forward in time—just at the same rate as everything else—but that *time had stopped within that volume of space-time*. As far as things in the box were concerned, they were jumping forward and would suddenly reappear at that date in the future. But for everyone else, that volume had become a bit of space that was completely unbreakable, unreactive, and impenetrable.

The time jump was important. He just didn't think, in the long run, the time jump would prove as important as the unbelievable material properties of the staded segment of space-time.

He blinked, realizing he'd been woolgathering during a crisis. He said, "Is it possible someone else could have come up with the same idea simultaneously? Or semi-simultaneously?" He shook his head, "No. That's about as likely as a coin coming up heads a hundred times in a row."

"Are you sure?" Arya asked apprehensively. "I gotta tell you, I'm worried."

"I see three possibilities," Kaem said slowly. "First, that they invented it simultaneously, an event less likely than winning two Powerball lotteries back to back. Second, and much more likely, that they *think* they've got something like stade, but they don't. Third, and most likely by far, they've somehow stolen the idea. Perhaps James Harris over at Harris Labs managed to..." Kaem shook his head, puzzled, "Though I have no idea how he could've gotten..."

Arya groaned, "We shouldn't have talked to *anyone* without getting patent protection first."

Gunnar cursed, stormed across the room and slammed out the door.

Lee caught the closing door and looked in questioningly. Kaem waved her off. Feeling weak all of a sudden, he grabbed a chair back, turned it, and slumped down on it. Dropping his head on his hands, he tried to think. "Did they say when they filed for their patent?"

Arya fell into the other chair. "No. But they did demand we stop work on stade and turn all notes, equipment, and models over to them."

Kaem lifted his head and frowned. "What?! Can they do that?!"

"*I* don't know."

"We need to call our lawyer."

"And pay him with what?!"

Kaem sat, staring into space, saying nothing.

"And pay him with *what*, Kaem?! The way we've been spending, my bank account's vapor!"

Kaem's vacant expression turned to a startled one. He said, "They *don't* know how to make stade! *That's* why they want our notes and models."

The Thunder of Engines

Arya gaped at him. "They *have* to know how to do it. They've filed for a damned patent!"

"No, they don't. We sent them samples, right?"

Arya slowly nodded.

"And they may have stolen some of my notes. Or, though I think this is doubtful, maybe they hacked them out of my computer. They could somehow have gotten into Gunnar's place to take pictures of the molds. Or into my dorm room to take pictures of the electronics. So, they have some vague idea of how it all works. And a sample of the product."

Arya looked doubtful.

"Patents aren't long on specifics, Arya. I'll bet if we saw their patent application, we'd be able to tell that they *don't* know how to do it. They're just filing a patent on making stade because they know it can be done and they think we're too small to fight them."

"Kaem! We *are* too small to fight them. Besides, patents take a long time! If they've got a patent, they do know how to do this and filled out their application a long time ago. Possibly years ago! Face it. They did beat you to it somehow."

"I'll bet they don't have a patent. I think they've *just* now applied for one. Yesterday or the day before."

"They *said* they have a patent, Kaem. They're a huge company and they wouldn't lie. Also, they have enormous resources. We can't possibly fight them. You're grasping at straws."

"You talked to multiple people? What'd they sound like? Could you recognize their voices?"

"No, wait... what?"

"You keep saying 'they,' as if a lot of people at Martin are involved. You need to consider that your nebulous 'they' might not be more than the one person you talked to and possibly one or a few others." He leaned forward, "I'm assuming you only talked to one person. What'd he sound like?"

"He... he sounded Asian, maybe Chinese." She shook her head, "But that doesn't mean anything, a lot of tech people are."

"Could you recognize his voice?"

She shrugged, "Probably, he sounds as if English is his second language and he's struggling with it. That's not uncommon either."

"Does he sound educated?"

"Well, no. But I think that's just because he isn't good with English."

"Or, maybe he's just a thug."

She leaned toward him, speaking slowly as if trying to control her temper. "Even if the guy that called us *is* some low-level grunt, Kaem; we can't fight Martin Aerospace. We don't have the money or the resources to take them on."

Kaem studied her a moment, "You're just going to give up, then?"

Her face fell. "What else *can* we do?" she asked plaintively.

"Call our lawyer. See what he thinks. Maybe he'll take our case on contingency. Or, hook up with Space-Gen. Tell them that Martin's trying to steal our IP and ask them for help fighting back."

Shoulders slumped, Arya said, "I don't know Kaem..."

"Come on, Arya. I can't believe you're just going to—"

The door swung open and they turned, Kaem hoping Gunnar had come back. Schmidt might be grumpy, but Kaem thought he'd put up more of a fight than Arya would. And, Gunnar had money, if he was willing to spend it.

Instead, it was Lee. She gave them a tense smile, "Check your account. The money's been deposited. So, we *do* have a contract." She looked at them a moment, apparently unsure what to make of their expressions. "I, uh, just wanted you to know… in case it made a difference regarding whatever you were deciding about Martin Aerospace's offer." She pulled her head back and let the door close itself.

Arya looked at Kaem's sudden smile. "No! You're not thinking of…"

"Damned right I am. You can quit if you want, but I'm gonna fight. And it sounds like there're a million little helpers in our account."

"You can't use Space-Gen's advance to pay our *legal* costs!"

"It's not an advance. They paid that money to gain the right of first offer. We're still planning to give them that right. We need to use that money to protect the IP they want to buy." He waved at her phone, "Check to see if the money's there."

Shaking her head, she spoke some commands to her phone. Looking up at Kaem, she nodded.

He decided that if he acted like she was still on the team; she might resume functioning rather than turtling up and quitting. He started giving orders, "I'm going to make nice with Lee. I'll do some more demos for her. You call our lawyer. See if we can talk to him today. Call Gunnar, tell him we're going to fight this and we need him. We especially need him to help us make more of your bulletproof vests. The way the bastards at Martin are acting we each need a vest for protection. Call Martin and tell them we think they're lying. Say we need to see their patent so we need their patent number. Otherwise, we can't know if we're infringing them or they're infringing us. Or, whether no one's infringing anyone else. They'll hem and haw because at best they've made an application—they don't actually have a patent. Make them admit it's just an application if you can. Then demand to see a copy of the application. Tell them we don't think they know how to make stade. That we think they're just trying to appropriate our invention. *Record everything!*" Kaem turned and walked toward the door to talk to Lee.

Wretchedly, Arya said, "Kaem..."

Kaem kept walking. Opening the door, he leaned out into the anteroom and said, "Lee, sorry. Come on in. I've kinda forgotten what we were doing when we were interrupted?"

She held up the stade testing sample. "You'd just made this for me. I've been wondering if you could make me a denser one?"

"Sure," he said, motioning her into the room. "Can I make one that's water density? Doing other densities would take a lot of setup time."

"That'd be great."

As they approached the worktable, Arya was on her phone saying, "Mr. Morales, this is Arya Vaii. We need to—"

Kaem interrupted her with a firm grip on her elbow and started her out to the anteroom. Morales was their patent attorney and Kaem didn't want Arya saying anything in front of Lee about how they needed to apply for a patent. When Arya flashed him a look, he cut eyes toward Lee.

Arya got the idea and started for the door to the anteroom.

The Thunder of Engines

Kaem smiled at Lee. "Now, let's make you that denser testing specimen." As he poured water into the mold, he asked—in his best affably unworried tone, "Have any other questions or concerns come up?"

"So, as I understand it, we need a mold that we could quote-unquote, pour our engine's combustion chamber and nozzle into. It should be made out of glass that can be silvered because you need a reflective surface facing the engine's structure, both inside and out?"

Kaem nodded, "Uh-huh."

"And the parts of the mold can be assembled out of tightly fitting smaller parts because stade won't form in gaps smaller than one millimeter, right?"

Kaem nodded again.

"Um, do you mind making suggestions? Like, how *you'd* make the mold?"

"Well," Kaem said thoughtfully, "if you think of the engine as a bell with a can on top i.e. the nozzle bell with the combustion chamber on top..."

"Yes?" Lee said, sounding eager.

"Then I'd be thinking that I'd make the inner mold—the part that will form the inside of the bell and chamber—in two parts. The bell section and the chamber section. The bell piece could be solid for a small motor, or thick-walled for a large motor. The chamber piece would be thin-walled, probably formed by blowing glass into a mold. The two pieces would fit together well enough that they wouldn't have any gaps bigger than one millimeter." Kaem looked at her to make sure she was getting it. She didn't look confused, so he said. "I'd be planning to reuse the heavy piece that formed the inside of the bell, but the blown glass piece inside the combustion chamber would be disposable. Once the engine was cast, you'd get the blown glass piece out of the engine by breaking it. So, you'd need a new piece for the interior of the combustion chamber for each engine."

"Um, okay," Lee said, "I understand that part, but how would you make the outer shell? The part that'd form the outside of the chamber and bell?"

"Ah, that part should be a lot easier. You can make it as a split mold. Two halves that fit around the inner molds leaving the right amount of gap for the casting. You wouldn't have to worry so much about keeping gaps between the two halves down to less than a millimeter because a few bumps on the outside of the engine wouldn't cause many problems."

She waved off that concern, "We could just grind..." She paused, looking embarrassed.

Kaem gave a little laugh, "Yes, you see the problem, eh? You can't grind or shape stade in any way. So, the mold has to be right," he shrugged, "or you have to accept a few bumps."

"Does it have to be glass?" she asked wistfully. "It's damned hard to work with."

Kaem shrugged again, "Maybe not. According to the theory, it just has to be a transparent material, so maybe you could do with a plastic like acrylic. But the surface against the engine would need to be reflective. I think it can probably be done, but we haven't tried it yet."

Lee gave him a look. "You really *are* just getting started, aren't you?"

"Uh-huh," Kaem said. He got up from the electronic setup he'd been working at to make her test sample. Stepping to the mold, he unlatched it and popped out

The Thunder of Engines

another testing stade. It looked just like the other one but it was much heavier. He handed it to her.

Lee pulled the first air-density stade out of her pocket and clawing her fingers around them to keep them from getting away, held them up to compare them. "They look identical, except this one's heavier. If their physical properties in terms of strength and heat tolerance are even close, we'd want the lighter stuff."

"Those material properties should be identical."

"Really?"

Kaem nodded. He stepped over to the cube that Gunnar had been setting up before he left so precipitously. Peering into it, he tried to see what Gunnar'd accomplished.

Lee said, a pleading tone in her voice, "Can you tell me *anything* about how this all works? It's just killing me that I don't have any idea. I mean, it's so cool that you have something this strong and even cooler that I'm gonna be helping build rocket engines out of it, but I can think of so many other things it'd be amazing for..."

Kaem laughed, "Can't tell you anything unless you come to work for us." He lifted an eyebrow, "We could use a good engineer."

Lee looked thunderstruck. "Really?"

Kaem looked down into the cube. "Really. Though we aren't ready to start hiring yet. Soon, though." He moved the foil-covered glass and saw the silvering had been removed in a ring where the inverted glass would make contact. Looking at the glass he could see the foil had been neatly trimmed. "I've had an idea we could try. It might answer your query about making more complex shapes. Would you like me to try it? It's pretty rough and ready. And... there's a good chance it won't work."

"Uh, sure! That'd be great."

"I'm afraid I'll have to ask you to step out into the anteroom again, then."

She frowned, "I can't watch to see how you do it? That could be very helpful in designing the, um, forms."

Kaem grinned, "Sorry, a boy's gotta have his secrets you know. Let me walk you to the anteroom, I need to talk to Arya again anyway."

~~~

Having swapped Lee into the anteroom and brought Arya back into the big room, Kaem asked Arya what she'd learned so far.

Looking a little frazzled, Arya said. "Mr. Morales says we can come over at four o'clock. Gunnar won't answer his damned phone. I talked to the guy at Martin and he was completely hostile. Kept demanding we turn over the working models we'd stolen. Wouldn't tell us their patent number. Wouldn't send me a copy of the patent application. Swore they'd *destroy* us in court." She made finger quotes, "'Make a you sorry! Veddy sorry.'" She looked at Kaem with frightened eyes, "Kaem, I'm scared."

He stepped toward her, wanting to put his arms around her and comfort her, then realizing she'd be pissed if he did. He backed up a step, "Arya, I'm scared too. But we've worked too hard to let them take this away from us..." He paused on a sudden realization, "He asked for the 'models we'd stolen'?"

She nodded, "Kaem, did you get some of your stuff from them?"

Kaem snorted, "Arya, listen to yourself! You had me give you receipts for the components I bought for our first setup. You *know* I got some of it from the physics equipment room—it had the physics department's tags

The Thunder of Engines

on it. *What* piece of equipment did I get from Martin freaking Aerospace?!"

She stared at him a moment, "*I* don't know! Yes, I know some items had physics department labels on them. Yes, I saw receipts for the equipment you bought. But the most important piece in the whole stack might have been the flangeron you got from Martin."

"The *what*?!"

"Flangeron. You know," a sly smile crept over her face, "that critical part you stole from Martin."

This time he stared at her. "Did you just try to make a joke?!"

She nodded snorting softly and looking embarrassed, "A bad one."

Kaem belly-laughed, looked at her, then laughed some more.

Arya sniffed, looking offended. "It wasn't that bad!"

"No, no," Kaem choked out, bending to brace himself on a knee, "It was hilarious. Just way, way funnier coming from someone like you who never jokes... someone who never thinks *anything's* funny."

She drew herself up. "I think some things are funny," she said indignantly. "Just not *your* stupid jokes." She gave him an entreating look, "Kaem, do you *promise* me this is your invention? You really didn't get it from Martin somehow?"

"Wait," Kaem said, turning to look at the rack of equipment he'd just used to form some stade. He started walking that way. He motioned her after him impatiently. "Come look at the rack of equipment we just used."

She came slowly, "I won't be able to tell anything..."

"Yes, you will. Look at the modules in this rack. Do you see that every single one of them has the trademark and logo of some company on it? And that *none* of them have a Martin Aerospace label on them?"

Arya studied the rack. After a moment she straightened, "I can see that, but what if you put someone else's label over Martin's."

"My God, Arya, what do you think of me?" He leaned closer, "Look at them again. All the company logos are screen printed directly onto the front plates of the modules. There isn't a single nameplate affixed afterward that I could've put over someone else's label."

She leaned in close again. "I guess…"

"You guess?! Come on!"

She straightened again, "No, you're right. But maybe you're just using all this stuff to do the same thing Martin's device does."

"I'm not, but there's no way I can prove that." He stopped suddenly, staring away into space. "Oh, that'd be evil…" he said, as if speaking to himself.

"Whatever it is, let's don't do any evil," Arya said.

"No. Listen. I've still got all those parts from the first version." Kaem was still staring off into space, but he could sense her nodding beside him. He continued, "So, I could kludge something together that looked like it'd been built to, to *staze* things, right? I mean, it wouldn't even be close to right but they wouldn't know that. We could send it to 'em and they could waste *months* trying to understand it and get it to work!"

"But… they'd be furious when they figured it out."

"Good! What are they going to do, sue us because they couldn't figure out how it works? Something they claim *we* stole from *them*." He blinked, "Oh, and I'll make a second version and keep it in my dorm room.

The Thunder of Engines

That's the one they'll get when they try to *steal* a working model."

Arya smiled at him. "That... *would be* evil..." she blinked, "but what if they take your rack of electronics?" she asked waving at the equipment she'd just examined.

"Instead of just disconnecting it the way I've been doing when it's not in use, I'll leave the wires hooked up, but all wrong. Maybe even remove a component and hide it somewhere. We'd lose the equipment, but they wouldn't get the secret." He glanced toward the anteroom, then started disconnecting the wiring and cables from the test sample mold and moving them to the mold for the cube. "And, thanks to Lee, we have enough money to buy another rack of electronics if they steal this one."

Arya asked, "What're you doing?"

"I promised Lee one more piece of stade. Let me just staze it for her." A moment later the capacitor snapped and he stepped to the mold. It took him a little work to get the piece of stade out of the cube because it was air density and he didn't think he could use gravity to help get it out. After some extensive prying with the knife, it came shooting out and right off the edge of the table. Rather than tumbling and floating the way air-density stades usually did, it immediately started falling and didn't roll, keeping its bottom face down.

Kaem grabbed it, not sure why it was falling.

Then the glass fell out of the bottom face, hit the floor and broke. It didn't shatter, the pieces being somewhat restrained by the foil. Kaem smacked his forehead, said, "I'm an idiot," and let go of the—*now* floating—cubical stade. He caught it again with a cluster of fingers around opposing corners and turned the bottom face upward. There was a cavity in that surface the same shape as the glass had had before it fell out and broke. He held the cube out to Arya, saying, "Hold this."

She took it and watched as he felt the inside of the cavity.

Saying, "Not bad," Kaem turned to the rack of electronics and started scrambling the switches and dials. Then he opened the back of the cabinet and scrambled the connections of all the wires. He used his toe to push a couple of pieces of broken glass under the table, then turned back to Arya, "Shall we go talk to Lee?"

"What're we going to tell her?!"

Kaem took the cube of stade with the cavity in it from Arya, lifted it a little, and said, "That my experiment with making something shaped like a rocket nozzle worked great." He started for the door.

"No! I mean, what're we going to tell her about this thing with Martin Aerospace?!"

"Nothing for now. The fact that Martin's trying to steal our IP isn't Space-Gen's problem, it's ours." He frowned a little, "It might be theirs too, someday. *That's* when we'll ask them for help." He stopped at the door. "Can you open it?" He held up the block of stade to show why he wasn't opening it himself.

"Oh, yeah, sorry," Arya said, opening the door. "It's easy to forget how many hands it takes to hold a piece of stade."

~~~

Lee gave them a curious look when they stepped out into the anteroom. Kaem set another cube of stade on the anteroom's table and said, "It worked!"

The Thunder of Engines

It bodes poorly if he's excited he was able to stade another block. How often does it fail? She wondered. Then Kaem stuck his thumb down into the top of the cube and Lee suddenly realized it wasn't just a cube, but a cube with a cavity in it. She stepped closer.

He said, "Have a look. I used a glass drinking tumbler wrapped in aluminum foil to make a cavity in this block of stade. A cavity that's not shaped too differently from the bell of a rocket nozzle."

"Aluminum foil? Are you saying it doesn't have to be a mirror?"

"The theory just says it has to reflect light. So, maybe you could make it out of clear plastic wrapped in foil, though a foil wrap's going to give you a rippled surface like you'll feel in here."

Lee gingerly reached in and felt the inside of the cavity. It was gently wrinkled, but not like you might get wrapping something with foil. Other than the roughness, it still felt impossibly slippery like stade always did. She said, "I feel little lumps, but they don't feel like the crinkles you get in aluminum foil."

Kaem shrugged, "Stazing doesn't form small features, so it smooths out those crinkles."

"Ah…" she said thoughtfully. "Um, I know you can "aluminize" some plastics. Would that work for casting stade?"

Kaem shrugged. "I think so. If you send us some small test molds, we can check that out for you."

She narrowed her eyes, "At the price of gold by volume?"

Kaem produced a tight smile. "We'll do those for free. After all, we need to know those answers too. We aren't charging you for these samples we made today either. We *will* charge for your test engines though.

Don't want Space-Gen getting us to make them hundreds of different test versions on our dime after all," He waggled his head, "Once you decide to do business with us, then we can work out a deal to do test versions for less money. Then two million per engine for the final versions of the engines you're going to use to launch rockets."

"Um," Lee said, "while you were in the other room, I got to wondering whether we could make the combustion chamber and the nozzle separately, using a threaded connection to screw them together?"

Giving her a contemplative nod, Kaem said, "I think so, though we haven't made any threaded devices out of stade to know the difficulties you might face. But remember, normally when you screw something together hard, it holds because of friction between the parts. Those parts also deform to fit together more closely. That isn't going to happen with stade. I predict that, no matter how tight you screw it, stade'll come unscrewed unless you come up with a non-stade mechanism that keeps it torqued. Also, because its surfaces won't deform to fit together better as they come in contact, it's going to leak through little gaps along the threads. Rocket exhaust is going to seep out between two surfaces a threaded mechanism is forcing together—because they fit together imperfectly, leaving tiny gaps where the surfaces didn't deform to fit together better. If I were you, I'd try to put a tungsten or carbon gasket in the interface, near the outside so the exhaust has to travel a long way through the tiny gap between the threads to get to the gasket."

Feeling better about herself for thinking of these problems on her own, Lee said, "I've already been giving consideration to some of those issues. I have some ideas for a mechanism to keep them screwed together and how to position the gasket. Are you saying that if we made up some test models to learn about threads and gasket positioning, you'd… what do you call it…? *Staze* them for us?"

"Sure, we need to know how that kind of technology works."

"I'm assuming that the fuel feeds to the combustion chambers can be made out of normal materials?"

"Mm, I'd build the chamber so it has the last part of the feed tubing integral to it and therefore made out of stade. That way heat in the chamber can't melt your feed pipes." He frowned, "You should consider that there won't be any flex in the stade parts of the piping, either at the engine, or up at the cryogen tank. That could lead to high stresses in the non-stade piping material at the junctions when the rocket body deforms under the stress of launch. I'd think that building the body of the rocket out of stade would prevent any flexing and shifting between the tank and the engine that might overstress the joints between the normal piping and the stade piping."

"Oh, good point," Lee said thoughtfully. "Um, how much are you going to charge for making the body and tanks out of stade? We only have your price on the engines so far."

Kaem glanced at Arya, then back to Lee, "We'd… have to negotiate that." He jerked his head at the main room of their new facility. "We obviously don't have room to staze even a single cryotank for one of your boosters. I've been thinking it'd be easier for all of us if you built the molds for big things like those near where you wanted to assemble the rockets. Then we could just show up and staze them on-site."

"The stazing equipment would be portable?" Lee asked, surprised.

Kaem nodded.

Whoa! That changes things. Lee thought. She said, "I'd been thinking stade's light weight would be nice for transportation, but it'd be even better to just cast it where we want to use it. Because of the size of finished rocket parts, transporting the 'base liquid' in a tanker would be a lot easier. If we set up reusable molds at the launch facility and just cast the big parts, all the rest of the small, normal-material parts could be brought in for assembly on site." She shook her head, realizing she'd been thinking out loud. "Thank you so much for sharing all this information with me. I'm going to call myself an Uber and get out of your hair. Can I call you with more questions?"

"Sure…"

~~~

After Lee left, Arya and Kaem stepped back into the big room. Not for the first time, she noticed a shiny birthday balloon tethered to a weight and hanging near the table. Pointing at it, she asked curiously, "Did you get us a birthday balloon because this is kinda the birth of Staze?"

Kaem looked surprised, then looked up at the balloon. "Um, no, sorry. I wanted it for an experiment."

"Experiment?"

"Uh-huh," Kaem said, pulling the balloon down. He took a knife out of his pocket and cut into the balloon, deflating it. He extended the cut and peered inside. "No such luck."

"What do you mean?" Arya asked, thinking that cutting into the balloon wasn't much of an experiment.

"I was hoping, though not very optimistic, that the Mylar was metalized inside and out. Turns out it's only on the outside."

"Why would you want that?"

"So I could try using it to make stade."

Arya drew back, "Is this the 'clear plastic' and foil thing you were talking about with Lee?"

Kaem nodded, "Yeah, then I was thinking of hard plastic. But using Mylar would be even simpler since you could just buy the Mylar with reflective surfaces already on it. Mylar's transparent and the reflective surface on shiny balloons like this is aluminum, same as most mirrors. I think it might work. Then we could just put something in a reflective Mylar bag and staze it."

"But... how would you make it into the shape you wanted?"

"Oh, I'm thinking about the rest of your pizza, or a doggy bag from a nice restaurant. Just staze it for twenty-three hours and have it for dinner tomorrow night. Or, forty-seven or seventy-one hours if you want to eat it in a few days."

She stared at him. "You wouldn't even have to refrigerate it, would you?"

Kaem shook his head. "I'm going to order the thickest Mylar film I can get that's metalized on both sides so we can try it out."

She frowned, "I think we'd better figure out what we're going to do about the Martin Aerospace debacle first, don't you?"

Kaem sighed, "Maybe. That's not as much fun though."

The door banged open. Gunnar stood there. "I'm back," he said resignedly. "Arya's message said you're going to fight. What the *hell* is the deal?"

Kaem explained how he thought Martin Aerospace was just trying to intimidate them into giving up their secrets. When he got to the part about making fake stazer machines, Gunnar's eyes brightened. "Oh, yeah! I could get behind that! And you could design a real, purpose-built one and we could staze it so they can't get at it!"

Arya felt confused and from the look on Kaem's face, he was puzzled as well. "If it's been stazed, how are we supposed to use it?"

"Just set the stade to last until you're going to need it."

"And if we need it sooner?"

"Oh, well, then you're screwed. Maybe you'd have to set it to come down every day. If you didn't need it, you could just staze it again."

"But, Gunnar, if we do that and they steal it, they'd just have to wait until it comes down tomorrow."

"Well, crap. That wasn't such a great idea, was it? He looked thoughtful. What if…?" Gunnar paused.

After a few moments, Kaem said, "What if what?"

"What if you made a stade box and put your stazer electronics in it. It'd have a hole for the cables and wires to come out through. It'd be booby-trapped so if anyone opened the box, boom." He clapped his hands together to emphasize the explosion.

Arya stared for a moment, "And if this booby trap kills someone? I don't want to go up on murder charges."

Gunnar tilted his head in thought, then said, "Maybe just a little thermite under the important bits. Something to melt the secrets beyond retrieval. The thermite goes off as soon as they start to unscrew the lid while the stade's still protecting everyone."

Kaem sighed. "Maybe. I think that kind of protection comes later too. We need to work on more immediate problems. Can you help me make us a bunch of the thin stades so Arya could assemble more of her bulletproof vests?"

Chapter Three

They made big stacks of the testing stades for Arya to build vests out of. Then Kaem and Arya Ubered to Attorney Morales office. As they described their invention to him, his eyebrows had first gone up in astonishment, but he eventually started looking doubtful. Kaem thought Morales felt they had to be fantasizing.

When Morales started to shake his head, Kaem reached into his pocket, clawed his fingers around the test stade he had there and pulled it out. He tossed it to Morales.

The attorney reached out to catch it, but—being an air-density stade—it tumbled in the air and came to a halt without reaching him. Throwing air-density stades felt like throwing balloons or feathers—they just didn't go very far.

Looking much more interested, Morales stood and reached out to grab it. The usual comedy of his repeatedly grasping after it when it slipped away ensued.

Kaem finally stood and trapped it in a basket of fingers.

Wide-eyed, Morales reached to take it in the same fashion. "This is..." he looked up at Kaem and Arya. "This *truly is* unique, isn't it?"

Restraining a strong impulse to accuse the man of ignoring them, Kaem merely nodded. Morales probably hadn't believed a word they'd said until confronted with the specimen.

Morales looked down at the piece of stade, then back up into Kaem's eyes. "And this'll be useful for building rocket engines?"

Kaem tilted his head. "It'll be useful for tens of thousands of things. Rocket engines are just *very* expensive things which stade's properties will make *far* better than existing tech. Thus, it should be able to gain nearly 100% of rocket engine market share." He shrugged, "So, that's where we're starting."

Morales blinked, "Can you give me an example of something else it could be used for? Something high value?"

"Bridges."

"Um, how would you use it for bridges?"

"You were listening when I told you about its strength, right?"

Morales nodded.

"If the Golden Gate Bridge failed, a quarter-inch thick sheet of stade holding up concrete pavement could replace the entire span of the bridge without any posts, pillars, or suspension cables. And, do it cheaply."

Morales stared, "That's hard to believe."

Kaem nodded slowly. "But it's true."

"Okay," Morales said slowly. "And you say Martin Aerospace invented the same thing and they're suing you for infringing their patent?"

Kaem shook his head. "They *claim* to have invented stade and already patented it. They haven't."

"And how do you know that?"

"If they had they'd be launching rockets and talking it up in the news. If they did have someone call us, it'd be a lawyer, not a thug making threats."

"Perhaps they just haven't finished building their first rocket." Morales snorted, "And some lawyers *are* thugs."

"If they knew how to make stade, they could've built a rocket in a month or two. It's my understanding that applying for a patent and getting it issued takes several years, right?"

Morales shrugged but nodded, "Sometimes less. Often substantially longer. But for something as obviously unique as," he glanced at the sample of stade he'd corralled between some pencils on his desk, "as this stuff, maybe less. There wouldn't be any argument about whether it was sufficiently different from existing art to justify a patent."

"Still, if they *have* a patent, they should've been flying stade rocket engines for a while now."

"Maybe they have been, but they've just been keeping it on the down-low until they had their patent in hand."

Kaem rolled his eyes, "I tell you they *don't* know how to make it. It's just such an unlikely process…" He shook his head, "The chances that it'd be invented twice in the same hundred years are so low they're laughable."

Morales slowly shook his head, looking sympathetic, but said, "I'm sorry, young man. You may not know that inventions tend to occur in clusters as soon as the technology necessary to build them has been created. The history of invention is replete with literally thousands of things that were invented almost simultaneously by more than one, sometimes many, inventors. Inventors who didn't know anyone else was working on the same idea. The telephone, the telescope, the airplane, the thermometer, calculus, the typewriter, the steam engine. The list goes on and on."

The Thunder of Engines

"*This* isn't one of them!" Kaem exclaimed. "The tech needed to build it's been around a long time. The math needed to work it out's been around for a long time too. It's just *so* unlikely…" He stopped at the expression on Morales' face. "Okay, see I'm not going to convince you. Give us legal advice then. Do they have a right to demand we send them our working models? If they know how to do it and *have* been doing it, why would they need our version?"

Morales frowned. "Their patent prohibits you from making, using or selling stade, or a machine that makes stade. But, they don't have a right to your property. You could destroy the machine that makes it yourself, you wouldn't have to turn it over to them."

"I did a search for patents or patent applications assigned to Martin Aerospace. None of them were for anything like stade."

"Patent applications often aren't published for eighteen months—"

"But," Kaem interrupted, "we know they don't actually have a patent as they claim. At best they've filed an application, right?"

"Unless you missed the actual patent with your search. Or, if it was patented but the patent wasn't assigned to Martin Aero. Maybe someone else invented and patented it and they licensed it to Martin after the patent was in force. Martin could still be responsible for defending the patent."

"Can we hire you to do a search for us? Maybe you could find it even though I couldn't."

Morales shrugged, "Sure. I'd be happy to. It's one of the ways I earn money. But, I'd have to ask you what keywords to search for because my expertise doesn't lean that way. What I'd be doing for you is checking all

91 | Page

the patents that come up from your search to see if they describe something like stade then asking *you* if I'd found it. I'd be doing tedious work for you that you might want to pay me for, *if* you have more remunerative ways to spend your time."

Kaem glanced at Arya, "Maybe we should try some more searches on our own first?"

She nodded, but he could see she was losing faith in his assertion that no one else could've come up with the idea.

Kaem turned back to Morales. "So, let's say Martin Aero may have a patent, even if we can't find it. It seems to me that if they're saying they have a patent and are trying to force us not to infringe, we should have a right to see their patent, shouldn't we?"

"If they've been granted a patent," Morales said, "the patent is public knowledge and can be looked up. Where's the letter claiming that you've infringed? It should specify which patent they think you're infringing."

Kaem looked at Arya.

She shrugged, saying, "They've only contacted me by phone."

"Ah. I certainly wouldn't do anything until you get a letter. If they call again, tell them to send you one. And, demand to know the number of their patent."

Arya looked uncomfortable. "I already called them back and told them I needed the number. They wouldn't give it to me."

"Oh…" Morales said, "That *does* seem fishy. You definitely shouldn't cooperate until they send you a letter with a number." He looked at Kaem, "You may be right. Perhaps they only have an application." He grimaced, "While they *can't* sue for infringement on an *application*, it'd markedly decrease the value of your idea if they had one for stade. If their patent's granted, Martin'll be able to sue for damages starting back at the date their application was filed."

Kaem studied Morales for a moment, then decided they had to have his expertise. "I'd like to tell you what *I* think they're doing and get your advice on how to fight it, okay?"

Morales leaned back in his chair and laced his fingers over his stomach, "Sure."

"Along with a bunch of other space launch companies, we sent Martin Aerospace a sample of stade." He turned to Arya since she'd sent out the samples, "Right?"

Arya nodded.

Kaem continued, "They tested that sample, then absolutely *shit* themselves when they realized it made a couple of their patents for high-temperature metals worthless." Kaem waited until Morales also nodded, then went on. "They immediately filed a patent application for a method to create stade, though they called it something else." Kaem looked Morales in the eye, "Because an application can be modified up till when it's granted, right?"

"Um, yeah," Morales conceded, "though it can't be a completely different app. The modifications should be minor."

"We told you about James Harris and how he'd tried to force his way into our business, right?"

Morales nodded.

"Harris might have had some contact with Martin. After giving it a lot of thought, I think Harris might've paid someone to get into my dorm room and take pictures of the electronics I use to create stade. Or have gotten photos taken over at Gunnar Schmidt's place. He could've shared this information with Martin."

"Who's Schmidt?"

"The guy who builds the forms we create stade in. He's a minor partner in Staze."

Morales took a deep breath and let it out slowly. "I hope you know how paranoid you sound?"

Kaem smiled at him, "You didn't already think that because I insisted on meeting in this interior room?"

Morales snorted softly, "That wasn't really because you didn't like the bright lighting in the other conference room?"

"No, it's because I'm afraid someone's painting your windows with a laser mic."

Morales nodded and spoke with an amused expression, "You *are* paranoid."

"Doesn't mean they're *not* after me," Kaem said with another tight smile. "Also, even if Harris didn't give information to Martin, they could've hired their own PI to hack my computer, search my dorm room, or otherwise try to get design information on the invention."

"The law restrains PIs from illegal searches."

"And all PIs follow the law?"

Morales gave a small one-shouldered shrug but didn't say anything.

"In any case, I think they're presently busy trying to get sufficient information to modify their patent app for a device that they've found is nonfunctional. They want to get their application to the point that it'll produce a device that does work. And *that's* why they're insisting we send them our working models."

Morales scrutinized Kaem a moment, glanced at Arya, then said, "In a paranoid way that makes sense. I find it hard to believe that a major corporation would—"

Kaem interrupted, "Did you know Arya got *shot* over this invention already?"

Morales gave her a startled look. When she nodded, he asked, "You're okay? They missed?"

She said, "I'm okay, but Harris did hit me."

"My God! Where?"

Arya laid a hand on her chest, "Here, but I was wearing a vest made of stade plates. The bullet bounced off."

"Oh… Wow!" Morales said thoughtfully glancing at the stade on his desk. Kaem thought he hadn't considered some of the possible applications for the patent.

Kaem said, "And that was just Mr. Harris, not all the aerospace companies we sent stade samples to. Admittedly, it seems that in his case the stress resulted in a psychotic break, made worse by his decision to go off his meds, but… I think people who give stade much thought realize how much it's worth. Then they tend to do some things they wouldn't normally consider." He shrugged, "The way you read about people doing crazy stuff in the pursuit of treasure."

Morales sighed, "Okay. Let's assume all your paranoia's justified. You should keep all your records of the invention in a safety deposit box or somewhere else where it'll be safe. The computer you use to work on it should be disconnected from the internet. Your actual devices should be kept in a secure location…" Morales paused thinking. "Could they have already hacked your computer to get design drawings or other descriptions?"

Kaem sighed, "I'd like to think not. I'm pretty good with computers and I've developed some of my own security and encryption, but," he shrugged, "there may be someone out there who's better than I am."

"If so, they really could've patented *your* work," Morales said, sounding dismayed. "Do you have printed and dated versions we could use to prove priority?"

"By priority, I assume you mean prove *they* copied me rather than me copying them?"

Morales nodded.

"No. But I think I have something better."

"What's that?"

"None of my drawings or descriptions will work as they stand. I inserted mistakes that're easy for me to keep track of. So, *I* can use the drawings and specs to build devices because I know the implanted errors, but no one else can. Whatever *they* built would be nonfunctional." Slowly he said, "Seems to me that if their patent won't make stade and ours will, that'd serve as proof of who invented it."

"Oh!" Morales said, sinking back into his chair. "I *like* that! So, then, all you have to protect is your hardware. Do you have a place you can lock it up?"

"No, but right now it consists of a bunch of commercially available electronic devices that I only patch together when I want to make stade. I disconnect all the wiring and reset all the devices whenever I'm not using the setup. So, just like the drawings, someone taking the equipment couldn't build a working device either."

Morales stood and peered over his desk at the suitcase Kaem had wheeled into the office with him. "The stuff's in there? Can I see it?"

Kaem lifted the rack out of the suitcase and showed him how all the switches were off or flipped downward. All the rotary pots were turned all the way clockwise.

"Where's the wiring?"

Kaem turned the rack around and opened the doors on the back.

"That's quite the tangle of wires. Um, I thought you said you disconnected them when not in use?"

Kaem smiled thinly, "I did. Starting today I've started hooking them up wrong instead."

"Ah," Morales said, producing a smile of his own. He grew thoughtful. "I think you're pretty well protected if you're right that they don't know how to make it and are only trying to shake you down for the correct method. If they really do have the same invention and have already filed for a patent, you're pretty much screwed. The question now is, do you want to protect your intellectual property with a patent so that if you're right and they don't have the same invention you'll be the owner?"

"Damned right I do."

"It'll be expensive."

"How much?"

Morales got out a pricing sheet describing his fee for writing it up with increments depending on complexity. Fees for filing, fees for working with the patent examiner. He pointed out which fees would be charged for sure, which things might be needed and which items likely wouldn't.

His explanation seemed quite straightforward and honest. Kaem said, "I thought lawyers charged by the hour?"

Morales gave a tiny shrug, "I'm fast, so I get paid more by fees than I do by the hour. Or I could lie about how much time I spend on your patent and charge you for more hours than I invest. I think this is more honest."

Kaem liked that. He'd been irritated when Morales was dubious about whether Kaem had a rightful claim on the invention, but he liked straight dealing. He knew how much it was going to cost upfront. He didn't need to worry that the attorney would be charging him for hours spent having "business drinks" with other lawyers. And, they could afford it now that they had the million dollars Space-Gen had deposited.

But... He looked up from the pricing sheet. "I'd prefer you were truly motivated to draw up the best damn patent you could. That you wanted to protect our IP to the best of your ability. That you feared someone stealing the idea as much as I do. That no one could buy you out. What would you think of being our lawyer for a tenth of a percent of our profits in the first three years after receiving the patent?"

Morales looked insulted, "A *tenth* of a percent?"

Kaem held up his hand. "We're talking about a business that's going to cast rocket engines in buyer supplied molds for two million dollars each. A business that won't have any expenses beyond a couple of thousand for sets of electronics that can cast engine after engine after engine. Electronics that can also cast bridges, dirigibles, or skyscrapers."

Morales narrowed his eyes, "So, you're saying that…"

"We should easily be able to do a billion dollars' worth of business that first three years. Your share of that would be a million. If we only did a hundred million dollars, you'd get a hundred thousand. If we did less than that, it'd probably be at least partly your fault. If you hustle and do your part right, we should do several billion."

"Unless your IP turns out to be worthless because Martin *does* have priority."

"They don't," Kaem said with conviction. "And if they manage to get that claim to stand up in court, you didn't do your job right."

Morales sat staring at them, his eyes flicking back and forth between Kaem and Arya.

Figuring we're too young and dumb, Kaem thought.

But then Morales stood, leaned over his desk, and extended his hand to shake, "I feel like I'm playing the lottery, but you've got a deal." They shook, then Morales said, "I'll draw up an agreement and email it to you. Come back tomorrow to sign it and bring all your information on the IP so I can draw up a patent application."

Kaem said, "Okay."

Arya said, "We'll be counting on your vaunted speed to get the patent in pronto, right?"

Morales grinned, "That'd be in my best interests. So, yes."

***

After the meeting with Morales, Arya went with Kaem back to his dorm the way she had back when they were worried about an attack from Harris. She surprised him by getting out of the Uber when it arrived at Kaem's dorm. He tilted his head curiously, "You're coming in with me?"

She nodded distractedly. "I want to talk some more. Not in an Uber, I don't think you can count on them to be… secure."

"Ah..." he grinned, "Congratulations. You're getting as paranoid as I am." He glanced around. No one was near. No shotgun mics in evidence. "What'd you want to talk about?"

"I don't want to spend, um," she glanced around the way he had, "our recent chunk of income. If they never get their product they may come after us."

Frustrated, Kaem said, "They didn't pay for a *product*. They paid for the right to *bid* on the product against other buyers!"

"Yeah, but if we're infringing, and therefore we never had any product we could sell..."

"Come on Arya. Look me in the eyes."

She stopped and turned to stare into his eyes.

Mustering all his sincerity, he said, "I did *not* steal stade from anyone!"

She shrugged and looked sad. "I'm not worried about that anymore. But you *cannot* be completely sure someone else didn't invent it first."

Keeping his eyes on hers, partly because he liked looking into Arya's eyes, but also hoping to display his earnestness, he said, "So, what...? You don't want to spend any of it? Please tell me you don't want to send it back. That'd pretty much say even *we* don't believe it's our product."

"No," she said, slowly. "Not send it back. But I don't think we should spend it."

With a long-suffering sigh, Kaem turned and continued to the dorm. He thought Arya would turn and leave, but she followed along. When they stood waiting in front of the elevator, he resignedly spoke without looking at her, "I won't spend any of it without your permission. You don't have to come upstairs and keep badgering me." Then he wondered, *I can't believe I'm trying to keep her from coming up to my room! I-I... don't know what I want,* he thought, disgusted with himself.

She didn't look at him either. "I want to talk to you about... other stuff."

On Kaem's floor, as they walked down the hall to his room, Kaem realized there were some campus police in the hall outside his room. "Oh, crap!" he muttered, walking faster, then slowing.

"Is that *your* room?" Arya asked.

He didn't answer since they were now close enough that the answer was obvious. Instead, he bumped the suitcase with the rack of electronics against her leg and, without looking at her, whispered, "Take this and head back to your place."

She said, "What?!"

He hissed, "Now!"

"Wait, give me your coat!"

Kaem set down the rack and slipped off his coat, handing it to her.

She took the coat, grabbed the handle of the suitcase, and kept going down the hall to the stairs.

Falling behind, Kaem stepped up to one of the policemen, "Hello, Officer," he said. "This's my room. What's happened?"

The campus cop gave him a suspicious look. "Your name?"

"Kaem Seba."

"Spell it please."

When Kaem did, the man asked to see ID. Kaem provided that as well. Finally, the officer seemed to accept that Kaem was who he said he was. Kaem told himself he should be grateful the man was making sure no strangers entered the room. But he couldn't help a niggling feeling that the man couldn't believe a black kid belonged in the dorm. *Probably thinks I'm most likely to be the perp.*

When Kaem was finally allowed to look into the room, the first thing he saw was that his desktop computer was gone. *Thank God my laptop's in my backpack!* They'd left Kaem's huge monitor, the main reason he had a desktop device.

Kaem noticed Ron Metz, his roommate, sitting on his bed looking pissed. Angry was Ron's normal state so it was a little hard to be sure he was more upset than usual. When Metz saw Kaem, he said, "For your sake, I hope your data was backed up."

Kaem felt surprised Metz had any thought for Kaem's problems. He continued surveying the room. He didn't see Ron's laptop and the guy didn't have a desktop. "They take anything but computers?"

Ron shrugged, "Of mine, just my laptop and my speaker system. Don't know if they got anything else of yours."

Kaem wasn't wild about his roommate, but he knew the guy was enamored of his speakers. He said, "Sorry about your sounds, man."

Ron nodded but didn't otherwise respond.

The cop in the room said, "You're the roommate?"

Kaem nodded.

"Have a look around. Let us know what they got of yours."

As Kaem walked across the room to his desk he asked, "They break into any other rooms?"

The cop said, "Apparently not. Metz here thinks they were after his sound system but I'm not sure it was worth more than that fancy monitor of yours that they left behind. How much did that monster cost?"

Kaem shrugged, "About nine hundred dollars."

The cop clicked his tongue. "You kids nowadays. You made of money or something?"

Kaem sullenly shook his head, "No, or I wouldn't be living in the dorm. It was part of my scholarship package."

"Wow, some *scholarship*," the policeman said, rolling his eyes.

Kaem checked the spot where his computer'd been sitting. Nothing there but the ends of cords. He knelt in front of the desk's footwell and peered up into the back of it. To his surprise, the external backup hard drive he'd screwed into the upper back corner was still there. He didn't mention it. Apparently, the CPU case was the only thing missing from his computer setup. He moved on, checking the rest of the room. When he pulled out his under-bed drawer he saw—without surprise—that all the electronic components of his version one stazer were gone. His initial reaction was that he shouldn't tell the cops about their loss, but then he decided he should. He wouldn't want whoever had done this— Martin Aerospace, he thought—to think he hadn't noticed or didn't care about the gear they'd gone to such lengths to get. He turned to the policeman and said, "I had a bunch of electronic gear from one of my projects in this drawer. It's all gone."

"Valuable?"

"About fifteen hundred dollars."

"You got model and serial numbers?"

Kaem sighed, "I might be able to get model numbers from the websites where I ordered them. But not until I can get on a computer. I'll have to see."

The cop spoke to his phone's AI. "I just sent you my contact info. Send me all the info you can about your gear. Sometimes we do better catching crooks who're trying to pawn weird gear than common stuff like computers." He gave a little shrug, "Though, to tell the truth, our success rate getting people's stuff back ain't great. Any chance you had insurance?"

Kaem shook his head glumly. He thought, *And there's no chance you're gonna find my stuff in a pawn shop.* He said, "You downloaded the hallway security cameras, right? You want Ron and me to see if we recognize the people who did this?"

The cop unhappily shook his head, "Somebody stuck gum over the lenses."

Though Kaem wasn't surprised, he lifted his eyebrows as if he were. "This is sounding more and more like a professional job?"

The policeman shook his head, "Professional thieves don't hit dorm rooms. You guys known to have something more valuable in here than your computers or the electronics you mentioned?"

Kaem slowly shook his head. Then he went through the motions of checking his closet, though he was sure nothing would be missing.

Nothing was.

Kaem asked, "Doesn't one camera cover the other, since they're at opposite ends of the hall? Shouldn't you be able to see the person who put the gum on the first camera in the vid from the second camera?"

"Yeah. He backed out of the stairwell last night, wrapped in a sheet and wearing gloves and a stocking cap. Rose up on his tiptoes and stuck the gum on the lens. You never get to see his face or clothes or anything."

"Maybe we'd recognize him from his mannerisms or something."

The Thunder of Engines

Ron said, "I already looked. Doesn't look like anyone I've ever seen."

The cop said, "You want to look too?"

Kaem nodded. The cop brought over his phone and showed him the video. Kaem hadn't thought about how tiny the image of the person would be with him at the far end of the hall. "You're right," he said, "I've got no clue."

The police piddled around in a desultory fashion for a while longer. This mostly consisted of taking statements and pictures and interviewing other students to see if they saw anything. They did swab for DNA in a few places but said—since the perp could be seen to be wearing gloves in the video—it likely wouldn't pay off.

Kaem said, "So this person came up in the middle of the night last night and blocked the cameras. Then returned in the middle of the day today when Ron and I were gone to carry the stuff away? But *didn't* take stuff from anyone else on the hallway? That seems like a *lot* of planning for your typical drug-addled, non-professional dorm criminal."

The cop nodded slowly. He said, "Sometimes there's no accounting for what crooks do. Most of them aren't exactly criminal masterminds."

"How'd he get into the room?"

"The door thinks it was open all morning. We think when Metz left this morning, the guy caught the door before it closed completely."

"No shit?" Kaem turned to Ron. "If he was close enough to catch the door when you left, you must've seen the guy. Any recollection of what he looked like?"

Ron shook his head. "I was late. Took off out of here at a run. Sorry."

Kaem needed another computer, but he didn't want to leave until the cops were gone. He sat on the bed, put his phone on silent, and pulled up the video record from his desktop computer's camera. He left it on all the time with the video storing in his cloud account. It started recording over the file after seventy-two hours but a record of the theft should be there. With all the planning that had gone into this Kaem wasn't hopeful. Surely whoever robbed them had disabled the camera somehow.

I'll be damned! Kaem thought when he brought up the video from that morning and the camera showed it'd been recording. *They probably covered the camera after they came in, but I might get some images of them before they occluded it.* After some thought, he realized people wouldn't expect him to be recording from the camera 24/7. It was only because of his paranoia. The same paranoia that had him using his own encryption system for his data. The paranoia that, in addition to the encryption, had him creating diagrams and descriptions of the staze process with multiple errors so if someone did hack his computer and break his encryption, they still wouldn't be able to create stade. The paranoia that kept him from writing his theory down.

As the video fast-forwarded past Kaem getting up and leaving, he pondered the fact that recording it was an invasion of Ron's privacy. *If I turn this over to the cops, Ron's going to rake me over the coals for recording without his permission.*

On the fast-forward vid, Metz reached out from under his covers, picked up his phone and made a call. He got out of bed, whirled into the bathroom, then shot across the room to put on clothes. Grabbing his backpack, he put in his laptop, then knelt by Kaem's bed and loaded the backpack with most of the electronics out of Kaem's under bed drawer.

As Kaem thought, *Son of a bitch!* Metz whirled out of the room on video, stopping to stuff a wad of paper through the strike plate and into the box in the doorframe for the deadbolt. Kaem realized *that* was why the door thought it'd been unlocked all morning. The bolt's auto mechanism couldn't throw itself.

Stunned, Kaem forced himself not to make any audible exclamations. Nor to look up at Metz. Nor to call the cop over to watch.

But his mind worked furiously.

Meanwhile, on the video, Metz sped back into the room.

Kaem thought, *He wasn't gone very long.* That phone call was probably to someone who met him in the stairwell or downstairs. I'll have to re-watch this and get times off of it.

Metz got the last of the electronics out of Kaem's under bed drawer, then put his own subwoofer in on top of them. He sped back out of the room.

Metz reappeared on the video and put his small surround speakers in the backpack. He crossed the room to Kaem's desk, bent over it, and a moment later the video recording crashed, presumably when Metz unplugged Kaem's computer.

Metz had already put everything that'd been "stolen" in the backpack, so Kaem didn't expect Metz would've reappeared on the video even if it'd still been running. The cops were still in the room, so Kaem didn't have anything better to do. He restarted the video and started noting times.

The cop in the room cleared his throat. "Okay. We've got everything we can get. We'll let you guys know if we find anything, but don't hold your breath."

Kaem frowned, "You'll let us know either way, right?"

"No. Only if we find anything."

"Surely you'll tell us what the DNA shows?"

The guy shrugged, "If he wore gloves to do the camera, he almost certainly wore them in here. DNA isn't going to show anything. We're just being thorough."

"I meant the DNA from the gum on the camera," Kaem said, noticing Ron's flinch out of the corner of his eye.

"Um, yeah. I'll let you know if it matches any of our databases."

"And you'll go through the video for a day or so before the gum went on the camera?"

"Why would we do that?"

"Well, it occurs to me that if it was someone on our floor of the dorm, someone who knew about Ron's sound system, that the camera would've recorded them on their way off the floor some hours before they returned to stick the gum on the cameras. Likely would've had a backpack stuffed full of sheets."

The cop rolled his eyes. "You think I've got nothing better to do than sit around watching video?"

"Um, no. But I did think it was your job to catch bad guys."

"Right…" the cop said glumly. "I'll do it, but it isn't going to pay off. Whoever did this didn't rob his own dorm. He'd have to be crazy to do that."

"You haven't heard how good Ron's music system sounded," Kaem said drily.

***

Kaem called Arya as soon as the campus police walked out the door. He wanted to meet at one of the eateries on the meal plan. She told him to wait for her in the lounge on the first floor of his dorm so she could act as his bodyguard again.

When he left, he wasn't surprised to see one of the policemen standing on a chair at the end of the hall, distastefully pulling the gum off the security camera.

When Arya showed up, she had a bundle under her arm. She held it out. "Here's your coat."

Irritated, he said, "I've already got a coat on."

"Take that one back upstairs. You need to wear this one."

Kaem sighed and turned back to the elevator. While he waited, he gently probed the coat he held, feeling the lumps from the vest of stade plates she'd inserted into it. When he got up to his room, he hung up his other coat and put on the stade coat. While waiting for the elevator back downstairs he patted around to figure out where the plates were located. *There aren't any up near the top of my shoulders,* he observed, realizing that they wouldn't fit the curves there. There weren't any over his arms either. *They're only on the relatively flat parts of me, because we only have flat stades. If we put them over the rounded places, they'd make the coat lumpy.* He pondered inserting them elsewhere no matter how they looked, but realized that'd draw a lot of attention. Attention they didn't need right now. *We've gotta do better than this though,* he thought. *We should at least make some curved plates.*

They walked to an eatery they didn't usually go to—worried that their usual haunts might be monitored. On the way, Kaem told Arya what'd happened.

"Your *roommate* did it?!" she exclaimed. "That's almost a relief. I mean, I'm sorry you lost your computer but you'd stoked my apprehensions to the point I was thinking it was some evil people from Martin Aerospace did it."

Kaem studied her a moment, "Arya, the evil people from Martin Aero *paid* Metz to do it."

"Oh, come on Kaem. That's just... paranoid."

"Oh, come on Arya," he parroted back at her. "Surely you don't think Metz would steal his own laptop and sound system just so he could steal my computer and some electronics he has no use for? Where's the benefit to him? He'd have to be *insane*."

Her eyes widened. "Oh..."

Kaem nodded, "'Oh' is right. Besides, each time he left the room, he was only gone long enough to reach the stairwell. He must've been handing the goods off to someone he'd called."

Arya sighed, "Crap. What'd the police say when you showed them the video?"

Shaking his head, Kaem said, "I didn't show it to them."

"What? Why not?!"

They were in line to buy food. Kaem rolled his eyes and whispered, "I don't think the Campus Police are up to dealing with this kind of thing."

"You're going to call the city cops?" Arya whispered in return.

"No. First of all, they'd turn up their noses. They'd tell me dorm robbery falls under the campus cops' jurisdiction. Second, I'm pretty sure they wouldn't know what to do with this kind of crime either. Third, I don't want Martin Aero to realize we know it's them. They might do something even more drastic."

They got their food and went to an empty area to sit. Arya asked, "What *are* we going to do then?"

Kaem shrugged, "Got any ideas?"

"No! This kind of stuff isn't covered in business classes!'

"Not covered in physics either," Kaem said unhappily.

They ate, mostly in silence, then started back to Kaem's dorm. Arya said, "Maybe you should sleep over at my apartment. Someplace they won't know to look for you."

Kaem's heart leaped, then settled. "I think they know we're associated by now. It'd probably just put you at risk." After a moment he said, "Though I'd love to… stay with you."

She punched his shoulder. "I *meant* on the couch, idiot."

"I… know. Sorry."

She didn't respond, but as they walked, she slipped her arm around his waist and leaned her head on his shoulder.

Goosebumps running down his spine, Kaem lifted his arm and started to settle it around her shoulders, then stopped uncertainly with it hovering in the air.

His arm had started to ache from being held up when she said, "It's okay. You can put it around me."

Trying not to sigh with relief, he settled his arm companionably around her shoulders.

She looked up at him and dashed his hopes. "Just this once. And please, *don't* say something stupid this time, okay?"

Kaem said nothing. As they arrived at his dorm she deftly let go and slipped out from under his arm. She opened the door and walked with him to the elevator, riding up and walking him to his room. When he opened the door, she leaned in, looked around, then stepped back and said, "See you in the morning."

Kaem paused in the doorway to sneak a glance at her walking away. Worried she might turn and catch him at it, he stepped inside and let the door close. Nodding at Metz, he tried not to let his feelings show, "Cops tell you anything?"

Metz said, "No. But I'm sorely missing my tunes."

Kaem threw himself on the bed, *Methinks thou doth protest too much.*

***

Kaem woke when he heard his phone vibrate. Rubbing bleary eyes, he looked at the screen. *Bana's calling at five-thirty in the morning?* He wondered what could've gotten his sister up so early.

Oh! Something bad.

Kaem got up and padded into the bathroom. Metz would raise hell if Kaem woke him by taking a call. "Hello, Bana. What's happened?"

"Dad's sick," she said, sounding exhausted. "We've been in the ER all night."

"Oh, no," Kaem said, heart sinking. His family was already financially destitute and didn't have health insurance. ER bills would make it far worse. "It'll take me at least half a day to get home. Maybe a lot longer, depending on when the next bus leaves. Do we know what's wrong yet?"

The Thunder of Engines

"No...," she said, a catch in her voice. "But I don't think it's good."

Kaem waited for her to tell him more, but all he heard was an odd rhythmic noise. *She's sobbing,* he suddenly understood. Bana normally played it so tough it was hard for Kaem to come to grasp with the thought of his sister in tears. "Um," he cleared his throat to try to get rid of a sudden frog. "What's been wrong with him?"

Bana cleared her throat as well. "He's been really tired and Mama hasn't been able to get him to eat. Yesterday she took his temperature and he had a fever. Trying to understand, she took his shirt off and got a good look at him. When she did she realized that even though his belly's been getting bigger, he's actually very skinny. Oh, and he has these bad sweats. He out and out *drips.*"

Could it be AIDS? Kaem wondered. He didn't think his dad had any of the risk factors for getting HIV, but Kaem knew people usually hid such risk factors, *especially* from the people they loved. And he thought AIDS victims were tired and lost weight. He didn't know about the other symptoms of the disease. "Let me check the bus schedule. I'll call you and tell you when I'm going to get there."

"No," Bana said. She gave a sad yet amused snort, "No matter how bad the crisis is here, Mom and Dad don't want their golden boy to leave his studies. Mom just asked me to let you know... you know," her voice broke and she developed a fit of coughing—Kaem thought trying to hide how upset she was. When she resumed talking her voice was strained. "Excuse me. They wanted you to know, um, in case it gets worse. I'll call you back when we know more." I'd better go now."

113 | Page

"What?" Kaem asked, trying to make a joke to lighten their bleak mood. "No begging to switch phones with me?"

Bana didn't laugh. "I'll call you. Bye."

The phone's AI dinged to announce that she'd hung up.

Another stupid joke fallen flat, he thought. *Why can't I stop?*

Sitting on the edge of the bathtub, Kaem buried his head in his hands and wept.

When he had nothing left to cry, Kaem decided to take a shower. He was all wound up and showers relaxed him.

Standing under the hot spray, his thoughts drifted back to the time his dad taught him to fight. An event that had meant a great deal to him for the way it left him feeling loved.

Then to a time in grade school. A time after his brushes with Rob Sanders—the bully who'd never bothered Kaem after he got the bloody nose. Kaem had been left alone for a year or so after the Sanders incident, likely because the class bullies were worried about what'd happened to Rob. A kid had even asked Kaem whether it was true he held a black belt in some martial art.

But then two other boys had taken Kaem on together. First, it'd been a swath of ugly words uttered on the playground. Kaem had ignored them as he'd ignored others. The next day it happened again, this time with some shoving. The day after that they crowded even closer, Kaem took his position, left side toward them, knees a little bent, right fist down at his side—and wondered which boy he'd hit if it came to it.

One of them shoved him again. Kaem staggered back, caught himself, and resumed the stance. When the boys crowded close once again, he decided he had to act. He unleashed his punch, throwing it at the boy closest to the line of strike Kaem was set up for. Kaem missed the boy's nose but hit his right cheekbone a solid thump.

A blow hard enough his fist hurt.

That boy staggered back, bawling, but his more aggressive friend tackled Kaem, driving him to the ground.

Knowing he wouldn't have the endurance to win this fight, Kaem turtled up, curling in a ball, arms around his legs, face between his knees.

The boy on top of him flailed somewhat ineffectually at his back and legs. It wasn't hurting a lot, so Kaem settled down to ride it out.

There was a scream and suddenly the boy was no longer on top of Kaem. When he peeked out from between his knees to see what'd happened, Kaem saw the boy on the ground with Bana kicking him vigorously. She was shouting. "He's sick! Can't you see that?! Why would you pick on someone smaller than you? Someone who's too sick to fight back?!"

Kaem smiled at the memory. *The little sister that protected me. When I go home to see Dad I really should swap Bana my phone.*

He started worrying about his dad again. *If it's not AIDS, what could it be?* He started his phone searching for his dad's symptoms.

There were quite a few diseases that could produce those complaints.

None of them were good.

~~~

Kaem exited the bathroom as quietly as he could and started trying to find his clothes in the dim lighting.

Metz rolled over and snarled, "Goddammit, what're you doing banging around at this hour?"

Kaem stopped stock-still in the dark, staring down at the shadows of his despised roommate with complete loathing. After a moment he turned to sit at his desk and open his laptop.

When the laptop's screen lit, Metz groaned. "For God's sake! Go down to the lounge with that damned thing!"

Kaem ignored Metz as he picked his way through menus.

Metz said, "Did you hear me?!"

Kaem said, "Ron, there's something I need to show you."

Metz pulled the covers up over his head.

Kaem rolled his chair over next to Metz's bed, angled the laptop's screen at Metz's face, then ripped the covers off the bed. "Watch!" he commanded.

Even in the dim lighting, Kaem could see Metz's eyes widen as he saw himself on his knees, taking Kaem's electronic gear out of the under-bed drawer and stuffing it in his backpack.

"Kaem, uh, I can explain."

"Oh, *this* I've gotta hear," Kaem said, sarcasm dripping from his words.

"This guy came... He, uh, threatened me."

"Which, no doubt, you reported to the police."

"No, uh, he said if I went to the police, he'd... he'd—"

"Having trouble thinking of a suitable threat he might've used?"

"He said you'd stolen that stuff from his company, and, and you'd taken some programs or designs or something."

"Uh-huh. And, of course, you believed some stranger over your roommate, did you?"

"Well, you and I haven't exactly been getting along, you know?"

"And who's the asshole there?" Kaem shook his head, "Never mind, I already know the answer to that question. This guy or his company have a name?"

"Screw you, Seba!" Metz turned his face away sullenly.

"Okay, I'll just send this file to—"

"No...!" He turned back resignedly, "What do you want?"

"The guy's name?"

"Kim. Wouldn't give me a last name."

"The company he worked for?"

"Wouldn't tell me."

"How much did he pay you?"

"He didn't. I did it because he convinced me you'd stolen that stuff."

"*Sure* you did. Ron Metz the saint. You even stole your own laptop and sound system to set things right with the world, didn't you?"

"Well, he paid me for *my* stuff. That was only fair."

"Show me the deposits."

"What?!"

"Show me the deposits from when he paid you."

"No!"

"Okay, Ron. I'm sure, with a warrant, the police can—"

"Arggh! Okay! Damnit!" Metz got out of bed and stumped over to his laptop. It took him a moment to bring up his bank account, then he pointed out a deposit.

He'd pulled the window partly off the screen. Kaem said, "Move the window so I can see the date."

Metz scoffed, but did move the window.

"So, that forty-five hundred is the payment on the day you stole my stuff."

"I *thought* I was returning *their* stolen property!"

"Keep telling yourself that, Ron. Show me their initial payment."

Putting on a puzzled look, Metz asked, "What do you mean?"

"I know you wouldn't have done the dirty work without getting a prepayment. I'm thinking half before you took anything and half on delivery. Show me that first payment."

"No, just the one payment," Metz said, scrolling back a few days without showing any deposits.

"Go back further."

Metz scrolled back a few more days.

"Come on Metz. Scroll back until I can see the other deposit."

"There's another deposit, but it's some money from my grandmother."

"And I'm sure she'll know what I'm talking about if I call her and ask if she'll vouch for you?"

A few lines farther another forty-five hundred-dollar deposit became visible.

"You really should've just kept the cash for a while, Ron."

"Okay, smart-ass. I'm not a criminal genius like you."

"I'm not a criminal at all, Ron. Transfer the money to my account."

"What?!"

The Thunder of Engines

"I don't think you should get to keep your ill-gotten gains. Transfer them to me. Oh, and I'll need a picture of this 'Kim' guy."

"No!"

"Okay, we'll see what the police have—"

"I'll tell them you're blackmailing me!"

"Ron," Kaem calmly lied, "I looked this up last night. It isn't blackmail to insist on getting the money you were paid for stealing *my* stuff."

Metz stared at Kaem, his face working. Finally, he said, "Four-thousand of that was for my laptop and sound system."

"Okay then. What models were they?"

"What? Why?"

"Because there's *no* way they were worth four thousand dollars."

"They were! And I don't know what their model numbers were!"

"Okay. Show me the receipts for the new models you replaced them with. Replacement cost is probably fairer anyway."

Metz's eyes flashed wide. He opened his mouth to object but then his shoulders slumped. He turned to his computer and he pulled up the charges for his new laptop and sound system. They totaled thirteen hundred and ninety-six-dollars.

"Okay," Kaem said. "You probably wish you hadn't bought your replacements right away, huh? Transfer seventy-six hundred and four dollars to my account."

Metz stared at him for a moment. "You're an asshole, you know?"

"Says the man who stole my electronics and computer."

Metz turned back to his laptop and made the transfer.

"While you've got it open, send me a picture of Kim."

"I don't think it's his real name."

"Send me a picture, not his name."

"I don't *have* a picture."

Kaem tilted his head and scoffed, "Ron, I know you would've snuck a picture of him. You're a cover-your-ass kinda guy."

Metz turned back to his laptop and a moment later Kaem's laptop notified him of an incoming message.

"And," Kaem said, "I need that old phone you keep as a spare."

"That'll cost you a hundred dollars," Metz said.

Kaem stared at him until he sighed and got the phone out of his drawer. Kaem reached in the drawer and took the charger himself.

Well, now I've got a little money to help out my parents, Kaem thought. *But I need to keep a bit of the money to buy a SIM card for that phone.* He asked his AI to try to find the guy in the picture of "Kim." Then he opened his browser and started checking bus schedules to figure out how long it'd take to get home.

Chapter Four

In the afternoon, Kaem—not having heard from her—called Bana. "What's the diagnosis?"

"Hi to you too brother."

"Sorry. Hi Bana. I'm worried about Dad."

"They gave him some medicine and sent him home. It's making him feel better."

"What's the diagnosis?"

"They don't know," Bana said in a flat tone. "They say they'll call when they do. I'm betting I'm going to have to call them a hundred times to get the results."

"Did they give you any ideas?"

She sighed, "No."

"I had my phone's AI look up his complaints. The… possibilities aren't good."

"Must be nice to have a high-end phone," Bana said bitterly.

Thinking of his regrets, Kaem said, "I've decided to swap phones with you when I come home to see Dad."

"No." Bana sighed, "You need it for your studies."

Kaem produced a chuckle, "Not as bad as you need it for your social life."

"Keep it," Bana said bleakly. "I don't have a social life anymore."

Oh, now that she's out of high school, her social life probably has dropped off. Kaem knew she'd taken a job doing clerical work in an office but didn't like the other women that worked there. She still lived at home to save money. *And now she's probably expecting to help take care of our dying father.* Full of remorse, Kaem said, "I want you to have it. Maybe it'll jazz up your social life."

Bana sighed, "Nothing's gonna fix *my* social life. You keep it until Dad's..." she cleared her throat, "till Dad's better."

Kaem didn't know how to respond to that. Instead, he tried a bit of good news. "I came into some money. I've transferred it into Mom's account."

Bana said nothing, so after a moment, Kaem said, "Bana?"

"I heard you. 'Came into some money?' Is that code for, 'I've been keeping some aside'? That no matter how bad off things were up here, you've had a little fund you keep for when *your* social life needs a boost? When you've had a hot date?"

No! Kaem thought. His mind flashed through several retorts including telling her the truth. Or even telling her about Staze and all its possibilities. He heard his mother's voice, *Don't count your chickens before they're hatched.* He sighed, "Yeah. That's what it is. My hot date money. Tell Mom to spend it however she needs. I don't need it back since I've never had a hot date." In a fit of resentment, he disconnected the call.

Kaem regretted hanging up on Bana but couldn't bring himself to call her back. He spoke to his phone again, telling it to call his mother.

"Hello, Kaem," she said. Despite the exhaustion and fear in her voice, she managed to sound delighted to hear from him.

"Hi, Momma. I just got some extra money. I put it in your account."

"You're sure you don't need it?"

"No Momma. And I know you do. How's Dad?"

The Thunder of Engines

"The medicine's helping some, but you're right, it's very expensive."

"Did you ask about cheaper options?"

Warmth suffused her voice. "Yes, Kaem. I learned that taking care of you. And, before you ask, I've already checked that website that tells you where to go for the best prices on the drugs. I bought enough to last a few days and mail-ordered the rest."

"Have they said...?" Kaem found it hard to go on with the sentence, but girded himself and finished, "what might be wrong with Dad?"

"No. They gave me a list of maybes. None of them were good. I'll bet you've already found most of them online."

Kaem didn't want to make her recite the terrible possibilities. "Yeah. I looked. When're they going to tell you more?"

"They have him scheduled for a bone marrow biopsy on Monday. We'll know more a few days after that."

"If I catch the late bus I can be there in the morning."

"No! Kaem, you need to stay and keep working on your degree."

"But... I've got to talk to Dad. If he's..." *Don't say "dying,"* he thought. "If he's sick... I want to talk to him." He finished in a whisper, "I'd never forgive myself if I—"

"Here, talk to him," his mother interrupted.

He heard his father's voice, "Kaem? Is that you?"

Trying not to sniffle, Kaem said, "Hi Dad. How're you feeling?"

"Much better. I don't know what this is, but the doctors are gonna figure it out. I'll be right as rain pretty soon."

He doesn't know! Kaem thought. He thought back on how his dad always said you had to face up to your problems. *Does he not know the possibilities? Or is he not facing up to them? Or is Mom hiding them from him? Or is he hiding them from me?* "I'm gonna leave tonight. I'll get home and see you in the morning."

"No, no! You need to stay there and study. I'm gonna lick this in a few more days and I'll be pissed if you get bad grades because you took a couple of days away from your classes to come visit me. Come home on your break. That way I can see you without worrying about how you're gonna pass your courses."

Kaem knew the university didn't send his grades to his parents. He thought, *I really should take my grades home with me when I go. Then he wouldn't always be worrying about me failing out.* "Okay Dad," Kaem said resignedly, "It's not long till the end of the semester. I'll see you then."

"Yeah!" his dad said. "We'll sit around and joke about how worried you were. 'I'll take the bus up here,' we'll say, imitating you. Then we'll have a good laugh."

"Yeah, we will," Kaem said, trying to sound sure of it.

After he hung up, he thought. *God, I hope Staze works out. Maybe I'll be able to take Dad to a real medical center.*

***

Ricard exploded, "What the hell, Wang!" He waved a hand at the apparently random and cheap-looking electronic components in the box Chen had brought to the meeting. "This box of loose junk isn't going to help us make stade!" He turned hopefully to Elgin Munger, "Is it? *Please* tell me this stuff means something to you."

The Thunder of Engines

Munger was staring at the box of modules in dismay. He shook his head. "I guess, if these are the components they used to make that sample, then they tell us we don't have to use high-quality stuff." He looked up and sighed, "But without knowing how it was hooked up or what the settings were..." he lifted his hands despairingly.

Ricard said, "Could you just have one of your minions hook them up in various configurations until something happens?"

Munger snorted, "Just as well sit a monkey down in front of a keyboard and see if he accidentally types out the script for Romeo and Juliet."

"Come on. You have some idea how it works from the diagrams we got off Seba's computer, don't you?"

Munger barked a derisive laugh, "Yeah, ideas like the power supply should supply power to the components. Obvious crap. The info you guys hacked off Seba's computer was for a purpose-built device, not for a bunch of separate components Seba may have used to accomplish the same thing. Or," he eyed the box askance, "components he might have been using for something else entirely."

Ricard narrowed his eyes, "Dammit Munger, this is *important*! Have one of your engineers *try* to match these components to what they might've done instead of some of the chips or other parts on the diagram for a purpose-built device. Tell him there's a bonus in it if he can figure it out."

"If *she* can figure it out," Munger said.

"What's that mean?" Ricard said irritatedly.

"The best circuit person I've got's a woman. I'll ask her to work on it, but there's still no chance we're going to build a machine that makes stade if we don't understand the theory behind it."

Ricard turned to Chen again, "This is *all* you got?"

"Got desktop computer case. Some call "CPU' because box contain central process unit, but also has hard drive an' other components. IT guy trying to decrypt drive now."

"How long is that going to take?"

"Not know. Last time took two days on supercomputer with quantum processor just decrypting one file. This Seba no joke with computers."

Ricard frowned, "Once you know how the disk is encrypted, can't you decrypt the whole thing?"

"Last time hacker stole two files while Seba is logged on computer but not watching system. That way, file computer sent was already decrypted when taken from hard drive. So, we no expect encryption at all. But, that time turns out file *separately* encrypted in addition to hard drive encryption. Decryption of one file containing diagrams took two days. We stopped because second file has *different* encryption key and many people mad about us using supercomputer. This time we have Seba's whole computer but entire hard drive encrypted. Must decrypt drive first. Maybe take two day. Maybe longer. Hope shorter. Believe then each file separately encrypted like before." Wang shook his head, "Don't know how Seba keep many different encryption keys." Chen shrugged, "Maybe has photo memory."

Ricard turned his back to swear long and hard. Still fuming, he turned back and said, "Wang! For what we're paying you, you've *got* to do better than this! We need a working model, not a bunch of loose components he probably doesn't even use any more.

Get us what he's using *now*!" Ricard restrained himself from stamping his foot ineffectually, "Come on man!"

***

Teri Nunsen got a text from April Lee. "Plane has landed. Should be at Space-Gen in forty minutes. Team meeting then to compare notes. Sign up small conference room."

All business, isn't she, Teri thought, texting back an "Okay." She pulled the little conference room up online and signed up for it. Getting up, she walked over to Evan and filled him in. Evan didn't look happy but he nodded without complaint. Next Teri headed over to Stitt's desk. "Lee's getting back at five. We're gonna meet in that same small conference room."

Stitt's eyes widened, "No way! I'm on my way out to drink beers with a couple of my buds!"

Teri studied him a moment, then turned and walked away. "I'll ask Lee who's taking your place," she said back over her shoulder. "Meantime, write up what you've learned."

"No! Wait!"

Teri kept walking.

"Teri!"

She heard his chair scrape back, then his footsteps coming rapidly after her.

"Teri! Dammit!" He grabbed her elbow and pulled her around. "I'll *be* there," he said disgustedly.

Teri looked pointedly down at her elbow until he let go.

"Sorry," Stitt muttered self-consciously.

"Get your notes and let's you and I go to the conference room. I'd like you to fill me in on what you've learned in case Lee wants you off the team."

"Come *on*, Teri! I was just upset about my plans is all. I *will* be there."

"Get your notes and let's go. I'm planning on you being there. But I need a backup plan..." she gave him a look, "in case you touch me without permission again." As she walked on, Teri couldn't help feeling a little surge of triumph, but she cautioned herself, *Don't throw Stitt off the team out of spite. His competence is not in question.*

Teri got her stuff and headed into the conference room. Stitt was only moments behind her, a relief because she didn't have to worry about whether he was slow out of insubordination.

Then he impressed her with what he'd learned and his thoughts about how they should proceed.

Really impressed her.

When Lee arrived, she started showing them pictures and describing the forms or molds the people at Staze used to create their super-material. Because the forms were mirrored inside, it was hard to grasp their shapes in the pictures. Lee said, "It's kinda hard to understand them even when you're looking at them in person. Like funhouse mirrors."

Lee spent quite a bit of time explaining what she'd learned, especially focusing on how you needed a clear material—with both surfaces mirrored—surrounding the volume you wanted to cast stade into. She pointed at the mirrors surrounding the cube-shaped mold. "These mirrors surrounding the cavity the cube is cast in are silvered, both on the side next to the cube and on the outside. Seba said you could think of it as if you

The Thunder of Engines

needed the mold form to hold light within its walls, but keep that light out of the cavity you're casting stade in."

Stitt pointed at the black man in one of the pictures. "Who's this?"

"Kaem Seba. The guy who invented stade."

"Really? He looks… unwell."

Lee nodded. "I think he's sick somehow, but it's not something we talked about."

"And what makes these forms work? You just pour the liquid in, close them up, and voila?"

Lee shook her head. "After the form's closed, Seba does a bunch of stuff with electronic gear in this rack," she brought back a picture that showed a rack for electronic gear, "that finishes with what sounds like a capacitor charging and discharging. *Then* voila."

"What's he doing? Do you have a picture that shows what kind of electronics we're talking about?"

"He wouldn't say. Wouldn't let me look at it or take pictures of it either."

Irritated that Stitt was asking all the questions, Teri broke in, "And what's the liquid substrate?"

"Looks like water." Lee said, "He acted like it wasn't though. I wondered if it might be water with something dissolved in it."

Stitt frowned, "You sure he wasn't doing some kind of sleight of hand. Distracting you with the electronics while a piece of stade just got slipped into the form?"

Lee studied him, "What good would that do them?"

He looked abashed, "I don't know. I'm just a suspicious sort, I guess."

Lee reached into her suitcase and carefully lifted out a six-inch cube of stade. "Here's one they made in front of me. It's water density." She two-handed it to Teri,

"Don't let it get away from you, 'cause it's over seven pounds. If it lands on your toe it'll hurt."

Evan asked, "Did they put something different in the mold to come out with water density?"

Lee shook her head, "Poured in the same stuff as far as I could tell." She went back into her suitcase and pulled out another six-inch cubical block. "This one's air density." She turned it over, "Notice it has a cavity in the back, shaped a little bit like the bell of a rocket nozzle. Kaem said he'd just wrapped a drinking glass in aluminum foil and set it in the form to create the cavity."

"So, it doesn't *have* to be mirrored glass?" Teri asked.

"Apparently not. I'm pretty sure Seba figured that out by trying the glass and foil while I was there. He said his theory predicts we can use any transparent solid with reflective surfaces on both sides, but he hasn't had time to try others out. When you're feeling the inside of the cavity the glass left in the stade cube, you'll notice you can kind of feel wrinkles left by the aluminum foil. They're smoothed out by the fact that features under one millimeter don't form."

"Geez," Stitt said, "it's like these guys are amateurs!"

"Yeah," Evan responded, "but, amateur or not, their product's... freaking unbelievable."

At that point, Teri, Jerome, and Evan took turns telling Lee what they'd accomplished while she'd been flying to Virginia and back.

Teri'd found two glass fabricators she thought could make suitable molds. She'd been planning on solid molds but knew they blew glass too. She thought they'd be able to blow a hollow mold for the inside of the combustion chamber. They claimed they'd be able to

The Thunder of Engines

grind and polish the junctions between the mold segments so the fit would leave defects smaller than a millimeter. For a premium, they said they'd be able to rush the production to complete the molds in less than a week.

Jerome Stitt had found designs for a thirty-six-centimeter-tall hydrogen-oxygen motor and modified it for stade.

Lee interrupted, "What modifications?"

"It was designed to feed a layer of unburned fuel against the inner surfaces to prevent engine rich exhaust. I eliminated those design factors, so we should get more efficiency."

"Engine rich exhaust?" Evan asked.

Teri impatiently answered, "When the walls of the engine melt and join the exhaust flume." She turned back to Stitt. "Are you sure this's going to improve efficiency?"

Stitt shrugged, not looking offended. "Pretty sure. Even if it doesn't generate more thrust, I'm almost positive the exhaust'll be hotter. That'll test stade's heat tolerance more thoroughly."

Lee said, "Okay. Evan. I assume you designed us a cryotank?"

Evan put up his design. He was planning a cylindrical tank cast in two pieces that would be screwed together.

Lee asked how he was planning to prevent leakage through the poorly fitting threads.

"The threads are only to force the surfaces together."

"The surfaces won't fit perfectly and won't be able to be forced into a better fit because stade's so rigid."

"We'll use an indium washer. Even at cryogenic temperatures, it's malleable enough to perfect the fit."

He shrugged, "If the threads won't do it, we'll have to use a crapload of bolts."

Lee said, "Redo it with a crapload of bolts. We want *this* one to work. We can try fancy stuff after we're not spending a million dollars a week."

Lee told them about Kaem's idea that the rocket body should be made out of stade as well to lower stress on the plumbing between the tank and the engine. "In fact, I've been wondering if the tanks could be integral to the rocket body." She waved dismissively, "But that's for version 2.0 as well. I've also been wondering if multiple engine nozzles could be cast into one block at the back of a bigger rocket rather than bolting on a bunch of separate engines."

Stitt got a distant look for a moment, then said, "That'd probably work except for thrust vectoring. Without mounting the engines on gimbals you'd have to try to direct the rocket with differential thrust by feeding less fuel to the engines on the side you wanted to turn toward."

Lee looked distant for a moment, then said, "Okay, send me your design drawings. I'm going to message Mr. Prakant and tell him I can talk to him at his convenience, tonight if he wants." She shrugged, "Probably tomorrow morning."

"You want us to come with you?" Teri asked.

"Good idea. I'll ask him. It'd be nice for you guys to get some face time with the man. That's if he's willing." She stood up, then sat back down. "I forgot. Seba said they'd cast testing objects for us for free. Bolts, nuts, pipes, fittings, ratchets to lock pipes so they'd stay screwed together. We can also make molds out of metalized clear plastics to see if that works. Start thinking and working up such items. Just get molds made for them and we'll take them out there next time we go. We especially need to know how we're going to join pieces of this stuff."

***

Mahesh Prakant arrived early for a before-hours meeting with April Lee. He was pleased to see she was already waiting and had the three young engineers of her team with her. She began with her preliminary assessment that Staze, the company making stade, likely *could* make rocket engines. She showed him a fifteen-centimeter cube of stade they'd made for her during her visit. It had a cavity in one side shaped somewhat like a rocket nozzle. She said it'd been cast using a drinking glass.

She said, "Looking at this block made me wonder whether there'd be an advantage to casting multiple rocket nozzles in a single large block across the five-meter base of the new launch booster. Then we'd just bolt combustion chambers on top of them."

Prakant shook his head, "If the nozzles were all in one large block you wouldn't be able to gimbal the nozzles to correct the flight path."

Lee said, "Following the KISS principle, using stade, we could put vanes directly into the exhaust path of the engines. Angling them to vector the thrust would likely be much cheaper than gimbaling the motors."

Prakant blinked, feeling his eyebrows rise, "But when the boosters land..." He paused when his thought process caught up with what he was saying.

Lee nodded, "Made from stade, the vanes would be strong enough to support the booster, though I suppose they might damage the landing pad. It's hard to adapt to the phenomenal properties of this material, isn't it?"

Prakant nodded. Used to being the best and brightest, it was humbling to have a junior engineer point out such an—obvious in retrospect—thing to him. He said, "Undoubtedly it's going to change *all* of engineering."

Lee had the other members of her team report on how they'd found glass fabricators they believed would be able to create the molds for casting engines, and how they'd designed a small engine and cryotank that would enable them to be sure stade would function in those specific and extreme situations.

Slowly he said, "We don't need to know anything more. We need to buy an exclusive license for stade from them."

"For engines *and* cryotanks sir?"

"No! For the material itself. We'll want to be the company that brings it to the world. There are so many..." Prakant blinked. "This stuff's going to change the *world*. Not just rocketry. *Everything*. With the license for stade, Space-Gen would quickly become the most important company in the world, not just in space launch."

"Um, sir," Lee said, "I asked them about a license for all products and they gave me a definitive 'No.' Seba, the inventor, said they were going to develop everything else. They're only willing to give us a time-limited exclusive license because they need capital to be able to develop stade for other uses."

"Time-limited?!"

"Yes, sir. He said three years, though I got the impression he just picked that number out of the air. We could try to negotiate for more."

The Thunder of Engines

"If they won't license it for all uses, what *are* they willing to license it to us for?"

"Rocket engines and cryotanks for sure. He mentioned that if the rocket body was made of stade, it'd decrease strains on the fuel feeds. Strains resulting from deformations in the frame holding the tanks and engines in position relative to one another." She frowned, "So, from that, I'm assuming we could get them to make the rockets bodies out of stade. Or, perhaps we could make the tanks integral to the rocket's body." She shrugged, "He also mentioned we might want high-density, high-weight stade for a launch blast shield. So, maybe they'd be willing to cast anything we need for the entire rocketry program. But I'm pretty sure they don't want us building bridges or skyscrapers."

Feeling dazed, Prakant gave his head a quick, sharp shake to clear his mind. "We've got to go talk to Aaron. You've got your samples and spec sheets?"

Lee nodded.

As he got up and headed for the door of his office. Prakant said, "Let me have the spec sheets. Come with me, all of you."

Behind him, he heard one of the young engineers ask, "Aaron *Marks*?"

Looking back over his shoulder, Prakant said, "Yup. And you know you'd better be at the top of your game talking to *our* CEO, right?" All four of the young engineers nodded, "Yes, he's a genius. Yes, he's a hardass. But he's actually a nice guy. It's just that he will *not* stand for anything less than your best." As Prakant walked by Mary's desk he said, "Cancel my first two appointments this morning. Let Aaron know we're coming and we need some time to make a presentation. Tell him it's probably the most important thing he'll hear this decade."

Mary said, "Yes, Mr. Prakant."

He shook his head and spoke back over his shoulder to the young engineers, "Probably the most important thing this century. I hope we're in time."

~~~

Lee found herself hurrying just to keep up with Prakant. "In time for what, Mr. Prakant?"

"In time for us to get some kind of toehold in this tech. I blew it when you came to talk to me. I shouldn't have had you trying to prove stade was good enough for rocketry. I should've been moving heaven and Earth to get us in on the ground floor."

"Um, they got calls from Orbital Systems and Martin Aerospace while I was there."

"Dammit!" Prakant sighed as he rounded the corner into the CEO's suite. "I'll be lucky if Aaron doesn't fire me on the spot."

Prakant almost ran into Marks, who smiled and said, "I always knew I'd have to fire your ass someday Mahesh. Why's *today* the day?

Prakant held out the spec sheet with stade's properties.

Marks took it, eyes sweeping downward as his forehead furrowed. Lee estimated he'd only gotten halfway down the page before his eyes rose to focus on Prakant. "What the hell's *this*?"

Prakant squared his shoulders, "My reaction too. I was so stiff-necked I just trashed the first sheet I saw with these properties on it—"

"Well, of course," Marks interrupted, "but what the hell—"

The Thunder of Engines

Prakant interrupted in his turn, "Then they sent us a sample of the material and we tested it in our own lab." He held out a second sheet. Lee recognized the sheet she'd prepared for Prakant based on her own testing.

Marks looked over this sheet. "Who ran this up? It doesn't look different."

Prakant waved at Lee, "April Lee, one of our junior engineers. Prefers to go by Lee."

When Marks' intense gaze fell on her, Lee felt like stepping back. She forced herself to hold her ground. "There are some differences, sir. The density listed on the sheet they sent us was one gram per cc. The density of water. The density of the specimen we received was the same as air. All the other differences we found show the material's even better than they claimed. I think that's because the material's properties are beyond what their, or even our—presumably better—equipment can measure."

Marks frowned, "Beyond what we can *measure*?"

"Yes, sir. So much stronger than steel that the hardened steel in our testing fixture fails before it does. Melting temperature so high we can't generate such temperatures—"

"Wait," Marks interrupted, "what about electron guns or induction furnaces?"

"It's so reflective the electron gun just bounces off," Lee said. "Absolutely non-magnetic and completely unaffected by the induction furnace." She pulled out her test specimen on its string, "This specimen spent several minutes mounted inside the combustion chamber of the Z-5.1 test engine at full thrust." She glanced at her boss, "I didn't tell Mr. Prakant this, but the mount melted and this specimen got fired out the nozzle and bounced off the blast shield. It was completely undamaged. It did gouge a chunk out of the blast shield. That's where I came up with the heat tolerance number. From the known combustion chamber temperatures... but I'll bet it'll tolerate much higher temperatures than that."

Marks studied Lee a moment, then reached for the specimen.

She held it out, saying, "Its coefficient of friction's zero. Handling..." she broke off when he grabbed it and his fingers slipped off. "Um, sir, you might want to take it by this string," she said, holding the end of the string out to him.

Wide-eyed, Marks gingerly took the string. He stared at the three by six-inch plate as it floated in the air on the end of the string. "Holy crap!" he breathed. Holding it by the string he grabbed the other end with his fingers again, Lee thought just to feel it slip away. Not, as with so many others, because he just didn't believe what'd happened the first time. His next step was to trap the two ends of it with a cluster of fingers and put his thumbs in the middle so he could try to bend it.

Marks' eyes dropped to the datasheet and went over it more slowly. He said, "I'm resisting a *powerful* impulse to call bullshit." He looked up at Prakant, "I don't want to doubt Ms. Lee, but has anyone else confirmed her test results?"

Prakant nodded at the datasheet, "You'll see the test facility's engineers signed off on that. I, ah," Prakant glanced at Lee as if a little embarrassed, "called them to be sure they had seen the tests and stood behind those results.

Marks looked up from the sheet. "If this... 'stade' truly has these properties it'll revolutionize the world. Rocketry would benefit immensely, yes, but almost

The Thunder of Engines

anything could be made better with this stuff. How much does it cost?"

"Unclear, sir. They've said they'll make rocket engines out of it for two million dollars each. About the same price as our current engines."

"Ah," Marks said thoughtfully, "if it's that expensive that'll limit the number of applications where it'll be cost-effective. How's it made?"

"That's also unclear, sir," Lee said. "When I visited them, my impression was that they probably don't have a patent yet. They certainly did their best to keep me from getting any idea how the process works."

Marks turned to a table and chairs at the end of his large office. He gestured to the entire group. "Sit down." To Lee, he said, "Tell me exactly what you did see."

Lee carefully described her day with Kaem, Arya, and Gunnar. Marks didn't interrupt her description, but when she finished explaining everything she thought important, he had questions.

"You really think those three people are all the employees they have?"

"Yes, sir."

"Not having a patent would be insane. What makes you think they don't?"

"If they had a patent, they wouldn't have been so reluctant for me to see the details of their setup."

"This fluid they poured in the molds. You said it looked like water?"

"Yes, sir."

"Clear, non-viscous, no odor, right?"

Lee nodded.

"Did you do a search to see what other liquids match those properties?"

"Yes, sir. Water solutions, some with quite high levels of various chemicals dissolved in them. Some silicone fluids. Some hydrocarbons have low odor. I didn't get very close, so I might not have noticed the smell from one of those."

"Find anything so expensive it'd justify a cost of two million per engine?"

"No, sir. Um…"

"Um, what? Don't be afraid to speak your mind. Unless, of course, you're about to say something stupid."

"Sorry, sir. I don't have any evidence to back this up, but I think they're starting with rocket engines *because* they can charge so much and we'll pay it. I don't think it costs them very much to make stade. It's just that they're trying to accumulate capital so they can develop other products."

Marks turned to Prakant, "We'll just fly out there and buy the whole damned company. Tell your people we're going to be gone a day or two." He turned to Lee, "Call… what's the company called?"

"Staze, sir."

"Call Staze and tell them we're on our way. Ask if we can meet with them late this afternoon. We'll talk more on our way." Marks lifted his phone and told it to connect him to his admin. Once the admin came on, Marks said, "Cancel my meetings for today and tomorrow. Call Cary Lark and Saul Izzo. Tell them I need them to come with me. Have them prep the plane. We're flying to…?" Marks looked at Lee.

"Charlottesville Virginia, sir."

Marks frowned at her, "Have you already talked to Staze?"

"No, sir."

The Thunder of Engines

"Get on it! If they can't meet, I don't want to have mobilized all these people for nothing."

As Lee backed away to a corner of Marks' office to call Kaem, Marks turned to Prakant, "We'll take these junior engineers with us but pick out a couple of seniors too. Will Goran for one. Why is it that I should fire you?"

Lee shook her head. Marks was famous for making rapid-fire decisions and moving quickly but this was the first time she'd seen it in action. "Kaem?" she asked when her phone made a connection.

The phone said, "He's replying by text."

She pulled it from her face and looked at it. The text said, "Am in class. Can you text?"

She entered a text. "Aaron Marks wants to fly out to meet with you. We'll be there this afternoon. Would you be able to meet?"

"Yes," was his only response.

For a moment she felt surprised. Marks was such a celebrity that surely Seba would've recognized the name. If Lee'd gotten a call like that while she was still in school, in a heartbeat she'd been out of class and taking the call. *But, then, I hadn't invented stade.*

***

In Space-Gen's private jet on its five-hour flight to Charlottesville, Marks had Lee review the story of how she'd evaluated stade for the other senior engineers as well as for Cary Lark, Space-Gen's CFO and Saul Izzo, their chief legal counsel. Lark expressed her doubts about the proposed value of stade, which brought grins to the faces of the other engineers, but Marks bent over in paroxysms of mirth.

141 | P a g e

Lee didn't like it that Marks had laughed at one of the other two women on the trip—and a senior one at that—but she couldn't help but find it funny that Lark couldn't see stade's value.

When Marks had stopped laughing, he said, "Cary, rest assured it's worth more than you can imagine. You're not here to evaluate its financial prospects, you're here to figure out how we can offer them so much money they won't be able to turn us down."

Lee told them what she knew about how stade was made. The other junior engineers contributed their bits on how they thought they'd be able to fabricate molds and the thinking that'd gone into the small engine and cryotank they'd intended to make as test runs.

Will Goran said, "Seems like a good idea to me. Why aren't we proceeding with the test runs?"

Prakant answered before Marks did, "Will, they didn't just offer stade to *us*. Presumably, they sent it to everyone in the space launch business. We know they've gotten a call from Orbital Systems. They got one from Martin Aerospace while Lee was out there."

"I thought we had some kind of legal agreement that they had to let us bid?"

"Yeah," Prakant said, "but it's costing us a million dollars a week just to hold that right to bid against anyone who beats us to it. What we want is to be the *first* bidder. The one who locks them up *before they get any other bids*. *And*, before we spend our second million just holding the rights. I do *not* want to be bidding against seven other companies!" He rubbed his neck, "What we want are the rights to stade itself. For everything that might *ever* be made out of it. Because if Lee's right and it's cheap... there are *so* many things it'd be better for than what we're using at present... it-it

The Thunder of Engines

beggars the imagination. So, everyone, try to think of leverage we might use to make *that* deal."

***

When Kaem left his last class of the morning, he sat and reviewed his notes a while, trying to distract himself from spiraling into worry about his dad. When that wasn't working very well, he turned to thinking about stade. That worked pretty well until Arya arrived to pick him up. It felt silly, having her once again protecting him everywhere he went. It seemed unlikely that whoever was trying to steal the secret of stade would take a chance on injuring him—as long as he was the only person in the world who knew how to make it.

But he liked being with Arya. Liked it a lot. So, it wasn't in his best interest to try to deflect her from her self-assigned mission to protect him.

Besides, even if the presumed bad guys didn't injure him, they might still *hurt* him, trying to make him spill his secrets. Kaem was not fond of pain.

Feeling antsy, he was glad when she arrived. As they started out the door, he said, "Can we stop by your place and pick up the electronics?"

She gave him a look—one he interpreted meant she *didn't* want him at her place. She said, "I can bring it by your place tomorrow morning."

"Oh, sorry, I forgot to tell you Aaron Marks is coming. So, I thought it'd be good—"

"Aaron Marks, CEO of Space-Gen?"

"Uh-huh, so I—"

"How could you *possibly* forget to mention that?!"

"I, uh, got a text from Lee while I was in class. I was distracted."

"When's he getting here?!"

"I'm..." Kaem shrank back, knowing she wouldn't be happy, "not sure."

Arya slapped his shoulder, "Well, *find out*! We are *not* going to take *Marks* to the Cavalier Buffalo."

Kaem frowned, "You're supposed to protect me. Not hit me yourself! Besides, Marks has a down to earth rep. He might like the Buffalo."

"Kaem, we can't take the CEO of a major corporation to a dive bar! Text your little girlfriend and ask her when they're arriving."

"Girlfriend?"

Arya huffed, "April *freaking* Lee. *Text* her!"

"Yes, ma'am," Kaem said, fumbling for his phone. Once he'd sent the text, he said, "Can we get the electronics? We might need them if Marks wants a demo. Besides, I've got some ideas I'd like to try."

Eyes straight ahead, Arya said, "I used some of the money Space-Gen sent us to pay rent on Staze's building."

"Good. What about the rack?"

"I don't feel good about doing it. I don't think we should be spending that money."

"I've heard that one of the first principles of business is that you have to spend money to make money."

"The principle right before that one is 'don't spend money that isn't yours.'"

"Come on Arya. Be bold. Don't get timid and screw up this deal. Let's get the rack of gear."

She stopped, turned, put her hands on her hips, and glared at him.

"I like the way you look when you're being fierce."

She shoved him back.

The Thunder of Engines

Kaem stumbled but caught himself. "I'm serious. Save that savage expression for negotiations with Marks. I hear he's a sharp dealer."

She turned and looked away, arms folded over her chest, "Dammit Kaem…"

Kaem stepped close, "Hey… I didn't mean to get you upset. You were looking like such a hard-ass… um, I didn't think there was *any* way I could throw you off your game." She didn't say anything, so he followed that with, "Miss 'kick-anyone's-butt' Vaii."

Her shoulders jerked a tiny bit. *Is she crying?!* Kaem leaned around to look at her, but she turned her head even farther. *Shit! She's in tears.* Saying, "Arya?" Kaem gingerly reached out and put his hand on her shoulder.

She spun violently away from the contact. "*Don't* touch me!"

"I'm sorry," Kaem said, surprised at the cracking sound in his voice. Then he thought about all the emotions that'd had him crying last night about his dad. *That stuff's probably spilling over into… whatever's going on here.* He dropped his hand to his side and stood stock-still, wondering how he'd messed up this time and what he could possibly do that wouldn't make things worse. *Is she this worried about the money? Afraid of what Martin Aero might do? Despite the way she pushes me away at every opportunity, could she be jealous of "April-freaking-Lee"?*

Kaem's phone spoke in his earbud, "You have a text from April Lee."

Kaem considered checking it. After all, Arya would want to know what it said. He decided now was not the time. *But what should I do? I can't just stand here doing nothing!*

Suddenly Arya spun and put her arms around him, burying her head in his shoulder. Little jerking motions confirmed she was definitely sobbing. *Maybe doing nothing was the right answer?* He slowly lifted his hands and carefully patted at her back. "I'm sorry," he whispered. "I shouldn't…" *STOP talking!* he thought at himself. *It only causes trouble.* Instead, he settled for enjoying the sensation of her arms around him.

After a minute or so, Arya's arms slipped from around him and her hands went to her face, Kaem thought to wipe at tears. That done, she stepped back and turned. As she started to walk away, she said, "Let's go get your damned rack of gear."

Kaem skipped a couple of steps, almost catching up. "I'm sorry—"

"Just *shut up*," she said hoarsely. "We're going to get your gear. Be happy with that."

"I am happy. Thanks," Kaem slowed slightly and looked down at his phone. "Um, Marks is supposed to land about four this afternoon."

Arya didn't answer, just walked even faster.

What's going on? he wondered. Why didn't she say anything? He reviewed the last things she said. Oh. She told me to shut up and—of course—I didn't. I must seem like a huge pain in the ass. He followed her silently until she started up a long hill. It wasn't terribly steep, but he soon felt short of breath. Not wanting to induce a sickle crisis, he slowed down until he wasn't having trouble, meanwhile, she got farther and farther ahead.

Arya was a full block and a half ahead when she turned left at a corner.

Oh-oh, Kaem thought, *If she turns again at the next corner, I could lose her.* He relaxed; *I can always call her if I do.*

The Thunder of Engines

However, a few moments after she turned the corner, she reappeared. She stood with her hands on her hips, presumably glaring at him for a couple of seconds, then suddenly relaxed her stance and started trotting toward him. Arriving, she gave him a quick, intense hug, then let go, leaned back, and said, "Sorry. I'm such an ass. I forgot about your anemia." She looked intently into his eyes, "Are you okay?"

Reminding himself to stay "shut up," Kaem merely nodded.

She said, "The thought of starting my life a couple hundred thousand dollars in debt to Martin Aerospace has me really scared."

Kaem opened his mouth to remind her of all the evidence pointing to the fact that Martin Aero didn't know how to make stade, therefore must not have a patent or even a valid application for one. Then he forcefully made himself shut his mouth. He swallowed, then softly said, "I know. I'm sorry."

She hugged him again and whispered in his ear, "Thanks for not saying, 'don't worry.'"

Did I just say the right thing?! Kaem wondered.

Arya let go and started back up the street at a more measured pace, asking him solicitously whether she was going too fast or not.

When they arrived at her apartment complex, she didn't invite him up, telling him to wait downstairs while she got the electronics. There wasn't an elevator, leaving him to wonder whether she left him downstairs to keep from stressing him going up the stairs, or to keep him out of her place.

She'd only been in her apartment a few seconds when she popped out onto the balcony, "Kaem. What time did you say Marks was going to be here?"

"About four."

She studied him for a moment, "You've *got* to change your clothes. Call us an Uber, then tell Gunnar to meet us at Staze. I'll make us a reservation at Argent for seven. How many people is Marks bringing with him?"

Kaem shrugged.

"Find out," she directed stepping back into her apartment and closing the door.

Kaem rolled his eyes, then sent Lee another text, asking the size of their party. He ordered an Uber, then called Gunnar. When Gunnar picked up, Kaem asked if he could meet Marks with them at Staze. As he'd suspected, Gunnar was an admirer of the superstar tech CEO, therefore quite excited. He asked, "Can you bring some aluminum foil and some old drinking glasses so we can make more demonstration stades with cavities in them?"

"Sure," the normally crotchety old man said, without complaint for a change.

He's gushing like a little girl, Kaem thought.

It was only about five minutes, but when Arya left her apartment, she looked stunning. She always looked good, but Kaem had no idea what she'd done to make herself look so... put together.

As the Uber pulled up, he dared ask, "You feel better?"

She nodded. "Did a brief relaxation-meditation technique my sensei taught me." She took a deep breath, "You'd probably say I 'got my shit together.'"

Kaem and Arya took the Uber to his dorm, where they had it wait while they went up to Kaem's room so Arya'd be able to be sure Kaem picked out his most suitable clothes.

The Thunder of Engines

As they walked into the dorm dragging the suitcase with the electronics—which they wouldn't think of leaving in an Uber—Kaem said, "Come on Arya. They won't care what I'm wearing. They just care what we're selling."

She shrugged offhandedly. "That may be true, but nice clothes make a subliminal impression. We need every advantage we can get if we're going to negotiate with Aaron freaking Marks."

"Maybe we need to make the impression that we're poor so he'll be nice to us."

Arya stared at him a moment, then said, "Shut up, Kaem. I don't tell you how to do physics, don't you try to tell me how to do business."

"You sure are telling me to 'shut up' a lot lately."

Imitating his tone, she replied, "You sure do *need* to be told to shut up a lot lately."

Arriving in Kaem's room, they found Ron Metz sprawled on his bed. He took one look at the suitcase Arya was pulling and raised an eyebrow, "What? Are you moving in?"

Arya stepped closer to Metz, bent, and spoke in a breathy voice. She said, "Kaem won a bet, and I owe him a *wild* sex session. Can you be a good boy and make yourself scarce for about thirty minutes?"

Kaem's hair stood on end. *What?!*

Metz looked stunned but scrambled to his feet. He stared at Kaem a moment, mumbled, "You owe me big time," and left the room.

Arya turned and saw Kaem's wide eyes, "What? It got him out of here, didn't it? Which closet's yours?"

Wordlessly, Kaem pointed. Despite being highly distracted by what Arya'd said, *and* by how good she looked, and somewhat by the way she cursed each time

149 | *P a g e*

she pulled another item out of his closet; he did notice that he had a package. *My Mylar?* he wondered. He glanced again at Arya, then tore open the package. *Yes!*

Kaem called Gunnar and asked him to bring whatever he thought he'd need to try using the Mylar as a form for making stade.

Arya turned to him. "That turtleneck and the black slacks you wear to Curtis's parties. Is that... the best you've got?"

Kaem shrugged, embarrassed, "I guess so."

"Are these the slacks?" she asked, holding up a hanger.

He nodded.

"Where's the turtleneck?"

Kaem pulled open a drawer.

"I've *got* to take you shopping," she muttered, but held up the turtleneck, looking at it from both sides before she folded it neatly and handed it to Kaem.

~~~

As they walked into Staze's freshly rented building, Arya asked, "How many in Marks' party?"

Kaem got out his phone, "Ten."

"Ten?! Crap! I'll bet we can't get a reservation for thirteen." She started making calls.

Gunnar arrived at Staze a few minutes after they did. He laid out his molds for the six-inch cubes and the three- by six-inch test plates. Kaem set up the rack of electronics and started plugging all the wires together correctly. That done, they made a hundred-second stade in each form to be sure everything worked. Those stades would be gone long before Marks and his people arrived.

Done, Gunnar turned to Kaem, "Is that the Mylar?"

Kaem nodded, "It's the thickest they had in stock that was aluminized on both sides. They can custom make thicker, but I'm hoping this'll work for proof of concept."

Feeling it, Gunnar said, "I've worked with Mylar a lot and this's way thicker than any I've ever seen." He looked around, "You just want to wrap it around some object and see if we can staze it?"

Kaem waggled a hand, "We could just form a bag, stick the microwave emitter head in the opening, tie it off and then staze the air inside the bag. I'm afraid the hard part'll be getting the laser emitter to fire into the Mylar *between* the reflective surfaces."

Gunnar cut out a four by eight-inch piece of the Mylar, folded it double, then ran a power tool down the two edges.

"What's that?" Kaem asked, surprised.

"Ultrasonic welder. Pretty good for welding plastics together." He picked up the piece of Mylar and demonstrated that the two sides had been firmly welded together, making a bag out of it.

He said, "You might consider getting Mylar that's only metalized on one side. You'd have them lay two sheets face-to-face, with the aluminized surfaces on the outside. Then they'd weld together the entire sheets, all but a strip along the edges. That'd make double-thick, double metalized Mylar with edges that are split apart a little way. To get the light inside the Mylar where you want it, you could stick the laser emitter head in between the unwelded edge flaps."

Gunnar turned the bag inside out so the seams were on the inside. Moving to the folded end, he pulled out a knife and scraped a little hole in the reflective coating. "Hand me the end of the light guide for your laser."

Kaem did and Gunnar held the end of the fiberoptic cable against the defect in the reflective coating. "Pretty good fit," he said after inspecting it. "Turn on the laser and let's see if we can see light leaking out the edges of the Mylar."

Sure enough, when Kaem turned it on, the exposed edges of the Mylar brightened.

Gunnar said, "Let me get a microwave emitter head to stuff into the end of the bag. You pass me your cable and we'll see what happens."

Kaem laid the cable out next to the Mylar bag, then set about adjusting the settings on his racked electronics.

Gunnar jacked in the emitter head, stuffed it a little way into the end of the bag, and wrapped the electrical tape tightly around it to squeeze the Mylar bag closed. He put the light cable for the laser against the hole he'd scraped in the reflective surface and nodded at Kaem. As soon as he heard the snap of the capacitor's discharge, he set down the light cable and poked the bag. "It's hard!" he said with a satisfied tone, starting to unwind the electrical tape.

A moment later he slid the bag off a lumpy, deformed stade the shape of the partially collapsed Mylar bag.

Gunnar's eyebrows went up as Kaem excitedly punched the air.

Arya asked what'd happened. Once Kaem explained, she said, "It's a doggy bag?"

Kaem nodded.

When Gunnar asked what the hell that meant, Arya explained how they thought they could keep leftovers until the next night by stazing them.

The Thunder of Engines

He turned to Arya, "There'll be a lot of other uses for staze bags though." Before she could start asking questions, he handed the lumpy stade back to Gunnar and said, "Put it in the cube-shaped stazer and hook up the cables. I've got an idea I want to try."

Gunnar took the ends of the cables over and hooked them up to the cube, then opened the door to put the stade inside. He halted, staring into the chamber and exclaimed, "Aw, shit!"

"What?"

"I forgot. We ruined the cube mold when you had me scrape out a ring of the silvering for that drinking glass trick of yours."

Kaem winced, but then said, "Tape a piece of aluminum foil over the scraped area. It might still work."

Grumbling about how the forms were looking more and more like kludges, Gunnar did so, carefully taping the aluminum foil down.

Kaem said, "Put the little stade in there."

Gunnar shook his head and closed the door with the box empty, "Let's do one thing at a time. First, we make sure we can make an ordinary stade."

Kaem rolled his eyes, but busied himself changing a lot of the settings on the electronics.

"You have to change it that much just because it doesn't have a stade in there?" Gunnar asked.

"You're just going to have to wait and see," Kaem said as the capacitor charged.

As soon as it snapped, Gunnar opened the door. Breathing a sigh of relief, he said, "It worked!" He started working his knife in between the walls of the cube and the stade that filled the cavity. A cube of stade popped out and he heaved it up and out into the room.

It stopped a few feet up as wind resistance, in combination with its lack of mass, caused it to halt, floating. "There, that'll be a nice conversation piece for when Marks arrives."

Kaem shook his head, "Sorry, it's only a hundred-second stade. It'll be gone before they get here. We can make another if you want, but first, can you put the stade from the Mylar bag in the chamber?"

"Okay," Gunnar said, trapping the lumpy little stade and putting it in the chamber. As he closed the door, he said, "I guess you're right, we *haven't* formed a stade with an existing stade in the chamber before. What do you think's going to happen?"

Kaem blinked, then slowly said, "I think another stade would form with the first stade inside of it."

"So, one big stade then?"

"No..." Kaem said, thinking furiously, "Because, if the first stade was set for a longer period of time, when the second, outer, stade disappeared, the first one would still be there."

"Oh," Gunnar said, eyes sightlessly staring at the mold. "Now that would be a *bitch* of a murder. Someone goes in a stade to wait ten years for a cure for his disease. His wife puts that stade inside a *slightly* bigger stade set to wait ten years and a month. His first stade collapses after ten years and he finds himself inside the bigger stade, quickly running out of oxygen. Or if there was an opening he could get air through, he'd slowly starve in complete darkness. Sad way to go."

Arya had appeared behind Gunnar, just as he started into this description. At the conclusion, she whacked the man's shoulder. *Hard.* "Gunnar! That's *terrible!* I can't believe you even *thought* of something like that!"

The Thunder of Engines

He crouched and shrank away from her, looking back over a shoulder at her as if trying to decide if she were truly angry or merely teasing. "*Hey...!* Um, we've got to consider the ways our tech can be used for evil so we can think of ways to prevent—"

"No! You sounded like a little boy gleefully pulling legs off an insect." Arya said, lifting her hand again.

Gunnar leaped out of the chair and stepped away from her, staying low with his hands up to fend her off. "You've never watched a horror movie where someone got bricked into a wall?"

"No!"

"Well, sorry, Ms. Goody Two-Shoes," Gunnar said, straightening haughtily, "other, perfectly fine human beings *do* think about such things."

"Would you two grow up?" Kaem asked as the capacitor snapped. "Open the door and let's see what happened."

Arya and Gunnar held their stare-down a moment longer, then Arya turned to the cubical stade mold and opened the door. She glanced into the empty chamber and said, "I guess it didn't work. What were you trying to do?"

Gunnar was gaping at the empty chamber. "What happened to the stade from the bag?" He turned to look at Kaem, "Did you take it out while we..." He glanced back at the chamber, "You didn't... did you?"

Exasperatedly, Arya asked, "*What* happened?" She looked at Kaem who was ecstatic.

Kaem punched the air for the second time of the day. "It worked! It freaking worked! I got to thinking about the theory and wondered if we could *undo* stasis with a frequency shift." He punched the air again, "Turns out we can!"

155 | Page

Arya said, "So, you could take your doggy bag out of stasis whenever you were ready to eat?"

Kaem laughed, "Sure. Or your gourmet five-star restaurant meal from Tuscany, prepared last year, put in stasis and delivered to you by boat. Take it out of stasis and it's ready to eat, still steaming hot." He grinned, "More importantly, remember how you were worried about how we might be littering the world with million-year stades?" At her nod, "Well, *I've* been worried about the situation where we made a rocket engine that'll only last five years but no one keeps track of its expiration date. Suddenly, in the middle of a launch, boom, the engine disappears and the rocket crashes!" Seeing them looking a little puzzled, he gave them a few seconds to catch up mentally. Then he said, "Problem solved, we make million-year stades for most things, then break them down whenever it's time to get rid of them."

Gunnar surprised Kaem by saying, "This'd be great for disaster relief. You could drop packages out of airplanes into a war-torn area where people were starving. They could break the stasis on the packages at their convenience."

Kaem looked at Gunnar for a moment, then said, "Gunnar, the only person who could break the stasis would be someone with a stazer."

"Drop one of those too."

"You don't think the person on the ground who gets the stazer is gonna demand a share of everyone else's food for his service in breaking it out of stasis? I think you've had a great idea, but wouldn't it be better if the packages were timed to come out of stasis by themselves, a few hours after they landed?"

The Thunder of Engines

Gunnar snorted, "Yeah. I guess that's why you're the boss."

"I'm *not* the boss!" Kaem said, jerking a thumb at Arya, "*She's* the *boss*."

Arya began, "I'm not—"

Kaem interrupted. "You're just the business boss. I know. Sorry to interrupt but we need to try another couple of things before the Space-Gen people get here."

Arya rolled her eyes and said something under her breath about how they were dodging the issue. However, Kaem had already started talking to Gunnar. "So, let's try making some short term stades with the Mylar trick and set them in the bottom of the cube. Then we'll make a longer-term stade in the cube. When the short term stades go away, if I'm right, we'll have cavities in the bottom of the cube. Space-Gen could use a trick like that to make their combustion chambers. Ones we won't have to break the glass out of."

Gunnar's eyebrows went up. He said, "Let's try it!"

This time Kaem had Gunnar make a longer Mylar bag. They dribbled a little water into the bag to give it weight, then inserted the microwave emitter a little way into the bag. Kaem pursed his lips around the end of the bag and the cable going to the emitter and managed to blow the bag up before Gunnar did his thing and wound the electrical tape around the emitter.

They stazed it while holding it vertically so the emitter—and the water—was on the bottom. The stade they pulled out this time was rounder and more like the inside of a chamber, not a lumpy deformed thing like the first one they'd made using the uninflated Mylar bag.

They made another, then set both of the stades from the Mylar bags on the bottom of the cube—where they stayed only because the water made them heavier than air—before stazing it. They set them on the square ends where the flat surface of the emitter had been and kept them from sliding frictionlessly around by blocking them with bits of tape applied to the mirror on the bottom of the chamber.

When they pulled the cube-shaped stade out of the chamber, it was flawless. There was no way to tell that the stades from the bags were inside the cube stade.

However, sure enough, five hundred seconds later, when the stades from the Mylar bags disappeared, the cube had two slightly wet cavities in the bottom of it.

After doing some high-fiving, they all calmed down to think. Arya said, "Being able to reverse stasis is going to let us do *so* many things! Not just food preservation, we could hold fully ripened summer crops until winter without *any* degradation. And, once they're in stasis, we can stack them as high as we want without the upper ones crushing the ones below. Rats and insects won't get into them. We could save members of endangered species until we have a way to resurrect them. Store sperm and eggs without freezing. I'm sure we'll think of a million other things."

Gunnar said, "Those are important, but this is also going to help with the fabrication of a lot of things we couldn't have made out of stade before."

"I think," Kaem said slowly, "we should stop thinking of pie-in-the-sky projects for a bit and consider how these changes apply to rocketry. We need to be ready when Marks gets here."

"Spoilsport..." Gunnar said, the grumpy tone belied by the gleam in his eye.

Chapter Five

Marks' assistant had arranged a couple of limos to take them from the airport to Staze. As Lee was getting in, she found the CEO right behind her. He said, "Lee, sit next to me. Tell me who I'm going to meet."

"There're only three people I've met." She glanced at him, meeting his intense gaze and feeling bowled over by the charisma people said he exuded. *It's not just what "they say," it's real,* she thought. She looked away to diminish its intensity, then shrugged, "I think those are all the employees they've got."

Marks nodded.

"Kaem Seba's the one who invented stade. He looks African-American. He's got a faint accent. Maybe he came from somewhere else, or perhaps his parents did. Also, he looks like he's… not well. As if he's got some kind of chronic illness. I'd say he's just a little taller than I am. About five foot eight."

"Nice guy? Jerk?"

"I…" a sudden realization struck her. "I really liked him. He's funny, and humble, and smart." *And he's going to be worth a fortune. Is that influencing me?*

Marks looked curious. "Smart, huh? How do you know?"

"Well… um, there's the fact that he remembers everything in the contract we've got with Staze."

"How do you know that?"

"I don't, but he remembered a lot of stuff I didn't. And when I looked those items up later, he'd been right.

I asked him if he had a photographic memory and he said, he did, 'for stuff that matters to me.'" She grinned, "Which is the kind of memory *I'd* like to have."

Marks looked thoughtful. "Having a great memory doesn't necessarily mean you're smart. Look at the autistic savants who can memorize entire books but can't even take care of themselves. Anything else make you think he's smart?"

"Other than the fact that he invented stade?"

Marks shrugged. "Might've been an accident. Just happened to mix the right two things in a test tube."

Lee narrowed her eyes, feeling a strong compulsion to defend Kaem. *Where's this coming from?* she wondered. *Both Marks' doubt and my compulsion to defend Kaem?* To Marks, she said, "Are you aware he's not a chemistry major?"

Marks looked a little surprised, "Materials engineer?"

Lee shook her head.

"What then?"

"Physics."

Marks looked thoughtful but not fully accepting. "Are you thinking he made some kind of fundamental discovery?"

Lee nodded, feeling a little tingle in her scalp when she realized how true it was.

"Like what?" Marks asked.

She shrugged, "I have no idea. I asked but he deflected all questions like that. He did say…" She stopped, suddenly struck by how important what she was about to say actually was.

"What?"

"He said it *wasn't* a material," she said slowly. "We got interrupted and I lost track of that in the ensuing conversation, but..." she looked Marks in the eye, "I don't know why he'd lie about that. And, I think it's *really* important. He wouldn't tell me what it was, but he did say what it wasn't. And you remember it comes in different densities. Or at least in two different densities. The density of water and the density of air."

Marks chuckled. "You think it also comes in the densities of earth and fire?"

She snorted, glad she remembered a little bit about Aristotle and ancient Greek history. "I don't think it's limited to the densities of the ancient Greek elements either. I think it can be just about any density he wants. He said it could be *lighter* than air. Lighter than *hydrogen*. He also implied they could make it with a higher density than water, though he didn't say how dense."

Marks' eyes had widened, "Neutron star dense?!"

Lee drew back in surprise, "I don't think so, but I didn't ask that one."

Marks leaned back, looking thoughtful. "So, not a material. Density's adjustable. Material properties are unbelievable." He shook his head, "Well, I may not know what it is." He smiled at Lee. "But I know we've *gotta* have it." He looked at the time, "Tell me about the other people I'm going to meet there."

"Arya Vaii. She looks as if her ancestors came from India. Short hair, slender..." Lee suddenly didn't want to describe Arya. The woman's looks weren't important to this deal after all. *Then why did I describe what Kaem looks like?* She shook her head to clear these random thoughts. "My understanding is that she's their business person. A search for her didn't confirm her major but she's a senior and she's in several University clubs aimed at business majors. She's even got a small business that guides tours of haunted houses."

Marks looked thoughtful. "What did you think of *her* intelligence?"

"I don't have much to judge her by but I thought she was smart... I just remembered, Seba and Vaii are both Curtis Scholars."

"What's a Curtis Scholar?"

"Richard Curtis is an immensely wealthy hedge-fund guy. Came from poor beginnings, so started a scholarship that looks for poor kids, not just from the US but from all over the world. Something she said made me think that Vaii's family wasn't as poor as most of them. They definitely weren't as poor as Seba's family. A lot of the scholarships go to kids who've done well in various non-traditional learning systems. Quite a few of them got online educations from a thing called the Khan Academy. They don't apply to Curtis, he finds them somehow. Curtis pays for them to take SATs and, if they do well, he pays for them to have full-ride scholarships at UVA, which is where he went to school." She shrugged, "I get the impression they have to do *very* well on the SAT."

Marks nodded thoughtfully. "Poor and book-smart. Okay. What about the third one?"

"Gunnar Schmidt. An older guy. I'd say late sixties to early seventies. Crotchety. Kaem introduced him as their fabricator. Called him an expert."

"You think he owns part of the intellectual property? Or is he just the guy that built their stazer and the molds they cast the stade in?"

"I don't know," Lee said thoughtfully. "I *think* he's just the builder, but he may have made important contributions." Out the window, she saw they were

The Thunder of Engines

pulling up to Staze's utilitarian metal building. "We're here," she said to Marks.

When he turned his head to look out the window, Lee felt both relieved and disappointed that she was no longer the focus of Marks' intense gaze. As everyone started getting out, Lee told her phone to send Kaem a quick text that they'd arrived. Then wondered why. *I want Kaem to succeed,* she realized. *So, I don't want him getting blindsided by our arrival.*

Arya opened the door and let them into the building's anteroom. Lee wasn't surprised when Marks graciously took Arya's hand and said, "You must be Arya Vaii? Lee's told me about you. A Curtis Scholar, eh?"

Arya looked flustered. Lee thought the young woman probably felt much like Lee had when she'd met the great man and become the focus of his regard. "Um, yes, I am. It's very nice to meet you. I've, ah, been a great admirer of your career."

Still holding her hand, Marks arched an eyebrow, "Well *I'm* a great admirer of your product. I hear you've been getting offers from Orbital Systems and Martin Aerospace? Have they been good?"

Vaii swallowed. "Um, their bids were... low. We feel they simply don't understand the value of stade to rocketry."

She shouldn't have told Marks that! Lee thought, stunned that Marks had drawn such an admission from the young woman.

"That's sad," Marks said, without showing an inkling of the triumph Lee thought he was probably feeling. He shook his head. "Some people just don't have the imagination." He released Arya's hand—which Lee thought he'd held far too long—and asked, "How much did they offer?"

"Uh," Arya looked like she was trying to resist the question but had been overwhelmed by his personality, "only ten million."

No! Arya! What're you doing? Lee thought. Then, *I'm supposed to be on Marks' side. I should be excited she's readily giving up information.*

Marks waved at his entourage, "I'd introduce you to all my people but perhaps it'd be better if we did the introductions where your other folks could hear them at the same time?"

"Oh... sure," Arya said, stepping to the door into the main area and opening it.

In the big room, Arya indicated Kaem and Gunnar, introducing them. To them, she said, "I'm sure you recognize Aaron Marks, CEO of Space-Gen."

Kaem and Gunnar shook Marks' hand, then Marks introduced his entire team, getting every name right as if he'd known them forever—rather than just having met the young engineers from Lee's team that morning. *He's just as impressive with people as they say he is,* Lee thought.

Marks turned to Kaem then, saying, "I hear you're the one the world has to thank for this amazing technology?"

Kaem smiled gently, "Only partly. Each of us played a part."

"Lee tells me that you might be willing to demonstrate how you make stade?"

Kaem nodded, "We can do that. We've developed a new method for forming complex shapes in stade that we think you'll be interested in as well." He turned to Gunnar, "How about if we make a cube of low-density stade for them?"

The Thunder of Engines

Gunnar said, "I've already got the mold set up and filled. I'll hook up the cables while you're setting up the electronics."

It only took a few moments for Gunnar to connect the cables, but—as before—took a while for Kaem to adjust the settings on the rack of electronics. Lee wasn't surprised when Marks started around the table to look at the equipment in the rack. She smiled a smile that never reached her face when Kaem closed the rack's door and grinned up at Marks. "Sorry, but our patent attorney says we can't let anyone see this stuff yet."

He doesn't want Marks to see it either, but blaming it on their attorney's a smart move, Lee thought.

Marks smiled, showed his palms, and stepped back around to the other side of the table. "Sorry. I should've known," he said magnanimously. "Don't blame you a bit."

After some more fiddling, Kaem looked over at the mold, "Ready Gunnar?"

Gunnar nodded solemnly.

Kaem flipped a switch, then set a timer on his phone.

When the timer went off, he made more adjustments and flipped the switch that snapped. "Check it Gunnar?"

Gunnar opened the door a tiny bit, then said, "It's stizzled."

"All right. Here we go." Kaem said, making another series of adjustments.

Lee heard the capacitor charge and discharge, then Gunnar opened the door and nodded. He got out his knife and started working the stade out of the chamber. Once it came out, he gave it a little push in Marks' direction.

Marks caught the cube-shaped stade in a basket of fingers, oohed and ahhed over it a bit, then passed it on to the other members of his team. As they began looking at it, he turned back to Kaem. "Sorry, but I'm sure you understand my compulsion to be thorough. It's occurred to me that you could've had that stade in the mold when we came in here. All the fooling around with the cables and electronics could've been a smokescreen for a magic sleight-of-hand event. I hope you don't mind if we ask you to do it again before we start negotiating over millions of dollars?"

Kaem smiled, "Not a problem. We'll make you a water density one this time."

Marks said, "Lee tells me you can make them with densities even lower than air. If you don't mind, I'd like to see that. Very low-density stade would, of course, be of great interest to the space industry."

Kaem and Gunnar glanced at one another. Kaem turned back to Marks. "We *could* do that, but Gunnar'd have to go back to his shop and get some equipment." He glanced at Arya, "I think Arya's arranged for us to have dinner somewhere. Perhaps later, while your team's checking into the hotel and getting a brief rest before dinner, Gunnar and I could make a low-density stade and bring it to you at the restaurant. Right now, we could make you a water density stade while you're watching for sleight-of-hand. That way you'd have three different densities to take home with you."

Marks hesitated a moment, then nodded, "Sounds like a good compromise."

Everyone watched while Gunnar turned the cube mold back on its back and filled it with the clear fluid from their bottles. Meanwhile, Kaem made a bunch of adjustments to the electronics. They went through the

The Thunder of Engines

three stages of stazing they'd gone through before. When they were done, Gunnar pried another stade out of the mold. It looked exactly like the one before, but this one was heavy. Because Lee'd been worried she might've missed some sleight of hand last time, this time she'd kept a careful eye on Gunnar and the mold throughout the procedure. At no time was there an opportunity for him to slip a premade stade into the mold. They had to have made it on the spot.

Marks nodded and said, "Amazing! Does it require a lot more power to create a dense stade than a light one?"

Kaem smiled as if thinking, *Nice try.* Aloud he only said, "I'm afraid I can't answer that question. Would you like to see some samples of how we think we could make combustion chambers without your having to break the mold to get it out after we've stazed the chamber? And, of course, without having to make another mold for the next engine."

Marks enthusiastically said, "Of course." He didn't even seem frustrated to have been denied again. Getting stonewalled couldn't happen to him too often.

Kaem showed them a group of several small stades. They were shaped a little bit like small baggies someone had blown up as if they were balloons. He said, "We've just tested a prediction of the theory that says if you form a stade around an existing stade, they remain separate to some degree." He looked up at the people watching him, "One of the most important ways they remain separate is that we can dissolve one of the stades and leave the other one behind."

Kaem reached over and took a cube-shaped stade from Gunnar. "So, we did that. You can see that after we dissolved stades like those," he nodded at the baggie-balloon shapes, "we were left with this cube-shaped stade that had a couple of cavities in the bottom of it." He stuck a couple of fingers into openings in the cube, then carefully handed the slippery cube to Lee so she could pass it to Marks.

Marks took the cube and digitally explored the cavities, but he was frowning. "Stades can be dissolved? With what?"

Kaem gave a little shrug, "Just another of the many things we can't tell you until we've got a contract."

Marks shook his head, "There's no way we're going to sign a contract to buy motors that might dissolve in the rain or something almost as ubiquitous." He managed to sound somewhat angry, concerned, and implacable all at the same time.

Kaem produced a reassuring smile. "You needn't worry. I can guarantee your motors won't dissolve without a purposeful intervention by our company."

"*No*," Marks said, forcefully. "We're not bidding without a better understanding."

Kaem shrugged. "Okay," he said, calmly.

After a moment of silence had passed, Marks impatiently asked, "Well then, what dissolves it?"

"Oh," Kaem said calmly, "Sorry. I meant, 'It's okay if you don't bid.' We're sure *someone* will. If you'd like you could maintain your 'right of first offer,' to be sure we'd have to let you know when someone else bids. Or if no one else bids and we decide we *are* going to have to explain how they're dissolved?"

At first, Lee felt Kaem had made an impressively ballsy move with what'd he'd said. Then she realized that, in fact, Marks had painted himself into a corner by claiming he wouldn't bid when he'd be a fool not to.

The Thunder of Engines

Marks—as if he'd just realized what Kaem had said, *not* as if he'd ignored it so he could try to back Kaem into a corner—said, "Oh, wait. You said you'd 'guarantee' they wouldn't dissolve?"

"That's correct," Kaem said with a faint smile. Lee, having seen him smile quite a bit by now, would've characterized it as a "knowing smile." She didn't think anyone else would've picked up on that though.

"So, if we bought them, then it turned out they *did* dissolve, you'd return our money?"

Kaem smiled. "Absolutely. Though the language of the contract would have to exclude someone purposely dissolving them once they understood the tech. It'd have to be non-purposeful dissolution that threatened the function of the engines during normal use."

Marks' eyes narrowed slightly. "How long do you think the engines are going to last under 'normal use'?"

Kaem smiled, "Believe it or not, we can sell you different types of stade. Some products we'd guarantee for a lifetime... some for shorter time periods. Right down to products that would only last for a few weeks, or even—"

Kaem was interrupted when Marks exclaimed, "What the hell?!" which echoed what was going through Lee's head.

Still smiling, Kaem spoke as if he hadn't been interrupted, "Though we've been assuming that you'd want stade that would last essentially until you wanted it disposed of. We've been pricing the engines at two million dollars each per that model."

Marks looked like he was about to explode. However, he took a deep breath, seemed to calm himself, and quietly asked, "And why would you think we'd want to dispose of engines?"

Kaem shrugged, "To be honest, I sincerely hope that several hundred years from now we'll have far better motors than the ones you design in the next few months. Ergo, you'll want to dispose of these so they don't accumulate as permanent landfill."

"You really think these motors will last hundreds of years, even under heavy use?" Marks said incredulously.

Kaem nodded, "Without a doubt. Well, unless you buy the ones with shorter guarantees."

Arya interrupted, speaking to Kaem, "If you and Gunnar are going to make that low-density stade and we're still going to be on time for our reservation at Argent, we'll have to break up pretty soon. Is there anything else you were planning to demonstrate for the Space-Gen people?"

"No," Kaem said. He looked around at the people from Space-Gen. "Anything else any of you wanted to see?"

Marks grinned, "A stade dissolving?'

Kaem laughed, "Maybe you guys had better check into your hotel while Gunnar and I make you a lighter-than-air stade. We'll meet you at Argent and you can have a go at browbeating us some more."

"Browbeat?" Marks said as if surprised. He smiled, "You haven't seen a browbeating yet. You just wait till after this dinner you're buying us."

"Wait!" Kaem said, "Arya, I thought you said Argent, but I'm pretty sure you *meant* the Cavalier Buffalo, right?"

Arya looked confused for a moment. When she didn't respond right away, Marks said with a suspicious tone, "What's the Cavalier Buffalo?"

Lee answered, "It's a college dive bar sir."

The Thunder of Engines

"Awesome," Marks said. "See you guys there at seven." He turned and walked out the door.

Arya fixed Lee with a pleading look. "Do you think he's serious?"

She turned to Prakant. "Would Marks really want to go to a dive bar instead of a nice restaurant?"

Prakant snorted, "Oh, *hell* yes. He loves low-class bars."

Lee turned to Arya and shrugged. "I guess he probably does."

Arya rolled her eyes, "Oh, well. It'll be better for our budget."

Lee frowned, "You haven't already spent the million dollars Space-Gen deposited in your account, have you?"

Arya had lifted her phone and said something to it. She gave a little shrug. "Not exactly."

"What's *that* mean?" Lee asked.

Arya shook her head and lifted the phone to her ear. "Hello. Is this Argent?"

***

Tipping liberally, Arya managed to arrange a back room for their dinner at the Buffalo. She cringed at the thought of holding a critical dinner in such a low-class place. This was not in alignment with what she thought she'd been learning in business school. Nor with her mother and father's business sensibilities. Her parents had started out very poor and were diligently working their way up, but they'd always held any meetings at places that strained their budgets.

However, she'd decided it'd be foolish to try to move this pack of—what she thought of as juvenile—men and boys to a better-quality establishment.

Arya'd been pleased when Lee, another woman, had been their first point of contact with Space-Gen. But, when the Space-Gen contingent had arrived with ten members; Lee, another junior engineer, Teri Nunsen, and Space-Gen's CFO, Cary Lark were the only women. Then, Marks, as she'd heard prior to his arrival, had proven to have such a dominant personality the rest of the Space-Gen team had seemed to fade into shadows. *Well, not Lee, but I think that's only because I feel like I know her.*

Arya made sure there were thirteen chairs while praying that these immature-acting men didn't have some expectation that she'd have arranged a stripper or some other humiliating entertainment. She knew such things still occurred in corporate America and had always thought she'd have the gumption to stand up to such idiocy. *But can I resist when there's so much money on the line?* she wondered. *Will I just roll over if they start asking for something offensive to women? Would Kaem expect me to lower myself to... such a level?*

Arya shook herself and turned to worrying about things she *could* control. She started checking the sturdy chairs for stains or stickiness. She was glad she did. She had to ask the server to replace two chairs.

She set to checking the silverware and glasses.

Arya decided everything was as good as she could hope for in a place like the Buffalo. She'd just started worrying about whether Kaem and Gunnar would arrive in time to provide emotional support when the door opened and the Buffalo's star-struck night manager ushered Aaron Marks in the door.

Marks made a beeline for Arya. The rest of his people were a little boisterous, as if they'd had a couple of drinks already. Marks, however, seemed fully in command of his faculties. *Of course, he's so brilliant, you could probably knock fifty points off his IQ without most people noticing.*

Arriving beside Arya, Marks said, "Thanks so much for setting this up. That demo this afternoon was…" he shook his head as if in wonder, "very informative. Have any other companies come for demonstrations?"

Arya, shook her head, resolving to be tighter lipped than she'd been earlier in the day.

"Was it Orbital Systems or Martin Aero that offered you the ten million?

"Um…" Arya said, still feeling like she shouldn't answer Marks' questions about their business, but unable to come up with a good reason why she shouldn't answer this one. "It was Orbital Systems. Um, Martin Aero…" Arya shook her head, stopping before she could say anything she shouldn't about their problems with Martin.

Marks said, "No need to say more. I know Ricard Caron, their CEO, and he's… not a pleasant man. I'd bet he's trying to apply pressure rather than making a sincere effort to negotiate, right?"

Marks just said, "No need to say more"! Arya thought, *Then promptly asked a question!* But maybe she could get useful information out of Marks. This doesn't have to be a one-way street. Just knowing Caron is difficult is helpful. To Marks, she nodded. "He hasn't called himself, but the guy who did has been kind of…"

"An asshole?"

Arya nodded again. "You could say that."

Marks shook his head in disgust. "And they haven't even made an offer, have they? I've heard of Martin using intimidation tactics before. Making ridiculously low bids. Telling vendors he'll *destroy* them if they don't play ball."

Arya shook her head. Which could've been an answer to the question about whether Martin had made an offer. Or not. She found herself feeling warmly toward Marks. As if they were a couple of girls with their heads together to discuss a hated bully at school. She pulled herself up short, *How did he do that?*

Marks gently patted her shoulder, giving her goosebumps. "Well, even if *we* can't make a deal, I'd love to help you guys stand up to Ricard. I don't like him either."

I was pissed at Kaem for touching my shoulder without permission. Now I'm getting goosebumps when Marks... Before her thoughts could go any farther, the door opened and Kaem came in with Gunnar. Incongruously, they had a Mylar party balloon with them. *Oh,* Arya thought with a sudden realization, *it's a stade on a string!* she thought. *It must be the lighter-than-air cube they promised to make.*

Marks stepped closer, focused intently on the floating stade.

Kaem pulled it down so the CEO could see it better. "Definitely lighter-than-air," Marks said. "How'd you attach the string?"

"Tied the string to a nut and put the nut in the chamber before forming the stade. The string's under the one-millimeter limit, so, small enough to get out the door of the mold without causing problems."

The Thunder of Engines

"What size nut?" Marks asked.

Marks' question seemed innocent to Arya, so she was surprised when Kaem smiled and said, "Just one we had handy," which *wasn't* an answer to the question posed. After a moment she realized, *Ah, if Marks knew the size of the nut, he could subtract its probable weight to infer the density of the stade itself and realize it's close to the density of helium. From that, he might deduce that the density depends on the stuff in the chamber when the stade was formed, not some wizardry Kaem's doing with his electronics...* She had a warm thought. *Marks may be brilliant, but he's not getting any steps on Kaem.*

Arya looked around. Their server was taking drink orders and passing out menus. Teri Nunsen, SpaceGen's young female engineer, and Prakant, their CTO, were talking to Gunnar.

Lee and a couple of the other engineers had gathered around Kaem and Marks.

Ah, and Cary Lark, their CFO and Saul Izzo, their legal counsel are heading for me. I wonder if this is all part of a well thought out plan of attack?

When Lark arrived, she extended her hand, reintroducing herself, "Hi, I'm Cary. You're Arya Vaii, right?"

Arya nodded, shaking Lark's hand and saying, "Good to see you again, Ms. Lark." She turned and extended her hand to Saul, "And you, Mr. Izzo." She frowned and spoke as if in confidence. "Sorry we've got you here at the Cavalier Buffalo. It's not a very nice establishment. I don't know if you heard the byplay between Kaem and Mr. Marks that got us here?"

Lark chuckled, "Don't worry. This really *is* Aaron's kind of place. The rest of us have gotten *quite* used to

175 | Page

having dinner in the worst dives to be found in any of the places we visit."

"You can say that again," Izzo grumbled. He didn't seem to find his CEO's proclivities amusing.

"Well," Arya said as if divulging a secret, "actually, their fish and chicken sandwiches, though served on paper plates, are quite tasty. The Buffalo also brews its own beer. I'm told their wheat beer's quite good." Arya hoped this last was true, since she didn't drink beer and only had knowledge of a few online reviews.

Lark looked around, "Trust me. We'll be fine. Well, except for Saul here. He's more of a sophisticate than the rest of us." She turned her attention on Arya, "I tried to look Staze up online but didn't find anything. The impression I've gotten from some comments is that you're the business side of this enterprise?"

Arya nodded, wondering once again what she *shouldn't* tell these people.

"Is it just the three of you so far?"

Now there's a fraught question, Arya thought. She said, "Well, we've hired some legal counsel, but you're right, we're very small." *Implying we're bigger isn't lying is it?*

Lark smiled, "From what I hear, you don't need to be big when you've got a product as interesting as yours, right?"

Arya took a sip of her water, dabbed her lips, and smiled, "That's what I'm told as well."

"So, are you guys most interested in licensing your invention, or are you planning to develop some parts of it yourself?"

Arya resisted closing her eyes to ponder a question with so many implications. She cleared her throat. "I would think that'd depend on the offers we receive."

The Thunder of Engines

She didn't actually think so, since Kaem was dead set on developing most of stade's applications himself.

Lark leaned a little closer, "Well, I think you're going to like the offer Mr. Marks is going to make."

Lark's eyes were aimed across the room. When Arya followed her gaze, she found they were on Marks. What arrested *Arya's* attention was the way the attractive Lee was standing right next to Kaem, apparently hanging on his every word.

She realized she didn't like that. *But I shouldn't care, should I? He's not my… boyfriend or anything. He doesn't fit my parents'...* Arya cut off that line of thought. She was American enough that she didn't think her parents should control her destiny. *Am I worried she's trying to use her looks to obtain an advantage for Space-Gen? No! She's an engineer. She wouldn't do that kind of thing. Besides, that's such a last-century thing to worry about!*

The waiter took orders from their little group, which got Arya's mind off Lee.

Once the waiter stepped away, Saul Izzo discreetly cleared his throat. "I, um, did a search for your patent on stade but didn't find it. Could you give me the number?"

Oh crap! Arya thought. *And here I was upset because Martin Aerospace wouldn't give me* their *patent number.* She smiled at him and said, "I'm sorry Mr. Izzo. We've only just applied for a patent. I think we probably have an application number, but I'm afraid I don't know what it is." She thought, *I sure as hell* hope *Morales has the application in.*

"Could you give me your attorney's name?"

"Um, I don't know the ins and outs of this kind of thing. Let me check with him." She held up her finger and backed away from Izzo and Lark, asking her phone to connect her with Morales.

She was just beginning to despair of reaching Morales when his voice came on the line. "Hello, Ms. Vaii. I hope you're not going to make a habit of calling me at all hours?"

"I'm sorry Mr. Morales," Arya said, suddenly feeling like a child calling someone important rather than co-owner of what could someday be the largest business in the world. "We're meeting with possible investors and need to know if the application is in?"

"Yes. I sent you an email."

"Sorry, we've been busy. Can you give me the application number?"

"I can, but I would strongly urge you not to share it with anyone. Don't think of yourself as protected yet. Secrecy's still your strongest ally."

"Um, we're meeting with Space-Gen over dinner at the Cavalier Buffalo. Since you have an interest in our business, maybe you'd like to join us?"

"I would. When are you going to meet, and could I suggest somewhere… with a little more class than the Buffalo?"

"Um, I'm *so* sorry. We're meeting right now. I had reservations at Argent, but Aaron Marks said he'd rather go to the Buffalo."

Morales produced a long-suffering sigh. "You're calling me after this meeting's already started?"

"Sorry…?" she said pleadingly.

"Well, I do have an interest in your business and I would like to meet Marks… I'll be there in about fifteen minutes."

"What can I order for you?"

The Thunder of Engines

"Their fried pickle appetizer. I've already eaten, but I should have something to pick at."

"Mr. Morales!" Arya said teasingly, "If you know the menu that well, you must eat at the Buffalo yourself."

"I went to school at UVA Ms. Vaii. Of *course,* I've eaten at the Buff. See you soon."

Arya went to find their waiter and ask for another chair and the pickle appetizer. When she returned, she decided she should check on the conversation around Gunnar. Considering Gunnar's crusty nature, she felt worried about what he might say if he got irritated.

To her astonishment, when she arrived Gunnar, Prakant and Nunsen were talking basketball! At first, she was surprised Teri Nunsen was hanging around men who were talking about sports. After listening for a moment and recognizing the depth of Nunsen's knowledge and the eagerness of her participation, she chided herself for her own sexist attitude.

Since Arya had no interest in basketball, she turned to check on the others. Saul Izzo was right behind her. "Did you get permission for me to talk to your attorney?"

"Oh!" Arya said, covering her mouth in embarrassment. "He's coming to the Buffalo. You can talk to him here."

"Did you get the application number?" Izzo asked, producing a pen and notepad.

Arya smiled, "He said I *definitely* shouldn't tell you the number. I think you'd better reserve your questions for Mr. Morales."

Izzo grinned, "Can't blame me for trying, can you?"

"Why, of course I can," Arya said trying for a disarming smile.

When it came time to sit down for their meal, Marks and Kaem sat next to each other, near the middle of one side of the long table. Arya maneuvered to sit close enough to hear what they said, deciding that sitting across from them was best. Prakant sat on Marks' left. Cary Lark, the CFO, and Saul Izzo, Space Gen's legal beagle, sat on Arya's right. Morales sat on Arya's left.

Arya blinked. Lee was sitting on Kaem's right. *She just wants to be near the action,* Arya told herself. *Even if she is angling for a romantic attachment to Kaem, it doesn't matter because I don't want to be his girlfriend!* No matter how much she reassured herself on that fact, she continued to feel unsettled. Especially when Lee put her hand on Kaem's arm while making a point. To Arya's relief, Marks started talking to Kaem and he turned away from Lee.

Their waiter stopped to give Marks his hamburger, causing him to turn away from Kaem.

Lee said something and Kaem turned back toward her.

Kaem laughed.

Then Kaem said something and she laughed.

What if she's just trying to sway him? Maybe she's not that great as an engineer, just an influencer.

After all, no one could honestly laugh at Kaem's jokes.

Conversation remained light while people were eating. Arya got concerned at one point when the waiter brought Marks a beer and he tried to get Kaem to have one too. She was relieved when Kaem shook his head. Kaem grinned at Marks, "You're not trying to get me drunk and take advantage of me, are you?"

The Thunder of Engines

Marks grinned, "The thought had crossed my mind. The ethanol molecule has a time-honored place in seduction you know?"

Kaem laughed, "I'm planning to keep my virginity intact tonight."

Arya didn't think it was funny. In fact, she thought it was offensive. However, Kaem and Marks both seemed quite amused.

Marks quickly finished his hamburger. After a glance around the table that reminded Arya of a general reviewing his troop placements, he focused on Saul Izzo. "So, Saul, I'm assuming that if we make Staze an offer, you could write a contract that would protect us if it turned out that all these amazing things they've shown us were just ploys in some startlingly sophisticated scam?" Marks briefly turned to Kaem and said, "I hope you don't mind some straight talk. I like to put my cards face up so we all know exactly what we're doing."

Kaem produced a subtle smile, "We certainly don't mind, but we're going to have to keep some of our cards face down so Mr. Morales doesn't have a heart attack."

"Understood. Understood," Marks said, turning his attention back to Izzo and lifting a questioning eyebrow.

"Sure," Izzo said, "I could draft something with production and performance guarantees in it. I'd need some help with specifications, but if you can work out the broad strokes, I could turn out something with the detail needed."

"Great," Marks said and turned his attention to the rest of the table. "Have you engineers got any doubts about whether we want access to this product?"

Will Goran said, "If we're sure about the properties, because, after all, they're unbelievable, then, absolutely, the answer is yes. Has anyone but Staze or the redoubtable Ms. Lee confirmed those properties?"

Marks nodded, "The engineers in Space-Gen's testing lab signed off on Lee's results. Prakant checked with them and they fully understand what they signed off on. No 'sign here' events occurred."

Goran said, "Okay," then glanced up at the stade floating over Marks' head. "I also keep worrying there's some horrific flaw we haven't been made aware of. Like stade dissolves on contact with water, or a high pH, or organic molecules, or... I don't know, some pollutants or something."

Kaem smiled and said, "We'll be happy to guarantee it won't dissolve... unless we want it to."

Goran said, "Maybe it fails on contact with something you yourself haven't considered testing it against. Just the fact that you think you *can* make it dissolve scares the hell out of me."

Marks glanced at Izzo, "The contract you're going to write up will protect us from such fiascos, right Saul?"

Saul nodded.

Marks looked around again, "Any other objections to beginning negotiations?"

One of the young Space-Gen engineers, Jerome Stitt—whom Arya'd taken an instant dislike to—said, "I'm just thinking of the old saying, 'If it *sounds* too good to be true...'"

Marks finished the saying for Stitt, "It *is* too good to be true. Yeah, I've got that feeling in the pit of my stomach too. I think we're just going to have to count on Saul to provide legal protection against getting pulled too far down such a rabbit hole."

The Thunder of Engines

No one else voiced an objection. Marks looked at Cary Lark, so Arya turned to look at the woman next to her. Marks asked, "Cary, can we scrape together a hundred million to buy Staze?"

Arya had intended to watch the CFO's reaction but her eyes flashed to Kaem instead. Kaem had said he wouldn't sell Staze. *But a hundred million! For doing nothing?! Almost twenty million to me?!*

Kaem still wore the inscrutable smile he'd worn much of the evening.

Lark said, "It'd be difficult and would take a while, but we could come up with that much."

Marks turned to Kaem and said, "How about it? You told me about your family's financial difficulties. You could help them out and still retire a wealthy man."

Kaem said, "Respectfully, as I've said, we're *not* going to sell Staze. We will *make* things out of stade for you. If you provide the molds, we'll staze rocket motors for you for two million dollars each. We'll staze booster rocket bodies with integral cryotanks for twenty million dollars. We'll staze an upper stage body or delivery capsule for five million each."

Marks fixed Kaem with a steady gaze, then gave a quick shake of his head. "That's not a great deal. Assuming an entire rocket has seven engines in the booster and one on the upper stage. That's a total of eight for sixteen million dollars. Add on the twenty million dollars for the booster body and then add an upper stage body and a delivery capsule for five million each. That means you're planning to charge us forty-six million for a rocket that doesn't have any of the pumps, fuel feed plumbing, descent parachutes, landing legs, astronaut seats, computers, control systems, and on and on. Our current rockets only cost us about fifty-

183 | Page

seven million total, so by the time we added the rest of the stuff to the bare bones you provided us, going with yours would cost a lot more."

Kaem smiled back. "I thought you might want to include the plumbing as integral to the rocket's body. And, you won't need pumps."

Marks blinked, "Okay, I understand integral plumbing, though laying it out might be harder than you think. But we've got to have pumps. Fuel has to be delivered to the engines at high enough pressures…" Marks paused as Kaem lifted a palm.

Kaem said, "Squirt a little oxygen into your hydrogen tank and ignite it."

"What?! It'd explode!"

"Not if the tanks are made of stade," Kaem said calmly. "Stade'd hold in the pressure of such a combustion event. You just need to carefully calculate how much oxygen you're going to squirt into the tank so it generates the pressures you want. You'll need sturdy pressure regulators and valves to control the flows of fluids under such high pressures. There'll likely be benefits to fabricating those components from stade as well, but we could give you a deal on those."

Kaem paused, Arya thought he was giving Marks time to come to grips with the radical idea he'd just proposed. Then he continued, "Next. Landing legs aren't needed. Just drop the booster in the ocean. It won't be damaged by the impact or corroded by the seawater. If you limit the number of non-stade components and used lighter than air stade for the body and engines, it'd be so light it'd fall slowly, even without a parachute."

Marks looked completely dumbfounded, as did the other Space-Gen people at the table.

Silence reigned.

The Thunder of Engines

When no one said anything for a couple of moments, Kaem continued. "Computing. You'll mostly be able to use off-the-shelf computing components because stade blocks the ionizing radiation that damages semiconductors and memory components out in space. Therefore, very little in the way of expensive radiation-hardened computing components will be necessary. I should point out that blocking radiation will also be of great benefit to the astronauts themselves. Especially when they travel into high radiation environments beyond low Earth orbit on their way to the Moon, Mars or the asteroids. It could be argued that, now that stade's available, it's irresponsible to send people into space without such protection."

"Wait a minute!" Marks exclaimed, "You can't tell me stade will block *every* high GeV particle!"

"I can, and it will," Kaem said calmly. "If it doesn't," he grinned, "we'll sell it to you for 50% off."

Despite her focused attention on the principals of the conversation, Arya noticed Saul Izzo frantically making notes.

Kaem resumed talking. "As far as your control systems, fins made from stade won't break or burn up, even if you place them directly in the exhaust stream of the rocket engines, which incidentally is where they'll give you the most control. Personnel can be returned to earth in capsules that land in the ocean or in shuttle-like designs that land on airfields. Neither of those designs will need ablative tiles since stade will easily tolerate the heat of re-entry and won't transmit *any* of that heat to the passengers." Kaem smiled. "You've got me on the seats. Staze won't be able to save you money on those. I would like to point out, however, that the parts of your rocket that're made from stade will *never* need to be examined, tested, or refurbished. They won't need to be replaced until you design something better and want to upgrade. This means that, essentially, you'll only have to buy as many rockets as you intend to have in operation at any one time. You won't have to buy new ones to replace those that're aging out. Also, fuel costs will be significantly reduced by the decreased weight of lighter-than-air stade rockets." He looked Marks in the eyes, "*I believe we're giving you a deal that'll let you substantially lower the costs of orbital launch.*"

Marks glanced around at the rest of his team, most of whom looked as stunned as he seemed to be. But by the time his eyes returned to Kaem, he had his look of wonder in control. He narrowed his eyes, "Your pricing is for exclusive access to stade, right?"

Kaem managed to look astonished, even though Arya thought he'd expected the question. "Oh! Sorry. No. If you want exclusive use for rocketry, we could give you that for three years, but your rate would double."

"You're going to charge me almost as much for one rocket as I offered for your entire company?!" Marks asked incredulously.

Kaem drew back and gave Marks a reproachful shake of his head. He said, "You *did* make an offensively low bid, didn't you? Not even what you spend on two of your rockets? Trust me, Mr. Marks, we *do* have a handle on the value of our technology. We have great admiration for Space-Gen and for you personally, but we won't be taken advantage of."

You go Kaem! Arya thought. She almost immediately began having second thoughts. What if Kaem was overvaluing the tech? What if they missed out on this bid and never got another one as good? What if they slaved away for decades trying to turn Staze into the world-changing corporation Kaem envisioned, all without success? The expected value could be chipped away by claims of patent infringement by people like Martin. By some unanticipated failure of stade to perform as they hoped.

Marks had been studying Kaem. Now he glanced over at Cary Lark. Arya couldn't tell whether anything passed between them, but Marks turned back to Kaem looking resolved. "Okay," he said. "So, you won't sell your company and its IP for a hundred million. What about a *billion* dollars? You'd be unbelievably rich. The income from investing it alone would be enough that you'd just keep getting richer. You'd never have to work again."

Arya heard Cary Lark inhale sharply, as if this hadn't been part of the original plan.

Kaem only chuckled a little and shook his head. "All we have to do is sell you eleven exclusive rockets. We'd have that billion, with more rockets yet to sell. And, then we could use that capital to develop stade in the ways we want. Ways that'll make real differences in the world. The kinds of differences I've always dreamed of making."

Arya's earbud chirped, "You have a call from Green Launch Initiative."

"I'll take it," she said, pushing back her chair and rising to move to a corner away from the crowd at the table.

A voice said, "I hear Aaron Marks is bidding to buy your company?"

"Hi," Arya said, brightly, then hoping her tone wasn't too bright. "This is Arya Vaii of Staze Incorporated. Who's calling please?"

"Jerry Branzon, calling from GLI. Is Aaron Marks really there?"

"Um..." Arya said, wondering whether there was any reason to keep Marks' presence a secret. Meanwhile, her inner businesswoman freaked out to be talking to Branzon, the wealthiest man on the planet—and self-made to boot. Deciding there not only wasn't a reason to keep it a secret, but that telling Branzon might set off a bidding war to their advantage, she said, "Yes, he's here."

Branzon said, "And it must be about seven PM there, correct?" Branzon didn't wait for an answer. He said, "So, I suppose he's got you out for some wining and dining. When he makes an offer, make him wait and call me back. Whatever it is, I'll beat it."

"Um, he's making an offer right now."

"Crap," Branzon said, sounding irritated. "Let me ask a few questions then. Unfortunately, I'm way behind the eight-ball because the idiot who received and tested your samples didn't tell me about them until a few hours ago."

"Okay."

Rapid-fire, Branzon asked questions Arya had heard before: How long stade would last, whether it was susceptible to breakdown, whether it could be produced in anything but air or water densities, etc.

Arya told him the answers just as quickly, having heard Kaem answer them several times by now.

"Okay," Branzon said abruptly. "What's Marks offering for your IP?"

"He offered a billion dollars. But the IP isn't for—"

Branzon interrupted with a snort. "Well, *that's* a lowball offer. I could've predicted Marks would try to screw you. I'll make a starting offer of ten billion."

The Thunder of Engines

"Um, the IP's not for sale."

"Really? I've been told your company consists of three people. Isn't that right?"

"No," Arya said, consoling herself that it wasn't a lie if she counted Morales. "We're small, but... we want to develop Stade ourselves." When Branzon didn't respond immediately, she continued, "We're negotiating with Mr. Marks to provide Space-Gen with motors, rocket bodies, cryotanks and space capsules made from stade."

"How do you form them? Seems like stade would be impossible to stamp, form, or machine. None of the ways we shape metals should work."

"Um, you can think of it as a casting process, even though it isn't actually casting. You'd provide us with molds of your design, made from glass or other transparent materials with mirrored surfaces. We'd fill them with stade. We could even cast it at your launch site so you wouldn't have to ship the components."

"And how much are you charging for it?"

Arya went over the pricing Kaem had just given Marks.

"Okay," Branzon said, "I'll offer twenty percent more."

Startled by how fast Branzon was moving, Arya asked, "Is that twenty percent more for the exclusive or the non-exclusive deal?"

"Either one. I'd prefer the exclusive deal though."

"I-I'll let them know."

"Whatever you do, don't sign a deal without talking to me again. I'm gathering my people and we're going to fly out there. Sorry to say, we'll arrive in the middle of the night so you probably won't want to talk to us until morning."

"Okay..." Arya said, staggered by the way things were moving.

Branzon hung up and Arya looked around. Everyone at the table had turned to look at her. Kaem spoke to her, "Mr. Marks has agreed to our prices. I'm not quite sure what's next? Do we wait until morning, then look over whatever contract Mr. Izzo draws up?" Kaem looked at Morales, "Could you look over the contract with us too?"

Morales shook his head, "For a contract this big, you need a lawyer who specializes in contract law. I'd recommend Sylvia Contreras."

Arya started around the table to Kaem's side.

"Alright then," Marks said jovially, extending his hand. "Shake on it now. Then we can have a beer. We'll niggle the finer points in the morning."

"No!" Arya said when Kaem started to reach his hand toward Marks.

Kaem pulled back.

Arya leaned in to Kaem's right ear, happy that doing it put her between Kaem and April Lee. She spoke quietly as if expressing a confidence, but knowingly loud enough that people would be able to hear. "I just got a call from GLI—"

Kaem interrupted, "Who?"

"Green Launch Initiative. They want to bid."

Marks spoke sternly, "Tell them they're too late. We already have a deal."

Arya said, "They're offering twenty percent more than you're asking Mr. Marks. Or, ten billion to buy the IP."

"That son of a bitch," Marks said. "Wait, who'd you talk to? Branzon often reneges on what his people say."

The Thunder of Engines

"It was Branzon himself that called." Arya glanced around at the reactions of as many of the Space-Gen people as she could eyeball without making it obvious. They looked distressed.

Unhappily, Marks said, "I'll go twenty-five percent over your ask if you'll sign it tonight."

Arya said, "Mr. Branzon said he's flying here from the west coast tonight and will meet with us in the morning. He strongly urges us not to make a deal without talking to him again."

"Come on, Kaem." Marks said, "You don't want a bastard like Branzon rolling out the first rockets using your baby, do you?"

Arya couldn't see Kaem's face, but she could *hear* the smile on it. "I don't know him or whether he's a bastard or not. But I do respect him enough to listen to his offer."

"You know, they're pretty far behind Space-Gen in the launch business. You should consider the possibility that he might pay you more than we will per rocket, but then won't buy very many of them. Your payday could be considerably less."

Kaem nodded, "Good point. Thanks. We'll be sure to consider inserting a minimum order in the contract."

From there, the dinner event gradually steered away from uncomfortable business and became more of a social event. Marks in particular turned on his already charismatic personality, carefully taking time to charm each of the four people associated with Staze.

On a break in a conversation, Arya noticed a young woman she didn't know enter the room. The woman looked around, then approached Tom Morales. He talked to her a moment, got out his phone and gave it a few commands, then handed it to her. She left the room, taking his phone with her. *What was that about?* Arya wondered. Before she could give it more thought, Lee and her fascinating yellow-green eyes appeared at Arya's side. "Hello?"

Lee tilted her head away toward the emptier side of the room, saying, "Could we talk, off a bit away from the crowd?"

"Um, sure," Arya said, uneasily wondering what Lee could want, but following her a few steps away from the closest group.

Lee turned and gave Arya an intense look. "Is Staze really just you, Kaem and Gunnar?" She shook her head, "No, don't answer that. I shouldn't have asked because it's none of my business." Lee glanced around as if checking on whether people might overhear. Arya noticed how Lee's eyes caught on Kaem again. Lee turned back to Arya. "My first trip out here, Kaem made an offhand remark that..." she hesitated.

"What?" Arya said, trying to conceal her impatience. She wanted to find out what was going on with Morales.

"Sorry, I'm embarrassed. He said he couldn't explain how stade's formed unless I came to work for you guys. He said you needed an engineer. Um, the more I learn about it the more I *do* want to work for Staze. Are you really hiring?"

Does she want to work for Staze, or does she want to work on Kaem? Arya wondered uncharitably. She said, "What'd he say when you asked *him*?"

"I haven't asked," Lee said with an embarrassed grin. "I don't want to put him on the spot if he was just kidding around."

"I can't read his mind any better than you can."

"But, surely, as the business… person, you'd know whether you guys are looking to hire or not."

"I'm sure we'll want to hire eventually. I'm not sure we can afford to hire anyone right now."

"But, surely, with that million-dollar fee Space-Gen paid to hold the right of first offer…"

"Yeah, but there are some issues with spending it. Ones I can't share with you."

"What if I came to work for free? At lead till you had the money to pay me?"

She's sounding more and more like a gold-digger who's after a husband, Arya thought bleakly. She said, "I think you're going to have to ask Kaem."

"Um, are you and Kaem…?"

"Are Kaem and I what?"

Lee glanced away, "Romantically involved?"

"No! Why would you even think that?"

"Sorry. It's just that he's so nice. And he has such a great sense of humor. It's easy to see how you could've fallen for him. And…"

"And what?" Arya said unable to keep from being abrupt.

"And you seem to give me a lot of jealous looks when I'm around him."

WHAT! Arya's thoughts fairly screamed. She forced a smile. "No. Nothing romantic here. And, I hate to tell you this, but he actually has a *terrible* sense of humor."

"Um. Okay." Lee looked puzzled for a moment, then said, "I'll go ask him then. The more I think about stade, the more I want to be involved in developing it. If GLI gets the contract it'd break my heart if I was still working for Space-Gen." She turned and wandered off, probably trying not to make it obvious she was angling toward Kaem.

Arya thought, *I should've told her we didn't have any room for people who're trying to marry our CEO!* She started after Lee, then decided it'd be too embarrassing to confront Lee about it now. *But,* she resolved, *I will talk to Kaem about it.*

Arya looked around and found Morales. She headed his way. Arriving, she asked, "Who was the young woman that took your phone?"

He grinned at her. "Nothing slips past you, does it? That was Sylvia Contreras, the contracts specialist I mentioned. Kaem asked me to put her on your case."

"In the evening?!"

"It seemed like things were moving pretty fast and we'd need some expertise very soon." Morales arched an eyebrow, "She's young but *very* sharp. Also, she's single. Young, hungry, lawyers definitely come out at night if there's a chance to get in on the ground floor of something as big as this. I'm surprised young lawyers aren't oozing out of the floors."

"So, why does she have your phone?"

"I recorded Kaem and Marks' conversation about the proposed deal. She's listening to it now to get a grasp on what's been offered."

"Ah," Arya said, pleased to have five people on their team. *But how are we paying her?*

Shrugging off that question, she surveyed the room again. Gunnar came in the door, having left for home a few minutes earlier. He looked agitated. His eyes roved around and found Kaem, then he headed that way. Arya moved that way as well, hoping Gunnar was pissed about something unimportant—as usual—and not upset because something *bad* had actually happened.

Arya arrived just as Gunnar pulled Kaem away from Prakant, Space-Gen's CEO, and said, "It's *gone*!" He

The Thunder of Engines

hissed it as if he thought his tone would keep people from hearing, but he did it much too loudly for that.

"What's gone?"

"The freaking stazer! That's what's gone! Someone broke into my truck's bed-box and took it, forms, electronics, and all!"

In dismay, Arya thought, *Not here Gunnar! And not so damned loud!* But it was too late, people were turning to look. They started drifting over.

Marks appeared at her elbow as if by magic. "Someone stole your stazer?"

Kaem nodded, managing to look unconcerned. "It'll be a hassle, but we'll just build another one."

Arya studied Kaem, *I think he's beyond unconcerned and into the "glad" realm. How can that be?!*

Marks frowned, "You had the stazer here? In the parking lot?"

Kaem nodded. "We don't like leaving it in the building at Staze. Too easy to break a window."

"But here? In what, your car?"

"Gunnar has a bed-box in his truck. It's bolted in and pretty secure." He turned to Gunnar, "How'd they get into it?"

"Cut the padlock," Gunnar said grimly. "Must've been a hell of a cutter; that was a hefty padlock."

"They take anything else?" Kaem asked calmly, leaving Arya wondering why he didn't sound as frantically distraught as she felt.

Gunnar said, "No. Just the molds and the electronics."

"You had other valuables in there though, right?"

"Oh yeah. Some expensive tools."

"So, this was someone who specifically wanted the stazer. Some kind of industrial spy. Have you called 911?"

"No." Gunnar said disgustedly, "The cops *never* recover stolen goods."

Kaem shrugged, "I believe that's true of ordinary theft, but perhaps when we're talking about one-of-a-kind industrial secrets they'll make an extra effort. Besides, we need their help getting the recordings from the Buffalo's security cameras."

Gunnar's eyes widened momentarily. He turned and started calling the police.

Marks said, "You seem pretty calm about this."

Kaem shrugged. "Not our first rodeo. We've been robbed before. Getting upset doesn't get the stuff back."

"What'd they get the first time?!" Marks asked tensely.

"Someone broke into my dorm room and stole version one of the stazer a few days ago."

"Holy shit! So, someone out there *already* knows how to make stade and you don't even have a patent yet?!"

Kaem chuckled, "I don't think they know how or they wouldn't be stealing version two."

Marks rolled his eyes. "Or maybe *someone else* stole this version. Even if it's the same people, now that they've got version two, they're definitely gonna know how to make stade in a few hours."

With his inscrutable smile, Kaem said, "I don't think so."

"Come on! They've got the machine, don't they? Don't tell me they stole a decoy or something."

The Thunder of Engines

"No. They've got the right machine. It's just that the settings needed to staze something are... complex."

"But can't they just fool around with the settings until they start getting something!"

Kaem shrugged unconcernedly, "I'm sure they'll try... I doubt they'll succeed."

"I wouldn't count on *that* bit of luck if I were you," Marks said. "Who do you think it is?"

"Well, all the major aerospace companies received samples of stade and so any of them *might* have gotten excited about it."

Marks narrowed his eyes. "I hope you're not accusing Space-Gen."

"Not Space-Gen the company, no. It'd be more likely some individual in your company I'd think. Someone who thinks he's figured a way to make a killing without having to share it with the rest of you." He sighed, "Though, at present, our most likely suspect *is* a company. One whose CEO has a... reputation."

"Ricard Caron," Marks said, disgustedly.

"Ah, you've heard of his reputation too?"

"Oh yeah."

To Arya's utter disbelief, Kaem calmly said, "His people have been calling us and saying they've got a patent on stade but—"

"*They've* got a patent?!" Marks interrupted incredulously.

"They *say* they've got a patent," Kaem said in a reassuring tone. "They don't. They've been demanding we turn over all our working models, drawings, descriptions, etcetera because they *don't* know how to make stade. They're desperately trying to figure it out in time to modify their patent application so the device they submitted actually works."

"Oh... I don't know about this..." Marks said, looking dubious.

Arya looked around to take in the reactions of the others. Her eyes caught on an appalled looking Lee.

Gunnar came over, "Kaem, the cops are here. You wanna help me talk to them?"

"Why, yes I do," Kaem said cheerfully. "I've got some important info for them."

Chapter Six

Arya woke just before her phone started chiming. She had a hangover from overindulging after everything had melted down the night before. "Hello?"

"Hi, this is Rami French, Mr. Branzon's assistant. I'm hoping to set up that meeting with Staze this morning?"

"Um…" Arya said, so many questions swirling in her mind. *Should I tell them about the theft and Martin Aero's claims? When could the others be ready? Where would we meet?* She checked the time, 9:00 AM! *How'd I sleep so late?! Wait,* she thought with some relief, *that's late for us, but, having come from the west coast, early for them.* She asked, "When did you want to meet?"

"Mr. Branzon wondered if we could meet somewhere for breakfast? Perhaps here at our hotel, unless you have a better place you'd recommend?"

Glad not to have to recommend a place and hoping that breakfast at the hotel would go on Branzon's tab, Arya readily agreed. They agreed to meet in an hour.

Arya called Kaem who was sinfully cheerful, then she remembered he hadn't been drinking. *And I've probably never had that much.* She said, "I just got a call from Branzon's people. They want to meet. I told them we could be at their hotel in an hour."

"I have class," Kaem said as if surprised she'd agreed to the meeting. "You're supposed to be picking me up in five minutes."

"Kaem! This is Jerry Branzon! Billions of dollars hang in the balance! Watch the video of your damned class later!"

He sighed, "Okay. But I *like* asking questions. Getting a degree's important to me. It'll make my dad unbelievably prou—"

"Kaem! Focus! Getting a degree and all is nice, but..." She sighed, "A deal for stade's starting to seem unlikely, but I don't want to wonder for the rest of my life whether we *could've* done it if we'd just put in a *little* more effort. Do you *really* want me to call and tell *Branzon* you can't meet because you have class?"

"I *said* 'okay,'" Kaem said in a surly tone. "Are you getting an Uber and coming by here?"

"Yes. Should I invite Gunnar to the meeting?"

"Of course... Wait, why not?"

"He tends to get excited and say... things I'd rather he hadn't."

With a little laugh, Kaem said, "Like telling Marks our stazer was stolen?"

"Uh-huh. Like that."

"I'd been trying to figure out how to tell Marks about Martin, so I felt relieved when Gunnar opened that can of worms and gave me a way to bring it up."

"Could've been done more... smoothly," Arya grumped.

"Well, there is that," Kaem said with another laugh. "Maybe you could ask Gunnar to come to the breakfast *if* he's not too busy checking with the police about how they're doing with the break-in to his bed-box?"

"Okay, I'll talk to Gunnar. I do think we should ask Morales and Contreras to come."

"Agreed. I'll call them.

The Thunder of Engines

"Should I tell Branzon's people the Stazer got stolen last night?"

"Absolutely. Don't want them asking for a demonstration."

~~~

It turned out that Gunnar much preferred following up with the cops. He wasn't as much a fan-boy of Branzon as he'd been of Marks.

Morales had appointments, but Contreras met them for breakfast. Branzon only had his assistant, Rami French, and an aerospace engineer, George Meade, with him, so there were only six people at the breakfast. Arya thought she was going to prefer that to the circus they'd had the previous night.

The entire character of the meeting was different. Almost immediately after they placed their orders Branzon turned to Kaem and said, "A little birdie tells me you not only had your stazer stolen, but that Martin Aerospace is suing you for patent infringement?"

While Arya wondered who the hell the birdie was, Kaem nodded calmly, "Correct on both counts."

Looking thoughtful, Branzon leaned back in his chair. "You don't seem terribly worried."

Kaem shrugged, "I can build another stazer and Martin Aero doesn't actually know how to make stade. This is a setback, yes, but not a very big one."

Branzon looked at Sylvia, then at Arya.

Arya hoped he couldn't tell how worried *she* felt.

Branzon looked back at Sylvia, "How do you feel about this quote-unquote, 'setback?'"

"I've only known them since yesterday," she said, "so I'm probably not the right person to ask. But Thomas Morales, the patent attorney who put them in touch with me, feels very confident that they own the rights. If it's good enough for Tom, it's good enough for me. He's *very* smart about intellectual property law."

"Hmm," Branzon said thoughtfully. He turned to Arya. "I understand that Kaem here's the inventor, right?"

Arya bobbed a nod, afraid of tripping over her tongue if she spoke.

"How confident are you that he's truly the one who invented it? That he didn't steal it from Martin Aerospace like Ricard claims?"

Has Branzon been talking to Ricard Caron? Arya wondered frantically. Nonetheless, she schooled her features to calmness. Taking a breath to relax, she said, "I met Kaem when he first arrived at UVA as a freshman almost three years ago. He told me about his theory, the one stade's based on, the day he arrived. He wanted to major in physics so he could learn enough to check for flaws in his theory, then was disappointed when his professors didn't seem to know enough about that area of physics to be of much use." She took a breath, "Martin claims they have a patent but won't give us a number. Our searches of the patent databases don't turn up a patent in the field Kaem's version of stade is based on. If Martin has something similar to stade it almost certainly doesn't have Stade's phenomenal properties. It seems likely that the best they have is a recent application since apps older than eighteen months are published and searchable. That would mean Kaem has priority."

Branzon put his hand out, palm down and waggled it, "Priority of invention doesn't mean much if he didn't apply for a patent but they did."

"We believe Martin applied for a patent even though they don't know how to make stade. That they're

The Thunder of Engines

hoping to amend the application to one that's functional as soon as they get our stazer."

This time Branzon narrowed his eyes, "What makes you think they don't?"

"The fact that they've been trying to steal the secret from Kaem."

"You're saying Martin's the one that stole your stazer?"

Arya nodded. Their food arrived and there was a break in their conversation as it was distributed and they started eating.

Branzon looked up at Arya from his omelet, "You realize that blaming your problems on Martin sounds... paranoid?"

"They've stolen stazers from us twice. The first time they just got a bunch of loose components. They obviously didn't know how to hook those up correctly to make a functioning stazer." Arya felt surprised to be—she thought successfully—defending Kaem against the same questions that were worrying her.

After more discussion with Arya, Branzon turned to Kaem, "What makes *you* think they can't make stade?"

Kaem shrugged, "Like Arya says, if they did, they wouldn't be trying to steal working models from us."

"How do you know Martin Aerospace is the one that's stealing your stuff?"

"They're the ones who're making angry calls about how we're infringing. They're the ones who're demanding we send them all our working models, diagrams, descriptions, and etcetera. They're the ones who're panicking because they can't figure out how to do it. It only makes sense that they must be the ones who're going a step further and stealing our stuff." His phone buzzed. He looked at it a moment, then leaned forward and held it out, "And, the tracking device I installed in version two of the stazer says it's just arrived at Martin Aerospace's South Texas facility."

Arya's eyes widened in astonishment. *Why didn't he tell me he was tracking it?!*

Branzon's eyes stared at the phone's display a moment, then he grinned, "Holy shit! That was smart." He frowned, "Though, I suppose you could be faking this display."

"I could," Kaem agreed equably. He stood up. "I'm sorry. Even though I told the police about the tracker, I'd like to check in with them to make sure they're paying attention to its current location. Don't want them to take so long the tracker's battery goes dead. Do you have any more questions, sir?"

"Sit. We'll all keep wolfing our food while I ask just a few. For instance, how do I know *you* can make stade? Maybe you just managed to steal some from Martin Aerospace and sent test samples out to everyone. Now I show up and, suspiciously, you suddenly can't make any because someone stole your stazer. Do you even *have* any stade?"

Kaem turned to Arya, "There was some in Staze's building. If the guy that stole the stazer didn't also steal all our samples, maybe you could give a couple of them to Mr. Branzon?"

Arya said, "Actually, I have some in my jacket." She looked at Branzon, "Would those do?"

"Um, sure," Branzon said, holding out his hand. "I just want proof you have more than a few pieces.

Arya pulled her jacket off the back of her chair and looked at Kaem, "You have your knife?"

"You're going to ruin another jacket?" Kaem asked as he got out his knife and handed it to her.

Arya nodded, but Branzon looked puzzled, "Why would you have to ruin the jacket?"

"She made herself a bulletproof vest out of stade," Kaem said. "She's offering to cut the vest out from between the shell and the liner of her jacket. But if you'd be willing to go with her to Staze's building, maybe she could give you one of the samples we have there instead?"

"Sure. Um," he said distractedly, "can I feel your jacket?"

Arya passed it over.

Kaem stood again and turned to go, "I'm heading to the police station. Call me if you need anything?"

Worriedly, Arya said, "Kaem, I'm supposed to go with you! Can't you call Gunnar and have *him* check to make sure the police are aware of the location of the stazer?"

"I need to tell the police about a couple more tricks I have up my sleeve."

Branzon frowned, "Why's she supposed to go with you?"

Kaem looked embarrassed, "I'd rather not say."

Branzon looked down at the front panel of the jacket he'd been feeling. His engineer, Meade, was fingering the other front panel of the jacket. He looked at the man and said, "It *feels* like there's a crapload of plates in this jacket doesn't it?"

Meade nodded.

Branzon waved at Kaem's chair, "One second. We'll make a nick in the lining of the jacket so I can see and feel at least one of the plates to be sure it really is stade. If it is, I'll go with you guys to the police station. A few minutes isn't going to make a difference. After we see the police, we'll go over to your building and see the samples there."

~~~

Arya had been horrified by the way the three men gobbled their food. She, Sylvia, and Rami barely ate half of theirs before everyone was getting up to go.

It didn't matter much to her, she wasn't hungry. Her stomach was too roiled by all the excitement. And by her hangover.

At the police station, Arya got the impression the presence and fame of Branzon cut through a lot of red tape. Instead of being told to wait—the way she saw happening to other people—a detective was quickly found. From the way one of the uniformed cops had to explain things to the man, Arya thought the burglary of their stazer hadn't been elevated to the level of a detective until Branzon showed up looking interested. While Kaem brought the police up to speed on what was happening and where the stolen goods were currently located—as they should have known from checking his location app themselves, though he didn't throw it in their faces—the police kept glancing at Branzon.

He nodded wisely but said little.

When Kaem started angling to have Martin's Texas facility searched for Staze's property, Branzon nodded and commented that a search certainly needed to be done because the missing device had a multimillion-dollar value. As they were talking about liaising with a police department near the facility down in Texas, Branzon said, "I'm going that way anyway," and offered to fly the detective down with him in his private plane.

To her astonishment, Arya found herself in the plane with Branzon, Meade, Rami French, and several other people she realized she'd vaguely noticed in the background that morning. People that turned out to be Branzon's security people.

Kaem, a uniformed officer, and the detective talked to one another near the back of the plane for over an hour. Arya assumed they were getting their ducks in a row for the proposed visit to Martin Aerospace.

Meanwhile, Branzon carried on a breezy conversation with Arya. It wasn't until they'd been talking for quite a while that she realized Branzon had efficiently obtained her life history and learned almost everything there was to know about how Staze came to be formed. He didn't have the obvious, forceful charisma that radiated from Marks but something was compelling about his personality.

Something... intensely formidable

Done with the police, Kaem came up and sat with them. As if he were just looking for interesting conversation, Branzon worked through Kaem's history and dreams as well. Kaem was a willing participant in divulging his life story—but he revealed nothing about stade.

~~~

When they were about to land in Texas, Kaem's and Arya's phones began chiming. She was getting a text from Marks and had missed a call from Cary Lark. The text wanted to know where the hell she was.

When she checked with Kaem, he confirmed that he had much the same text from Marks. He said, "You reply to the Marks' texts, telling him we're talking to Branzon. That should keep them on the edge of their seats."

"Do I tell them we're in Texas or what we're doing here?"

"Hmm, be cryptic. Tell them we're getting the stazer back from Martin Aerospace."

She frowned, "What if we don't get it?"

He shrugged, "Doesn't matter. I want to build a better one anyway."

"Are you going to text him too?"

"No. I'm not eager."

"You mean you don't want to *seem* too eager."

"Well, of course. If I'm *not* eager, I shouldn't seem eager. They'll call and text some more. Ignore those."

Arya wondered if he was a savvy negotiator or was endangering their business by refusing to cooperate.

They were met at the airport in South Texas by a pair of local detectives and a small group of uniformed police. After some brief get-to-know-you conversation and an examination of Kaem's phone and tracking app, the police set out for Martin Aerospace, search warrant in hand.

Branzon's people rented a Chevy Suburban. It pulled up at the airport's private facility just as the police pulled out on their way to serve their warrant. When Branzon got in, Kaem piled in behind him. No one invited Arya, but she got in as well. They'd driven about a mile when one of the police SUV's pulled off the road and flagged them down.

They pulled off behind it. Arya worried that they were about to be told they couldn't follow the police to Martin Aero—something she actually couldn't believe was within policy. The man who trotted back to their SUV proved to be one of the Texas detectives. Opening the door, he said, "We got the warrant so you can start recording audio. There's some concern that a lawman needs to be in attendance while the recording's being made so I'm gonna ride with you guys, okay?"

The Thunder of Engines

Branzon nodded and the detective got into the seat beside Branzon and Kaem. Arya was wedged into the seat behind the two men with two of Branzon's guards, but close enough to be able to hear what was going on.

Kaem had his phone out. He tapped the screen a couple of times and voices began issuing from it. He plugged a cord into a USB socket to make sure the phone's battery didn't run down.

Not sure what was going on, Arya focused on the voices emanating from the phone:

> "...two and a half days on the supercomputer and there's *bupkis* to show for it!"
>
> "Yeah. I heard Caron's in a frenzy."
>
> The first voice asked, "Do you know whether he's pissed about how much the time on the supercomputer costs? Or is it about how long it's taking to break the encryption?"
>
> "Both, probably," the second voice answered, sounding distracted. Then he said, "Okay, trying it again." A moment after that, he said, "Open it up."
>
> The first voice said, "Nothing."
>
> "Dammit!"
>
> "I mean, I guess there's nothing," the first guy said. "It's supposed to have something shiny in it, right?"
>
> "Yeah," the second man said, "Like the samples I showed you. All mirrored surfaces."

"You wanna look? This damn thing's nothing but mirrors inside anyway. Maybe I'm missing it."

"No. You're not missing it," the second man said as if exasperated. "There's nothing in there. Feel, it's empty."

"It's okay to put a finger in there?"

"Yes! Dammit! Now, close it up and let's try it again."

Arya thought the man sounded glum.

A few moments of silence followed, so Arya leaned close to Kaem and whispered, "You put a *bug* in the stazer too?"

"What I put in is an old cellphone with an extra battery. It has a charger that runs when the rack's plugged in," Kaem said quietly. "I put it inside the shell of one of the components that has a plastic case. I installed an app that lets me control the phone. It auto-answers when I call but mutes the sound. No ring, no vibration, doesn't light the screen. My phone records the audio it sends."

"Holy crap! The phone's what's sending you the location data too?"

Kaem nodded.

Cursing came from the phone. Evidently, the men had failed again. From what they'd said, Arya assumed they were trying to make stade with the second generation stazer but—not knowing how to wire it up or adjust the settings—weren't having any luck.

"What was that about a warrant?" Arya asked.

Kaem leaned back to her but still spoke quietly. "In Texas, without a warrant, you can't legally record someone without their consent, so the police applied for one. It just got approved."

"So, we're hoping the people with the stazer will say something incriminating?"

Kaem shrugged, "Sure, but I think these guys are just underlings. I'm hoping someone important shows up and *they* say something incriminating."

The voices on the phone continued.

> The second man said, "Okay, open it up."
>
> "Still empty," the first guy said. "Hey, you know, it doesn't seem to me you can make something outta nothin'. Maybe we gotta have something in the compartment to be *changed into* the silvery stuff."
>
> "It's *not* empty," the second voice said, "It's full of air." Then there was a pause. "Still, that's not the dumbest thing you've ever said. Put something in there and close it up again."
>
> "What am I supposed to put in there? There isn't *room* for anything bigger than a scrap of paper!"
>
> "A scrap of paper and a paper clip'll be fine," the second guy said, sounding annoyed. "There're a bunch on the desk."
>
> After a brief silence—while the man presumably went over to said desk—the first guy said, "Okay, go." They heard a faint sound, then, "Nope, nothin' happened to it."

For about ten minutes, they heard nothing but repeats of words to the effect of, "Check it," and, "Nope, still empty."

Arya was starting to worry that they'd arrive at Martin Aerospace before anyone said anything definitively incriminating:

> Suddenly they heard the sound of a door banging open. An angry voice said, "For God's sake Munger, tell me you've got *something* happening!"

Branzon calmly said, "That's Ricard Caron's voice. He's Martin Aerospace's CEO. Elgin Munger's Martin Aero's CTO. Pretty surprising that the CTO'd be working on a device but Caron may be trying to limit the number of people involved."

> The second voice from before—presumably Munger—said, "Nothing yet." His tone implied he didn't have much hope. "There are literally thousands of ways to make these settings. If only one of them works…"
> "*SON OF A BITCH!*" Caron shouted, sounding like someone who'd dropped a brick on his toe. "Wang! Dammit! You're *sure* you didn't change the settings on this thing when you got it?"
> "No. When I got, everyt'ing turn' off. Dials all set on lowest setting. Switches all popped out or flipped down. I t'ink Seba know you might steal an' he scramble settings."

Hearing his name, Kaem looked up meaningfully at Branzon.

The Thunder of Engines

The CEO gave him a subtle nod in return. He turned to the detective in the seat ahead. "What we've heard is pretty incriminating. I assume you heard them mention Kaem Seba's name?"

The detective nodded.

"We're almost there. You might want to slow down and give them a few minutes to dig an even deeper hole."

The detective nodded and spoke to his phone. Soon all the vehicles were pulling off the side of the road:

> Sounding even more incensed, Caron said, "What about the wiring on the back? It's like a freaking rat's nest. You're *sure* that's the way it was when you got it?"
>
> No one responded. Arya got the impression the silence was quite uncomfortable.
>
> "Come on, Elgin," Caron said pleadingly, "the damn wiring looks like someone snarled it on purpose. Isn't there some obvious way these kinds of components *should* be wired together?"
>
> A chair scraped, presumably Munger moving to have a look at the wiring. After a moment, Munger's voice said slowly, "Some of the components are wired... counterintuitively. But if I started undoing those things, I still wouldn't know which one of the hundreds of ways such components might *normally* be wired together was the correct one."

> "You've re-read the diagrams and descriptions from the files on Seba's computer?" Caron asked.

Kaem abruptly straightened, looking alarmed.

Arya said, "I thought you said the encryption on your hard drive was unbreakable. That if they *ever* got into it, it'd take *years*."

Kaem didn't answer, motioning for silence so he could hear Munger's reply:

> With strained patience, Munger was saying, "...gone over that first set of diagrams and descriptions *again*. They still don't make sense... personally, I think they're just a smokescreen. I thought you got his whole computer now? Are there any better descriptions or diagrams on it?"
>
> To Arya's surprise, Kaem seemed to relax on hearing this.
>
> Caron spoke, sounding as if he were making a threat, "You *know* we haven't been able to break the encryption on Seba's goddamned hard drive!"
>
> Munger asked, "You *are* using the quantum processor on the encryption, right?"
>
> "Yes! I'm not *an* idiot!" Caron's tone became resigned, "Besides, even if I hadn't thought of it, the IT wienies would've insisted on using the quantum processor just because they like to get access to it. They say they have no idea how the encryption on that disc is holding up against quantum

> decryption. They think, if we can figure out how Seba's system works, we should try to patent his encryption scheme too."

Branzon glanced at Kaem. Arya saw respect in the man's eyes when he did so. The CEO turned to the detective. "That was pretty damning. We might want to move in. It'd be nice if we caught Caron there with the device."

The detective nodded. He'd been talking to someone in one of the other vehicles as they drove, reporting on what was being heard over Kaem's phone. Now he passed on Branzon's suggestion. The SUVs pulled back onto the road. It was only another couple of minutes before they turned off and stopped at a security gate with signs saying "Martin Aerospace."

There was a bunch of headshaking and showing of warrants, then some shouting. When one of the guards in the shack made as if to call someone, one of the uniformed officers arrested him. The other one stood down. Two of the uniforms stayed with the guards as the SUVs pulled onto the grounds.

To Arya's astonishment, Branzon's rental SUV followed along behind the police. They *did* still have the detective in their vehicle, so she wondered if they considered Branzon's car part of the police group because of his presence. *Or, maybe Texas police are more liberal in the way they follow the rules. Or maybe I just have no idea what the rules are?*

The police apparently had the location of the specific building the stazer was in from Kaem's app. The SUVs drove directly to a building on the Martin Aerospace campus and parked.

As the detective got out of Branzon's vehicle, he said, "Keep recording, but y'all need to stay in the vehicle." He quickly moved to join the rest of the police. As most of the police gathered in front of the building, several of the uniforms trotted around to the back. *Do they think someone's going to try to escape that way?* she wondered.

She saw one of the uniforms knock several times on what appeared to be the main door of the building. Finally, the door opened. After what looked like a brief argument with whoever had opened the door, several of the policemen pushed their way inside. The detectives followed.

They heard nothing on Kaem's phone. Evidently, Munger and Caron weren't in the room directly behind the entrance.

About a minute later they heard some banging and a muffled:

> "Police! Open up!"
> Caron's voice hissed, "Son of a bitch! Hold them while I go out the other door."
> Arya heard the creak of a door hinge, then an unmuffled voice cheerfully said, "Well, hello! Ricard Caron, I believe? Where do you think you're going?"
> In an ugly tone, Caron said, "What the hell do you think you're doing here?! This's private property!"
> "Ah, yes, you're right. But, you see here? This's a warrant to search this facility for property stolen from Staze Incorporated."

The Thunder of Engines

"Get that out of my face! I've never heard of Stade Incorporated and we *certainly* wouldn't have any of their property here."

"That's *Staze* Incorporated, sir. Now, let's see... Yes, I think that rack of equipment on the table behind you looks very much like the quotes 'stazer' pictured on the supplemental pages of this here warrant."

There was a moment's pause, then Caron said, "I've never seen that rack of equipment, but I'm sure it's merely similar. All those electronic racks are pretty much the same size after all, and once you start loading off the shelf modules into them—"

"Come, come now, Mr. Caron, I might not be a high-tech aerospace wizard like you, but I can still tell when someone's *lying* to me. You might claim you've never heard of a company called 'Staze' but we've got a recording of you taking Mr. Seba's name in vain several times this morning, so we're *sure* you know where that rack of equipment came from."

"Recording?!" Caron spluttered. "Munger, you bastard! You're gonna regret this!"

The policeman sounded amused, "What's he going to regret?"

"Wearing a wire!" Caron exploded, "Like some kind of scum-sucking asshole!"

"Now, now, Mr. Munger wasn't wearing a wire. But, from the look on his face I'll bet he wouldn't mind turning state's evidence, would you?"

Loathing in his voice, Munger said, "No, I wouldn't. In fact, I'd *love* testifying against this son of a bitch."

"Hmm," Branzon said musingly, "you've *gotta* stay on the good side of people you've got doing dirty work." He looked up at Kaem. "I've really enjoyed being here listening to Caron get what's been coming to him, but I think I've heard enough. You guys ready to take off?"

Kaem nodded.

Arya said, "What about the stazer? Shouldn't we wait to get it back?"

Kaem shrugged, "I'm sure the police consider it evidence. You remember how that goes."

Arya thought back to the way the police demanded her jacket when Harris shot her. She said, "I suppose by the time we get it back, if they ever turn it loose, you'll have built a better one anyway, right?"

Kaem nodded.

Branzon said, "Now that I'm convinced you're the real inventor and Caron isn't going to be able to cut you out of the patent, maybe we could do some negotiating on the plane ride back to Charlottesville?"

"Sure," Kaem said. He jerked a thumb over the back of his seat at Arya, "I gotta warn ya though, Arya drives a hard bargain."

***

Some discussion but little actual negotiation got done on the flight back to Virginia. Branzon wanted to make a deal during the flight, but Arya repeatedly reminded him that they were legally compelled to give Space-Gen a chance to counteroffer.

Even if she'd forgotten that fact, when she used the plane's Wi-Fi to check her messages she found several reminders from Marks to that effect. Her thought that Marks might've been driven off by the theft of their stazer and the possibility that Martin owned the actual patent didn't seem to be correct. It wasn't clear why he hadn't called until after noon, when they were already on their way to Texas, but it did seem Kaem's lack of concern about his level of interest had put him on edge.

She made an internet call to Marks, putting it on speaker. When she told him they'd been there for Caron's arrest he sounded delighted. *Just a little additional confirmation of all the evidence Caron was a jerk,* Arya thought.

"So, you've got the stazer back?" Marks asked.

"No. The police are keeping it as evidence."

"When'll you get it?"

"Maybe never. They'll want to keep it until any court cases are concluded. Kaem wants to build another one anyway."

"How long'll *that* take?"

Arya looked at Kaem. He said, "We'll need money before we can do it. So we'll need some up-front money from you or Branzon, whoever buys the rights."

Marks sounded incredulous. "What about that million dollars we gave you for the right of first offer?"

Kaem said, "Arya doesn't want to spend that until we've got a deal worked out."

"Speaking of a deal, where are you on any negotiations with Branzon?"

"We're on his plane. He flew us down to Texas."

Sounding startled, Marks said, "Is he there with you? Jerry, are you listening to this call?"

"Hi Aaron," Branzon said with a little chuckle.

"You *dog* you! Good thing I didn't verbalize any of my innermost thoughts about your character."

Branzon snorted, "None of those'd be news to me. But how about if you and I come to an agreement regarding the purchase of their rockets? I don't want to get in a bidding war so I'm gonna suggest we *both* get rights to have them exclusively cast rocket parts for us." He turned to Kaem, "What would you say to that? We'd both buy at your exclusive price and you'd have double the sales."

"So," Kaem said thoughtfully, "you'd pay four million for an engine, forty million for a body, etcetera, etcetera?"

Branzon nodded, then realizing Marks couldn't see him, he said, "Something like that."

Marks said, "I could go for that."

Arya said, "What's your minimum buy?"

Branzon said, "Minimum buy?"

"Yes. When you were bidding against one another, Mr. Marks pointed out that GLI's volume wasn't as great as Space-Gen's and so, even though you might pay more per rocket, you might not buy very many."

Branzon snorted, "Aaron? You *already* sold me down the river?"

"I was just trying to hold onto my shirt Jerry. I know you can outbid me."

"Okay..." Branzon looked thoughtful, "How about if GLI agrees to buy... Wait, over what period?"

Kaem said, "A minimum total number of rockets. Remember, you can reuse them forever, so if you aren't doing a lot of launches, our fear would be that you'd only buy one."

"Ah. Okay, how about if GLI and Space-Gen each promise to buy ten rockets?"

Marks said, "We can buy more if we want, right?"

"Uh-huh," Branzon responded.

Kaem said, "That'll get you exclusive rights for three years."

"Five," Branzon and Marks said almost in chorus.

"Four then," Kaem said. "But we'll need a million from each of you upfront so we can get started. A million you agree not to ask to have back, otherwise, Arya *still* won't let me get our business going."

The two tycoons agreed. Marks made a halfhearted attempt to have the million he'd paid to guarantee the right of first offer act as his up-front start fee, but gave in quickly when Kaem simply said "no."

Arya said she'd bring Sylvia Contreras up to date so she could work with the lawyers from Space-Gen and GLI while they hammered out the contracts.

***

Over the weekend, Kaem worked hard redesigning circuits for a new, purpose-built stazer. It'd be a heavy-duty one capable of generating the high-powered microwave and laser emissions he'd calculated would be required to staze large segments of space-time. Once designed, he again swapped around important components in the design, trading capacitors with inductors, and resistors with diodes. The new arrangement would produce a functional circuit, which would, however, be incapable of generating the proper microwaves or correctly exciting the lasers. It certainly wouldn't be able to induce stasis.

In fact, by his calculations, this nonsense circuit would blow itself out at most of the settings that could be chosen through its integrated controller chip. Yet, with certain settings, it would produce outputs he could use to confirm the board was functional. Once he was sure each board worked, he'd swap the components to make it functional for stazing, test its ability to induce stasis, then put it in the stade box that would protect Kaem's secrets from being discovered. To make the swaps easier, he specified that many of the connections wouldn't be soldered—until the board went into the stade box—relying instead on plug and socket connectors to that point.

Finished with the design, he spent a few minutes committing to memory the swaps needed to change it back to a functional state.

The design work helped take his mind off his father's illness.

Once he'd ordered the necessary parts and components, he went through the videos of the classes he'd missed during the negotiations and the trip to Texas. That done, he fell back to thinking maudlin thoughts.

To distract himself, he called Gunnar. "Tell me about your thermite idea."

"Whiskey Tango Foxtrot, Kaem! It's like you guys vanished off the face of the Earth! What the hell's going on! Last I heard you and Arya were flying off to Texas to try to get the stazer back. Did you get it?"

"Oh. Sorry. I was thinking Arya brought you up to date. She's probably thinking I did it."

The Thunder of Engines

"You guys treat me like the dumb ugly cousin you only talk to when you need something!"

"Sorry. You're right," Kaem said. He put a sly tone in his voice, "You want us to buy you out?"

"Buy me out?! Hell no! I made an investment; I want to reap the rewards... if there ever are any."

"Sorry," Kaem said, "I was trying to make a joke... Arya says I'm not a comedian. You definitely *do not* want out. Let me bring you up to date." Kaem described what'd happened with Caron, Branzon, and Marks and how they now had three million in the bank that Arya finally agreed they could spend. "... and she's agreed that each of us can have our share of one and a half million to spend. Your one percent means you should have fifteen thousand in your account on Monday sometime."

"Big whoop. That's about what I invested."

"So, you've broken even already. And, a lot more'll be coming in. Don't cry in your soup."

"Yeah, yeah," Gunnar said grumpily—no change from his usual demeanor.

"You can imagine, after getting two versions of the stazer stolen, I'm liking your idea of protecting the secrets of the stazer with something like thermite. Can we meet at Staze's building to talk about it?"

***

When Kaem entered Staze's big room, Gunnar was already there. He said, "So, you've decided to go ahead and pack stazers in thermite to keep anyone from stealing the tech?"

"Yeah. Something like that."

"What about Arya's fear that we might go to jail if someone got hurt?"

"I was counting on your idea of putting only a little bit of thermite under a few parts of the circuit board. Just enough to destroy the board so no one could figure out how it worked."

"Hmm," Gunnar said, sounding as interested as he typically did when confronted with technical problems. "We'd probably want to use a thermate…" He trailed off thoughtfully.

When he didn't say anything more, Kaem stimulated him, "And the difference between thermite and thermate is…"

"Hmm…? Oh, thermates are various nonstandard mixes of thermite. Usually, they have some added chemicals to accomplish various goals. Thermite's really hard to ignite, so we'd want a modified version that's easier to light… Or maybe just part of it would be easy to light. We wouldn't want the whole thing going up just because your circuit got hot."

"I saw something about using magnesium to light thermite?"

"Yeah, but even though magnesium burns like hell, it isn't all that easy to light either. Maybe we could have something easy to light that starts the magnesium. Then the magnesium lights a thin slab of regular thermite right under the circuit board?"

"It'd be nice to rearrange the stazer's components after they burned. Wouldn't want the thieves analyzing the arrangement of the crisped parts and figuring out how the stazer was built from that. Maybe something that explodes once the board's burned enough to lose its structural integrity?"

"This is getting pretty complex. Besides, you know Arya's not going to go for something that explodes. Prison, remember?"

The Thunder of Engines

"Here's what I'm thinking. There're outer and inner stade boxes. When you start trying to open the outer box, it ignites a fuse that sets off the thermite in the inner box."

"So, the thermite in the inner box burns, generating a lot of heat and pressure and nasty gas. The stade doesn't let any of that escape, not even the heat. Then they open the inner box and, *boom*!"

"No, we've got to put in some pressure relief holes that let the pressure escape the inner box before they can open it..." Kaem hesitated. "The thermite reaction's *supposed* to convert aluminum and iron oxide into iron and aluminum oxide, plus heat. The chemical formula ($2Al + Fe_2O_3 \rightarrow 2Fe + Al_2O_3$) doesn't call for anything else to be produced. Where's this nasty gas you're talking about coming from?"

"Well, the reaction's so hot it vaporizes some metal. Breathing aluminum or iron vapor isn't healthy. Plus, if we want our thermite to be a solid rather than a powder you need to stick it together with something, usually something organic. The heat of the thermite can turn organic binders into toxic fumes. And that's not counting the circuit board and all its components that might release toxic byproducts when they burn..." Gunnar cocked his head, "Um, the safest explosive might be a steam bomb."

"Steam bomb?" Kaem asked.

"Yeah, you put a capsule of water in the middle of your circuit board. When the thermite gets it hot enough, the steam explodes the capsule, blowing the board's components apart, without adding any more toxic products."

"Crap. I thought this was gonna be simple."

Gunnar suddenly sounded eager, though a little embarrassed. "Um, I... kinda like this kind of stuff. You give me a budget and I'll do some experimenting until we get something that works without being too... dangerous, or toxic, or whatever. It'll still need a lot of warning labels on it though. 'DANGER, DO NOT OPEN!' That kinda thing."

"Okay, you've got yourself a project. Ask Arya for money to do it."

Gunnar said, "Wait. What if they use your... whatever it is you figured out how to do to break down a stade?"

After a moment's hesitation, Kaem said, "That *would be* a problem, wouldn't it? It'd break down the outer stade, and then, you're wondering, what if they just ran the sequence again to break down the inner stade while the stazer was still in the chamber from breaking down the first one?"

Gunnar nodded.

"And then the burning thermite's exposed...," Kaem said slowly, "We'll need a steel box inside the two stade boxes. That way, if they quickly destabilize the outer two stade boxes and the thermite reaction's in full bloom, busily destroying the electronics, they'll still be protected from it by the steel box. To hurry things along in that event, we could even put an ultracapacitor in the outer box. As soon as they destabilized the stade, the capacitor's electrodes would make contact and send power to the inner box to jumpstart everything by blowing out all the electronics and igniting the thermate."

Gunnar shook his head, "That's not going to work. Capacitors don't hold their charge very long. Even a battery'd probably be dead by the time, a couple of years later, someone stole the stazer and started taking it apart."

"The capacitor'd still have its charge if it was *part* of the outer shell stade."

"Oh!" Gunnar grinned. "Yeah. You'd charge it up right before you formed the stade the outer box was made of. Then as soon as the big cap comes out of stasis, boom, it discharges into the circuit board, frying everything and I mean *everything*. A big ultracap can deliver so much current the conductors in the board and a lot of the components on it'll just vaporize. It'll have plenty of juice to ignite the magnesium that lights the thermite…"

Gunnar halted because Kaem had been motioning for him to slow down. "Don't forget that if the crook *doesn't* break the stasis, but just starts disassembling the boxes, that ultracapacitor won't come on line. We need a mechanical way to light the thermite in that situation."

"Ah, yeah. I'll keep that in mind."

"You should think about how we're going to assemble the stade boxes. I'm thinking of a box with a lid that's bolted on. If those bolts are made of stade they'll just come undone, but if they're made of something else, they'll be vulnerable. Maybe we could have the head end of the bolt be made of stade, while inside the case the thread end of the bolt and the nut itself are made of steel?"

Gunnar frowned, "How do we make a bolt that's stade on one end and steel on the other?"

"We start with a steel threaded end that has a rough shaft surface and cast a stade head around that shaft."

"Will that work even though stade's frictionless?"

It was Kaem's turn to look puzzled. "I was thinking it would. That if the steel part of the bolt had a reflective surface with little divots in, or even outright holes, that the stade would form into the irregularities and an interlocking effect would hold them together. We'd have to have a mirrored mold the shape of the head end of the bolt that clamped around the shaft of the threaded end of the bolt. I was thinking stade would only form inside the mold up to the point where it clamped on, but we haven't tried it and we definitely need to. Maybe the shaft of the bolt that's sticking into the mold will get stazed as well, in which case we wouldn't need a reflective surface or any roughening or divots." He sighed, "There're *so* many things we need to try so we can find out how or whether they'll work."

Kaem's phone spoke in his earbud, "You have a call from April Lee." Eagerly, he stepped away from Gunnar, saying he'd take it.

~~~

Lee felt relieved when Kaem took her call. "Hi Kaem, sorry to bother you on the weekend."

"That's okay. I can use the distraction. My dad's sick and I keep worrying about him."

"Oh! What's wrong?"

"Sorry, we don't even know what it is yet. I shouldn't be bothering you with my personal problems. What's up with you?"

"Gosh," Lee said, not knowing what to say. "I'm so sorry to hear about your dad. My call's not urgent. You could call me, um, um… when you know what's going on with him?" She immediately felt regret. *Why'd I say that?! If he doesn't call, I won't know if he just forgot, but also won't feel comfortable calling in follow-up.*

The Thunder of Engines

To her great relief, he said, "No, no. Talk to me. Distract me. What can I do for you?"

"Well, maybe Arya talked to you?"

"About you?"

"Uh-huh."

"Not that I can think of."

"I mentioned to her how you'd said you could only tell me more about the nature of stade if I hired on. Um, do you even remember saying that? You also said Staze needed an engineer,"

"No, I remember. I was half kidding, half-serious. Are you thinking you'd like to jump ship? Space-Gen's pretty cool."

"It is. It's been my dream job forever. Even though there've been some hassles since I started working there, I've been really happy. But… I think Staze is going to be far cooler. There're so many things you could make with a material having stade's properties. It's… going to let us build… astonishing things." She sighed, "So, yes, Space-Gen's great, but I think Staze'll be even better and, and… I want to be in on the ground floor. I think we could change the world."

She could hear the smile in Kaem's voice. "Yeah! That's what I'm always talking about. Changing the whole damned world! Not just making money but making things better. We'd love to have you here. Just say the word."

"Um, I think you should check with Arya. I talked to her about it the night of the dinner and… I don't think she's too keen on the idea of me joining you."

"That was probably because we didn't have the money to be hiring anyone back then. We're solvent now."

"I... I kinda got the impression that she might not want any... any other women around."

Kaem sounded astonished. "Why not?! She's big on equality for women. 'Equal pay for equal work' and all that."

"I, uh, think she might have a thing for you. Have you guys been dating?"

This seemed to surprise Kaem even more. "No! I mean... I'd like to because she's pretty, and smart, and *really* capable. But she pushes me away at every opportunity. I don't think she's at all interested in me and never will be. She's never laughed at a single one of my jokes. I think she just puts up with my personality for the sake of our business."

Lee laughed, "That's funny, sad, and true. I told her I liked your sense of humor and she said I was misinformed, that you actually have a *terrible* sense of humor."

Kaem cackled, "Sounds like her. She *does* hate my jokes and... I tease her, which I know I shouldn't. I'm trying to stop, but now I'm thinking I should insist we hire you just so there'll be *someone* around who thinks I'm funny. It'd be *so* good for my ego to occasionally get a laugh."

"Well, I'd like to work for you guys, if it doesn't cause too much friction. Or you could just keep me in some dark room where Arya never has to see me. As long as I get to work with stade I'll be happy."

"Great! You're hired."

"I am? Don't I... need to formally apply or something? I'm sure there needs to be some kind of contract, right?" *What am I doing?* she wondered. *Don't look a gift horse in the mouth! He just offered me the job. Take it!*

The Thunder of Engines

Sounding abashed, Kaem said, "Sorry. You're right. I'm getting ahead of myself. You'd need to know what you're getting paid and what the benefits are and things like that. I haven't even thought about that stuff 'cause you'd be our very first hire. Let me talk to Arya and she'll get back to you."

"I hope she's okay with it."

"I'm sure she will be. All I'll have to do is tell her you've promised to laugh at my jokes, so you'll be easing *that* burden for her."

Lee said, "I'll be out there in a few days with our mold for a small rocket engine. Maybe we could talk then?"

"You know I'm having to build another stazer?"

"You didn't get the one back from Martin Aerospace?"

"The police are keeping it as evidence, so I'm having to build another. I don't mind. I wanted to make some improvements anyway. But you'd better call before you come to make sure I've got the new one built and working."

They said a few more words then ended the call. Lee hung up, wondering whether Kaem was right, and Arya wouldn't actually object.

And whether he actually could build a stazer?

~~~

When Lee signed off, Kaem put in a call to Arya, "Hey, April Lee wants to come work for us. What do we need to do to hire her?"

There was a brief silence, then, sounding stiff, Arya said, "You offered her a job?"

"Well, yeah. But then I realized I didn't know anything about how to generate a contract, or how much we should pay, so I figured I'd better ask you for help."

"What's her degree and where'd she get it?

"Um, I don't know," Kaem said, feeling a little embarrassed

"What kind of grades did she get?"

"Don't know, but I'm sure those things must be pretty good or she wouldn't have been able to get a job with Space-Gen."

"Is she licensed as an engineer here in Virginia? Or even in California? And what kind of engineer is she?"

"They license engineers?"

"Each state does. I'm not sure you have to have a license if you're working under another supervising engineer, but if she's going to be our *only* engineer for a while, it seems like we'd want her to be licensed here. Or, wherever you want to set up Staze as a business to begin with."

"Um, I was thinking here in Virginia."

"You didn't talk to her about salary?"

"No," Kaem said, starting to feel badgered.

"Benefits?"

"Well, I said she'd probably want to know what the benefits would be before she signed on and that you'd get back to her on that."

"Do you know she offered to come to work for free?"

"What?! How would she support herself?"

"Not permanently. Just until we could pay her."

"She's *really* interested in stade."

"Are you sure that's all?"

"What do you mean?"

"I think she's interested in *you*, Kaem."

The Thunder of Engines

"What's really funny is that she thinks *you're* interested in me. I told her nothing could be further from the truth. That you push me away at every opportunity and that you *hate* my jokes."

After another brief silence, Arya cleared her throat, "That might be, but we *shouldn't* be hiring you a girlfriend. Mixing business and romance is a bad idea."

Kaem snorted, "Girlfriend! That's ridiculous! I like her, but not *that* way. And, and… I'm sure she's not interested in me." He gave a little laugh. "Though, she did say she likes my jokes, so there."

"We shouldn't be hiring you an audience either Kaem."

"So you're saying that if I get along with someone and they think I'm funny we can't hire them? Does that apply to guys too, or just to women? It's going to be hard to live up to your ideal of providing equal opportunities for women if we have to reject every woman I might get along with."

This time the silence went on for some time. Eventually, Kaem said, "Are you still there?"

Sounding like she was gritting her teeth, Arya said, "Did you check this decision out with your partners in Staze?"

Kaem's thoughts stumbled, then he replied, "I'm doing that now, by talking to you."

Arya gave a long sigh, then said, "I'll contact her and find out whether she's qualified. But, personally, I think we need to hire someone with experience. We shouldn't run this business with nothing but newbies like you and me."

"*Gunnar's* not a noob."

"You're *still* not funny Kaem," Arya said, immediately disconnecting the call.

Kaem wondered how they'd gotten on such a bad footing again.

Chapter Seven

After the last of his classes Monday, Kaem was anxious to get to a private corner so he could call his mother and ask how his dad's marrow biopsy had gone. A little research had convinced him that the only reason they'd be doing a marrow biopsy would be if they suspected a blood cancer like leukemia—since those originated in the marrow. However, as he made his way to the front of the classroom, he realized Professor Turnberry's eyes were on him. Kaem made to go on by, but Turnberry said, "Mr. Seba?"

Kaem stopped. "Yes?" he asked, trying not to sound impatient.

Turnberry hesitated, then said, "I was very impressed with the way you explained the WKB approximation when I called on you a few weeks ago."

"Oh," Kaem said, glad to be complimented but anxious to move on. "Thank you."

"I wanted to ask what your plans are...? For after your graduation?"

"I've... got an idea for a business," Kaem said, uncomfortably, feeling like he shouldn't talk about Staze at all until it was on solid footing.

"Because I've been talking to several of the other faculty. They're all just as impressed as I am," Turnberry said.

"Thank you."

"Have you ever thought about trying some research?"

Kaem stared uncertainly. "Into what?"

"Into anything. The best research is done by people who generate their own hypotheses. For instance, if you've ever wondered whether something worked differently than conventional knowledge proposes. Then if you also had some ideas about how you could test to see if your hypothesis was correct, you could do some research to find out."

Kaem was so surprised he didn't answer immediately. His mind was racing trying to decide how to respond, but it wasn't getting much traction.

Finally, Turnberry said, "I and the other faculty have noticed that you frequently ask... unusual questions. As if you might have different thoughts about the way things work. None of us know what those beliefs might be, but..." Turnberry paused, then rushed ahead, "Have you ever considered going on to grad school and testing some of your notions?"

"I..." have tested some of my ideas, Kaem thought. But I shouldn't talk about that now. "Thanks for the suggestion. I'll have to think about it." It might be a good backup if, for some reason, everything with Staze goes to hell, he thought. So I definitely shouldn't burn this bridge. "Um you might not know this, but I'm attending UVA on a Curtis scholarship. I couldn't possibly afford to keep going to school without it. Is there such a thing as a scholarship to go to grad school?"

Turnberry nodded, "There *are* scholarships for grad school. You'd have a good shot with several recommendations from the faculty. Also, you might get a paid position as a research or teaching assistant.

The Thunder of Engines

Personally, because I think you're so bright, I hope you're interested in research. But your brief stint in my class suggests you'd be an amazing teacher too. With a doctorate, you could pursue either career."

"I thought you *had* to do research to teach at a university."

"That's true at most of the big research universities," Turnberry said. He shrugged, "But there are a lot of smaller schools where all they want you to do is teach."

Kaem studied his professor. "What do you think of people who try to create things by working in industry?"

Turnberry shrugged again. "There are jobs for people with undergrad degrees in physics. But they usually aren't jobs where you're encouraged to be creative. They're more in the way of jobs for smart people who're good team players."

"Ah," Kaem said with a nod. "Thank you for your explanations and encouragement. I'll have to give this a lot of thought."

People were trickling into the room for the next class, so he and Turnberry said their goodbyes.

***

Kaem made his way into the atrium to wait for Arya—if she showed. She'd called this morning to say she couldn't walk him to class like she'd been doing. He'd immediately wondered whether she was so pissed at him she'd decided he'd just have to take his chances without her services as a bodyguard.

Normally he reviewed the lecture and his notes, but today the first thing on his to-do list was calling his mother.

She answered the call, "Kaem! Where'd you get all that money?!"

He'd been so focused on his dad's illness that at first, he didn't know what she was talking about. Realizing she was talking about the money he'd gotten from Metz and sent to her account, he said, "Someone... stole some of my stuff." Hoping his mother would think the authorities had made Metz do it—rather than Kaem committing blackmail to get it—Kaem said, "He had to pay me for it and so I sent the money on to you."

"But Kaem, surely you need to use that money to replace whatever he stole, don't you? Seventy-six hundred dollars! Whatever he stole must've been valuable. And important to you!"

"Um, we-I already got it replaced," *and stolen again,* Kaem thought. "I don't need the money right now, and you guys do."

"But could you need it in the future?" his mother asked suspiciously.

"Probably not," Kaem said, then realized that if she thought there was any chance he'd need it, she'd do her very best not to spend it. "I mean, definitely not. Don't worry about me. Use it however you need."

"Well," she sighed, "we *are* probably going to run short. Make that *very* short, but I'll do my best not to spend it if we don't have to."

"No! Mom! *Spend* it. That's why I sent it to you."

"I don't want you going hungry, getting bad grades, and getting thrown out of school."

"There's nothing to worry about, Mom. My grades are fine. I'll bring you a copy when I come home to see Dad." He couldn't keep the worry out of his voice as he said, "How is he?"

The Thunder of Engines

"Sore. He said that even though they numbed him up for the biopsy, it still hurt pretty bad. And, now he feels bruised."

"Um, could they tell anything yet?"

"No, it'll be a couple of days before they get results. They sent his marrow off to the lab for analysis."

"How're you holding up?"

"Worried. Worried about your dad. Worried about my job if I have to take much more time off to be with him." Her voice caught, then turned into a near whisper, "Worried about Bana."

"What's wrong with Bana?!"

"She hates the crappy, dead-end job she's got here, but she won't leave us to look for better jobs elsewhere."

"Mom, why haven't you and Dad moved away from Valen? Things are a lot better in other places, you know? Places without drug problems. Then Bana could move away with you."

"I don't know," his mother said tiredly. "First it was because this's where the Lutherans settled us and there were people here who were helping us figure out life in America. Then it was because I had a job and your dad was getting some work. Then it was because you and Bana were in school and we didn't want to take you out and make you start over somewhere else. Meanwhile, the town slowly went to hell around us. Meth was destroying the people, crime was destroying the town. We were like the frogs in a pan of water heating toward a boil; it all happened so slowly we just didn't realize everything was..." She cleared her throat, Kaem thought to cover the fact her voice had almost broken. "Maybe we should move as soon as your dad's better. Then Bana wouldn't have an excuse for staying in that terrible job. Dad could find a job somewhere, then once he had an apartment, I could follow him and look for a job of my own. Bana'd have to come then, right?"

Throat aching, Kaem managed not to croak as he said, "I may be getting a job at a place near here that could hire one of you. Then you'd be able to move for sure."

"That'd be great Kaem... Um, most companies don't want to hire more than one person from a family. They're afraid they'll do each other favors."

Kaem decided not to argue. He was already violating her rules by, in a sense, trying to count chickens that hadn't hatched. He said, "We'll just have to see. First thing's to get Dad better, right?"

"Right."

***

After his mother hung up, Kaem tried to study but his mind kept wandering back to his dad's diagnosis, stimulating him to do more and more web searches. And he kept wondering whether Arya would come and pick him up or not. Whether he should just head back to the dorm on his own.

He was still wondering about it when she appeared at his elbow, "You ready to go?"

"Um, sure," Kaem said, stuffing his laptop in his backpack. "I wasn't sure if you were gonna show."

She gave him an irritated look, "Why not?"

"You seemed kinda pissed about Lee yesterday. Then you couldn't come this morning."

"I told you, something came up. I have a life that *doesn't* revolve around you, you know."

The Thunder of Engines

Kaem put his palms up in surrender. "Just saying I was worried, that's all." He shrugged, "And, besides, maybe now that Caron's out of the picture, you don't need to babysit me anymore?"

"Yes, I do. Gotta protect my investment."

"Oh, that reminds me, have you sent us our shares of the three million yet?"

"Should be there. Check your account."

Kaem asked his phone to check his bank account. The phone displayed a balance of $767,355. Kaem blinked at it, startled. He remembered checking his balance at $1,618 yesterday which would mean his deposit had only been $765,737! *How can I be saying "only" when it's two orders of magnitude more money than I've ever had before?* Yet it wasn't the one point two million he'd expected. He turned to Arya. "I thought you were dispensing half of the three million?"

She nodded. "One and a half million."

"I only got $765,737. Do you think there's been some kind of mistake?"

Patiently, she said, "One and a half million, minus one percent to Gunnar and point one percent to Morales leaves..." she got out her phone to do the math.

"It leaves $1,483,500," Kaem said impatiently. "I can do the math."

Arya blinked at him, then said, "Take off my twenty percent."

"That still leaves $1,183,500."

"Take off your estimated US income tax of 30.5 percent and Virginia income tax of 5.75%, then take off another $9,500 for social security."

Kaem felt surprised, "*You* take that? Not the government?"

241 | Page

She cocked her head, "Haven't you ever worked a job with a paycheck?"

"Oh..." Kaem quickly calculated that after those subtractions he should get the $765,737 he'd received. "Are those what they call 'withholding'?"

She nodded. "If employers didn't withhold estimated taxes from employees' paychecks, most people'd spend it all. Come April fifteenth, they wouldn't be able to pay their income tax. Besides, the government wants that money to come in regularly throughout the year. If Staze *doesn't* withhold taxes from your paycheck, come next April, the IRS will want it all at once, *plus* interest, *and* assess a penalty for not paying on time."

"Ah. Thanks. It should be plenty anyway. I don't know why I'm worrying."

"It should be a lot more than plenty. You've been getting along on less than a hundredth of that much!"

"Um, my dad's sick," Kaem said with a catch in his voice. "Probably cancer. It may not turn out to be treatable, but if it is, a lot of the treatments are hundreds of thousands of dollars."

"Oh!" Arya gave him a horrified look, then gathered him into a hug. "I'm so sorry."

Kaem found her embrace far more comforting than he'd expected. "It's okay," he husked, thinking suddenly that it wasn't okay at all.

"It's not!" Arya said with a catch in her voice. She squeezed him harder. "If it were my dad, I'd be a blubbering mess."

Feeling as if he were melting, Kaem whispered, "Thanks for being understanding. I-I hardly ever get to see my family, so, I've been feeling really alone."

The Thunder of Engines

"You're *not* alone." Arya squeezed him again. "I may not want to hire girlfriends for you, but I'll always be here for you myself."

Feeling Arya making little jerking motions, Kaem wondered, *Is she sobbing? It's my dad that's sick.* He pulled back to look at her but she just came with him so he couldn't see her face. Finally, he actually pushed her away and saw the tears running down her cheeks. They were pulling little trails of mascara with them. "Arya? What's the matter?"

She swiped at the tears, sniffed, and said abruptly, "I feel bad for you. Is that allowed?"

Kaem pulled her back in. She resisted a moment, then folded into his arms, shoulders shaking. He said, "You're the best friend I've ever had and I care about you. We don't have to hire Lee."

She sniffed again, "Shut up, Kaem."

He just held her.

Eventually, she pulled away, wiped her face on her sleeves, and resumed walking toward his dorm.

Kaem opened his mouth to say something, realized he wasn't sure what to say, and closed it.

"Thanks," Arya said.

"For what?"

"For not saying whatever stupid thing you had on the tip of your tongue."

Kaem opened his mouth for a retort, then closed it again.

In his dorm's lobby, she waited until his elevator arrived, then turned to go.

"Bye," Kaem said.

She gave a little backward wave and kept walking.

When Kaem got to his room he threw himself face down on the bed, immensely gratified that his constantly annoying roommate was absent.

After a few morose minutes, his phone chimed. It was Arya. Clearing his throat so he wouldn't croak, he said, "What's up?"

"I checked. Insurance should pay for most cancer chemotherapy."

Embarrassed, Kaem said, "My family can't afford health insurance."

"Their employers don't provide it?"

"Their jobs are part-time."

"Oh..." Arya said, her voice cracking again. "Sorry."

Sometimes she hates me, Kaem thought.
Other times she cares... more than I can fathom.

***

The parts for the new stazer had come in by Wednesday. Kaem called Gunnar and they agreed to meet in the afternoon at Staze's rented building. There Gunnar could consult on and help with the build; he could especially assist with Kaem's consideration of how to make the new device susceptible to Gunnar's thermate.

Focusing on the build kept Kaem's mind off the impending results of his dad's marrow biopsy much better than studying.

Kaem was using a breadboard to set up a test version of the circuit. After he was sure the circuit he'd designed worked properly, then he'd design and order an actual custom circuit board. He'd left a gap in the tightly packed components where he intended to swap in a large induction coil—while swapping out a smaller capacitor—right before closing up the box. He'd do it when no one was around to see what he was doing. It was one of the several swaps only he knew about, that'd all have to be completed to make the electronics functional for generating stasis.

Gunnar looked over his shoulder. "Is that big gap where we're gonna put the exploding steam capsule?"

Damn! Kaem thought, *Forgot about that.* He said, "No, I need that gap for… another reason." Kaem felt certain Gunnar could see right through such a clumsy excuse. He said, "Wouldn't it be better if I left you a gap in the *middle* of the board?" Kaem waved a finger over the central area of the board, simultaneously trying to figure out how to reposition parts to leave a gap in the center.

"Sure," Gunnar said. "Hey, while you're working on that, do you mind if I mess around with some of the Mylar? I've been thinking about how we could use Mylar to form a stade dirigible."

"I thought about dirigibles too. If you made a huge vacuum stade it'd lift tremendous loads but the problem is that you'd have a hard time controlling altitude. As opposed to gas blimps, you couldn't vent the lifting gas. Of course, you could dump water to *increase* buoyancy, but when you wanted to go back down, you'd have a problem."

Gunnar grinned, "We make a *hollow* stade. Pump it down to vacuum when we want lift. Let air back in when we want to descend."

Kaem slapped the side of his own head. "Of course! Great idea!" He shook his head. "How could I be so stupid?"

"'Cause you're just not very smart," Gunnar replied with a snicker. "I don't have any idea why so many people seem to think you are."

Kaem snorted, "Thanks Gunnar. You're gonna give me a complex."

"Doubt it," Gunnar said with finality. He turned toward the other table. "I'm gonna work on *my* idea while you're working your magic with the electronic stuff."

Kaem rearranged the components and connected everything to set up what he thought of as "test mode." Ready, he powered the breadboard, applied certain settings through its integrated chip, and checked the outputs.

The outputs were all wrong.

Dammit! Kaem thought. He sighed, *Probably a loose connection somewhere.* However, the other possibility was incorrect assembly, placing components incorrectly, and that was more easily checked. So, he set about comparing the location of every part in the assembly against his circuit diagram.

Ten minutes later he was glad he'd started by checking the circuit against his plan since he'd found two mistakes. He powered up again, this time getting different outputs.

Different, but still wrong.

After some creative swearing, Kaem carefully went through the schema all over again. This time he didn't find any incorrect component placements. His circuit diagram was done on a software circuit emulator. He ran it again to check what the outputs of the board should've been under those settings—confirming that he wasn't getting what he should be.

The Thunder of Engines

With a sigh he set to work with a meter, checking connections and confirming that the various components met their specs and were correctly inserted—and not reversed, which mattered a lot with the diodes.

Hearing a hissing sound, he turned and saw Gunnar had just inflated his Mylar blimp. It looked about six feet long and almost two in diameter—Kaem thought it was likely as big as could be made from welding together the edges of two six-foot strips of Mylar off the three-foot-wide roll. The balloon was bobbing at the ends of a couple of taut strings so Kaem said, "You filled it with helium?"

Gunnar nodded, "You ready to staze the interior yet?"

Kaem shook his head morosely, "Circuit's not working. I'm checking for faults."

"You want me to do that?"

"No, it'd take a long time to explain all the things I've already checked." *And, I don't want you spending too much time looking at the circuit,* Kaem thought.

"How about if I run out and get us some gyros for dinner? There's a good place down the street."

"Is it that time already?" Kaem asked, checking his watch. Seeing it was almost six o'clock, he said, "That'd be great. Hopefully, I'll find the problem by the time you get back."

Gunnar'd only been gone a couple of minutes when Kaem found a bad connection at one end of a capacitor. When he inserted it more firmly the circuit produced the expected outputs.

He set to swapping components to the arrangement that'd staze.

This time, probably because he was more careful seating each connection, the board produced the correct outputs. He closed the cover of the breadboard's case, screwed it, and laid out the cables so their ends were close to Gunnar's blimp.

Kaem's phone chimed, "You have a call from Bana."

"I'll take it... Hello sister, what'd they say?"

It was his mother's voice he heard. "Hello, Kaem. My phone's dead and Bana's... She's upset. So, I'm the one calling. They say it's a B-cell lymphoma. That's a blood—"

"It's a blood cancer," Kaem said, the words bursting up out of him as relief flooded through his veins. "I know. I've read about it. You don't have to explain it."

"You already heard about his diagnosis from someone?"

"No, I just read up on the things that might cause his symptoms, especially the ones that they'd need to get a marrow biopsy to make a full diagnosis."

After a brief pause, his mother said, "You must've done a *lot* of reading."

"Not that much. What've they recommended for treatment?"

"Radiation and chemotherapy," she said, dread tinging her voice. Her tone changed to upbeat, but sounded forced, "They say it's not a cure but that it'll help a lot."

"Wait. What about CAR T-cell therapy?! It's supposed to cure most people!"

His mom sighed, "She mentioned that. But she said it's really expensive. Without good insurance, Emmanuel can't get it. She said he *might* get approved as a charity case, but only if regular chemo and radiation didn't work."

The Thunder of Engines

"Oh..." Kaem said, his mind spinning. *Why haven't I been checking into this already? I knew lymphoma was a likely diagnosis!* To his mother, he said, "Wait! Radiation and chemo aren't very good for you so you'd a lot rather just go straight to CAR T-cell. Don't do *anything* yet. Let me find out if they have a program at the medical center here at UVA. One that treats B-cell lymphomas with CAR T-cell therapy."

"Kaem," his mother said soothingly. "You're grasping at straws. We *might* be able to get on Medicaid here in West Virginia. That'll pay for a lot of Emmanuel's treatment. The chances that he could get any kind of charity care in Virginia is..." she sighed, "the chance of that's almost nonexistent."

"When do they want to start treatment?"

"As soon as possible, though we have to have applied for Medicaid first." As if speaking confidentially, she said, "I think they're worried that if they don't insist, we'll just run up a big bill without ever putting in the application."

"Okay. That should give me time to check into things. Just don't let anyone start treatment until I get back to you with what I find."

"You're wasting your time, Kaem. We *can't* get treatment in Virginia. You should be focused on your studies. Your dad and I'll work our way through this, never fear."

"Mom! Just promise me you won't let him start treatment without getting back to me?"

"Okay, okay. We appreciate your efforts, but please, don't waste too much time on it. I talked to the financial people here and they say there's no way."

Gunnar returned with the gyros shortly after Kaem hung up. Kaem was deep into Google searches on his laptop. Distractedly, he took a gyro and started eating while still reading.

"Um, Kaem? Did you get it to work?"

Kaem nodded without looking away from the screen. Then he turned to look at Gunnar. "I assume so anyway, as best I can test it. I didn't have a mold to test it with. Can we use your blimp?"

"Sure."

Kaem was back to reading. "Can you hook it up?" He waved at the cables he'd laid out.

"Okay..." Gunnar said, picking up the cables and starting to hook them up to the blimp. "What's so interesting there?"

"Um..." Kaem glanced at him, wondering if he should burden Gunnar with his problems. *We're a team,* he thought. "My dad's been sick. He just got his diagnosis and I'm trying to read up on it."

"Oh," Gunnar said, freighting the word with consequence. "What's his diagnosis?"

"B-cell lymphoma."

"Oh..." Gunnar said, standing stock-still a moment, then suddenly pivoting and walking to the door. He opened it and left.

"Gunnar?" Kaem said to the empty room. After a moment he decided he shouldn't go after the crotchety man. There was no telling what kind of mood he was in. Kaem returned to what he'd been reading.

About five minutes later, the door opened again and Gunnar entered. His eyes were red-rimmed and Kaem immediately knew the man had been crying. However, he didn't know whether to acknowledge it or not. In the best of circumstances, a conversation with Gunnar seemed to have a lot of land mines. When he'd just been so emotional... Kaem didn't know how to handle it. He sat, eyes on Gunnar, wondering what to do.

Gunnar crossed the room and dragged up a chair close to Kaem. "Sorry about your dad," he said in a raspy voice. "My wife... she died of lymphoma and I can have some trouble with my feelings when I think about... Sorry, that's not your problem. Does your dad have good insurance? There's this treatment called CAR T-cell therapy that *cures* a lot of people. Evelyn didn't get it until they'd tried a lot of other stuff and... things didn't go so well for her."

"Yeah, his insurance isn't so good, so they're wanting to start with chemo and radiation. I'm looking for other options."

"The CAR T-cell therapy guy you'll want to talk to here at UVA's a Dr. John Starbach."

"That's what I saw online. I'm trying to figure out how to get my dad an appointment."

"They have an online appointment system."

"Yeah, but when I go on it, my dad gets rejected for being uninsured and out of state. The appointment system's AI keeps saying he has to get his treatment in West Virginia."

Gunnar stared at him for a moment, then barked a sudden laugh. "And the system doesn't have any way for you to say you can pay cash for his care, does it?"

Kaem blinked a moment, then realized that probably *was* the problem. He said, "Ah. Now I think I understand."

Gunnar grinned, "You're gonna have to actually *talk* to someone over there."

"Huh?"

Gunnar shook his head, "You young people are so used to doing everything online you never think to try to *talk* to someone. Give it a try."

Kaem looked down at the appointments page on his laptop. Sure enough, a phone number was displayed. "Okay. I'll try it." He grinned, "Much as it pains my young self to do so." He gestured at the cables. "If you hook up your cables, we can see if this thing'll make some stade."

Gunnar started hooking up the cables while Kaem placed the call. He was immediately placed on a hold line that provided frequent verbal reminders that appointments could be made online.

He got up to study what Gunnar was doing. The Mylar was cinched around a microwave emitter on one end and Gunnar had already connected the cable to that. The older man tucked the other end of the blimp under his left arm and said, "I'm just gonna have to hold the light conduit up to the Mylar on this end."

"You're ready now?"

"Uh-huh."

Kaem stepped back over to his new stazer. He changed the settings so it should create a stade, specifying one that'd last a kilosecond (16.7 minutes), and depressed the switch that'd give it power. "Done," he said.

Gunnar squeezed his blimp. Even before Gunnar said, "Yup. It worked," Kaem could tell there was no longer any give to the Mylar.

Struck by a thought, Kaem asked, "How're you planning to cast a stade around that one?"

"I'll just blow in a little more helium. Stretch the Mylar a little. Shouldn't take much, we only need an extra millimeter all around."

The Thunder of Engines

"But how're you going to keep the old one centered in the middle of the new one? If you don't it'll probably be too thin on one side and the stade'll be incomplete."

Gunnar shrugged, "I'll worry about that if it happens." He picked up the hose from his helium tank saying, "Wait one."

A young man spoke in Kaem's ear. "Hello, how may I help you?"

"I've been trying to make an appointment for my dad with Dr. Starbach. We'd like to get him CAR T-cell therapy."

"Your dad's name?"

Kaem gave the man his dad's info. The guy said, "Let me just look... Oh, I'm sorry. Your father doesn't have insurance. He'll need to seek treatment in his home state of West Virginia."

"But we can pay."

"It says here you don't have insurance."

"That's correct. But we have money."

"I'm sorry. CAR T-cell treatments cost hundreds of thousands of dollars."

"I know."

"You'd *have* to have insurance."

Frustrated, Kaem said, "We *have* the money."

"Sorry, but even if you had enough money for the treatment, what if there was a complication? What if the cost suddenly doubled? No, he'd be much better off applying for Medicaid and seeking treatment in his home state."

"No! We *have* more than enough money. We want him to have his treatment here..." Kaem trailed off as he realized he'd been disconnected. "Hello?" he said, checking to be sure the other man wasn't just being unusually quiet. There was no answer. "Dammit!"

When Kaem looked up he saw Gunnar watching him, sympathy in his eyes. "Sorry. Sometimes the bureaucracy seems worse than the cancer."

"Got any more suggestions?"

"Try emailing the doctor from your university email account. If it comes from UVA and has a good subject line, he might read it. He might even sympathize enough to try to help." Gunnar shrugged, "On the other hand, he may be just as hamstrung by policy as the lady you just talked to."

"Guy," Kaem said.

"Huh?"

"I was talking to a guy."

"Oh. They're usually less sympathetic than the ladies. Sorry."

"You ready to try stazing your blimp?"

Gunnar hesitated a moment, then said, "Sure."

Kaem set the stazer for four megaseconds (46.3 days) and glanced at Gunnar. Holding the light conduit against the end of the blimp, Gunnar gave him a nod. Kaem pushed the button.

Gunnar squeezed the blimp and said, "It's hard. How long's the stade in the middle gonna last?"

Kaem looked at his watch, "About three more minutes. How are you gonna get the Mylar off that thing without destroying your pretty balloon?"

Gunnar chewed a lip. "I don't know. I need a Mylar zipper or something."

"That'd let your helium leak out."

"I'm planning to use air and a pump in the future. The helium tank was just an easy way to blow it up with some pressure."

"Yeah, but it's gonna cause some trouble."

"How's that?"

"Once you blew the balloon bigger around the first stade, the inner stade would've floated up to the top of your tied-down blimp because the extra pressure in the new helium would've made it denser. So, the inner stade would've been in contact with the Mylar at the top and you won't have formed any stade up there."

Gunnar stared at him a moment, then said, "I'll be damned. You're not as dumb as I thought."

"Unfortunately," Kaem said, "the fact I'm smarter than *you* doesn't mean I'm not dumb."

Gunnar snorted, "You got *that* right."

"A zipper with a Mylar flap over the inside of it might work. The pressure in the balloon'll tend to press it closed as long as it isn't too high."

Gunnar looked thoughtful. "I'll try that on the next one." He got out his knife and started carefully slitting the Mylar longitudinally. A minute later he pulled out a blimp shaped stade that promptly got away from him and shot up to the ceiling. "Dammit!"

They were still looking up at it when the inner stade vanished and the blimp suddenly moved up a little closer to the ceiling. A moment after that an irregular hole rolled into view as the blimp slowly turned on its axis. The interior of the blimp was just as reflective as the outside but the hole was visible because the interior of the blimp was somewhat darker.

"Looks like you were right," Gunnar said irritatedly.

Kaem shrugged, "If you're going to pump a vacuum inside that blimp, you needed an opening into the interior anyway. Think of that hole as serendipity."

Gunnar blinked, then smiled, "Yeah. That was my plan all along."

~~~

Having reset the components in the stazer back to a nonfunctional state, Kaem was waiting for an Uber to take him back to the dorm. His earbud said, "You have a call from Arya."

"I'll take it… Hi Arya."

"Where are you?"

"Over at Staze, working on the new stazer."

"Kaem! I'm supposed to be *with* you when you go places!"

"I, ah, took an Uber over here. Gunnar's been with me. I'm sure I'm safe."

"Is *Gunnar* supposed to protect you?!"

She really sounds worried about me, Kaem thought, getting in the Uber that'd just pulled up. "I just hate having you waste your time babysitting me. I know you need to study—"

"I could've been studying while you were working on the stazer. Besides, if I graduate with good grades but you…" It sounded like she was trying to decide what to say. She settled for, "If something happens to you. I could never live with myself." She changed tack, "It sounds like you're in a car. Are you in an Uber, coming back here?"

"Uh-huh."

"I'll wait for you and we'll go to dinner. You can tell me about your dad's… Wait, did you find out what it is?"

"B-cell lymphoma," Kaem said without telling her that Gunnar had already bought him a gyro and he wasn't hungry. He'd enjoy the time with her and could just force himself to eat a little.

"That sounds like…" Her breath caught, "Is that a cancer?"

"Yeah, but there's—"

The Thunder of Engines

"I'll read up on it while you're driving over," she said, disconnecting before he could argue.

~~~

When Kaem arrived in the Uber, rather than waiting for him to get out, Arya got in. She told the car to take them to Bistro Valentin.

He'd heard of Valentin but never eaten at it. Worried, he asked, "Is Valentin on the meal plan?"

Arya rolled her eyes, "I think you've got enough money for us to eat somewhere else now."

"Oh… Yeah, I guess we do," Kaem said.

"There's a pretty well-known doc here at UVA that treats B-cell lymphomas with this high-end therapy called CAR T-cell therapy. I made your dad an appointment."

"What?!" Kaem said, flabbergasted. "I've been trying and *trying* to get him an appointment and—"

Arya interrupted, "You've just got to know who to talk to."

"Who?!"

"One of my many secrets," Arya said primly.

"They wouldn't even talk to me because my dad doesn't have health insurance! How did you—"

Arya interrupted. "I told them I was CFO of a new company just opening its Virginia branch. I said I was arranging the appointment at the behest of our reclusive CEO who needed the appointment for his father. Then I had the bank send them evidence of your line of credit. Pretty simple actually."

Kaem stared, "Not simple to me. Thanks!"

"He'll see your dad Friday afternoon at two."

"That might be too soon. It's going to be hell getting my dad down here. The bus makes so many stops it takes over twelve hours to make the trip and—"

"For *God's* sake Kaem. You're *rich*. Have an *Uber* pick him up at their house and drive them down here tomorrow afternoon. Get them a room at a nice hotel so they can rest. I scheduled the appointment in the afternoon so you could go with them without missing any of your precious classes. You should try to relax and enjoy some time with them while they're here."

"Oh," he said. After giving it a moment's surprised thought, he said, "I *am* rich." He rubbed his hands together like a movie villain. "That changes things doesn't it?"

Dryly, Arya said, "Try to give it a couple of weeks before you start acting like a *total* asshole."

Their meal at Bistro Valentin went by in a blur. He had a vague recollection that he enjoyed it though, not being hungry, he didn't eat much. He couldn't remember specifics.

Except toward the end, when Arya leaned closer and said, "I hired Lee."

Surprised, Kaem said, "You didn't have to."

She shrugged, "As you thought, she's highly qualified. School at Cal Tech with great grades and amazing scores. Licensed as an aerospace engineer in California and won't have any trouble getting licensed here. Agreed to start at half the salary she was getting at Space-Gen until we'd made fifty million—which," Arya shrugged again, "which will happen halfway through building our first rocket. You were right, she does *really* want to work on the development of stade. When I confronted her, she admitted she thinks *you're…* appealing as well, but has no idea whether you reciprocate that interest."

The Thunder of Engines

Kaem felt a flicker of excitement at the thought Lee was interested. *Attractive, smart, likes me, why wouldn't I be thrilled?*

Arya sighed and turned to look out the window. "I'll admit I still don't think we should hire you a girlfriend, but she's eminently qualified, so I want to help her achieve her goals."

I may like Lee, but not enough to upset Arya, Kaem thought. He said, "Hey…" he shook his head, "You don't have to hire her. I know you don't want to."

"No. You were right. I want to provide opportunities for other women. If I don't hire her, I'll be betraying myself."

Kaem gave her a sly grin, "Even if it gives you competition romancing me?"

"*Still* not funny, Kaem," Arya said rolling her eyes.

Dammit, he thought, *No jokes! How many more times am I gonna have to have this little talk with myself?*

~~~

Arya was walking him home after their—well, mostly her—dinner when Kaem heard a chime in his earbud, "You have a call from Aaron Marks."

"I'll take it… Hello, Mr. Marks?"

"What's this about you hiring away my favorite young engineer?" Marks said, as if upset.

"Um, yeah, sorry. She's really interested in stade."

"Yeah," Marks said, gusting a sigh. "I would be too if I were her age. In proving her sincerity, she tells me she's so interested she took the job at half what we're paying her here?"

"As far as I know, that's true," Kaem said slowly. "Though I don't know the exact numbers. We're wanting to be a little more certain of our cash reserves before we hire a lot of people." He produced a nervous laugh, "We don't want to be one of those flash-in-the-pan companies that burns through all its cash, then disappears."

"If that happens, give me a call and I'll buy a stake in Staze to give you more working capital. Unfortunately, most of the companies that burn out like that don't have a good product, much less an incredible product like stade. I won't hold my breath waiting for your call."

"Okay..." Kaem said, pausing because he didn't think Marks had revealed the real reason for his call.

"I'd like to offer to pay half of her salary. At least until you can afford to pay it all. She'd spend most of her time there with you, but she'd shuttle back and forth some, bringing parts out there for you to staze and helping us figure out how Space-Gen can get the most out of your product."

Uncomfortably, Kaem said, "Even if she were our full-time employee, I wouldn't be telling her how stazing works."

"I didn't think you would. But she's an aerospace engineer. I'm sure having even a part-time person on the ground there, someone who has the mental tools to think about how your product can be used for rocketry, that's gonna help me stay ahead of Branzon."

"Um, are you sure that's—"

"Yeah, I already had Saul review the contract and he says it's okay. But if Branzon complains, you can let him pay for half of another engineer and you'll come out even farther ahead."

Kaem glanced over at Arya, walking beside him and looking curious. "I'll, uh, have to have our legal people tell me for sure if it's okay."

"You do that," Marks said, then said his goodbyes.

The Thunder of Engines

Kaem explained the call to Arya and was pleased to see a smile spread over her face. *She likes saving money, which is a good thing in our business person.*

Chapter Eight

Later that evening, Kaem called his dad. After a moment his dad said, "Kaem! It's good to hear from you. How's school?"

"School's fine, Dad. I'm going to bring you my grades so you can stop worrying about it. It sounds like you're feeling better?"

"Oh yeah! I'm feeling good. I don't think I need all these treatments they're talking about. I'm thinking I'll just stay on the meds they've got me on. Those're cheap."

Stunned, Kaem said, "Um, Dad, you know this thing you've got, this B-cell lymphoma… You know it's a cancer, don't you? Kind of like a leukemia?"

"Well, that's what *they* say. But, I'm not so sure. I'm feeling fine now. Maybe I'm cured." He lowered his voice as if speaking confidentially, "I found an herbalist near here who had some dried bonduc-nut bark and I've been taking a preparation of that. It might be the bonduc-nut bark's that's making me better, not any of the medicines the doctor gave me."

Oh my God! Kaem thought. *My dad thinks freaking witch doctors' snake-oil remedies could be more effective than scientifically proven medications!* This was a possibility Kaem hadn't ever considered—though in hindsight he thought he should've. His dad's community in Tanzania had a lot of herbalists. Aloud, he spoke slowly. "You understand the medicines the

The Thunder of Engines

doctors gave you are intended to make you feel better, but that they won't do anything to cure you?"

His dad sounded surprised, "Are you sure? I admit I wasn't feeling very well when I saw them. I was sick enough I didn't listen very carefully."

"Hasn't Mom talked to you?"

"Well yes, but…"

But you don't listen to your wife either, Kaem thought. He wondered whether his father would listen to him. "Now that you're feeling better, I've arranged for you to come down and see one of the cancer specialists here at the medical center in Charlottesville. You can talk it over with him and, since you're not so sick, you'll be able to understand it better."

"I don't think that's necessary. I'm pretty—"

"Dad!" Kaem interrupted, "I used up a lot of favors getting you an appointment. You've *got* to come!" His father was a firm believer in the concept of owing and collecting favors, so Kaem felt pretty sure the loss of the favors Kaem had "used" would influence him.

"I don't know, Kaem. You've told us about those long bus rides. I may be feeling better, but—"

Kaem interrupted again, this time with a little lie. "I've already arranged for someone to pick you up at your house tomorrow at 2:30. He'll drive you down here and it'll only take about three hours.

"I don't know… tomorrow? When am I supposed to be seeing this doctor?"

"Your appointment's at two PM Friday. I've got a place for you to stay Thursday night. *Please,* Dad. *Don't* mess this up. I had to pull all kinds of strings to get everything set it up."

Worriedly, his dad said, "Seeing another doctor. I'm not sure I can afford—"

Kaem interrupted, "Already taken care of. Used another favor."

"But your mother won't be able to get off work."

"Don't worry. *I'll* go to the doctor with you."

"But..." Emmanuel dropped his tone hopefully, "Would your mother be able to come down with me if she *could* get the time off?"

"I'll make sure of it. You could bring Bana too if you want?"

"Bana wouldn't be able to get time off work."

"Okay. That's fine too. Bring extra clothes in case you have to stay more than a day,"

***

Thursday morning, Kaem cut one class and took a four-passenger Uber up to Valen to get his parents. He'd become convinced that if an Uber showed up without anybody in it, they'd refuse to get in. The Uber was expensive, but not as much as he expected, especially considering how much it cost to go across town in one. *Of course,* he decided, *it's in their best interest to have lower rates for long trips because their vehicles stand idle less.*

He hadn't gone far when Arya called to tell him that Sylvia Contreras said it was okay to share Lee with Marks. Then, sounding suspicious, she said, "Where are you? It sounds like you're in a car!"

He explained and Arya went off on him for going somewhere without her again. After a while, she acknowledged that no bad guys would expect him to be on the road to Valen. Besides, if she was in the car, they wouldn't have room for Bana if she could get off and wanted to come.

The Thunder of Engines

After Arya hung up, Kaem called Lee.

She picked up immediately, "Hi! Um, are things okay?"

"Yeah. I'm just calling to say we've worked things out for you to work, half for us and half for Space-Gen."

"Oh, that's great. I really appreciate it... Um, you're sure it's okay with Arya?"

"Yeah, she says you're quite impressive on paper. Besides, she's very dedicated to providing opportunities to women."

"I'd... rather *earn* my opportunities. I don't want them handed to me just because I'm a woman."

"Okay..." Kaem paused, not knowing what to do with that. "I think she thought you earned this one and you being a woman was only icing on the cake. But if you're worried, come on out here and earn the next one."

"I will. When can you tell me how you make stade?"

"Oh... Probably never. I'm starting to think keeping it a secret might be better than having a patent."

"Really?! What if something happens to you?!"

"I'll probably have to figure out some way for Arya to decrypt my files in case that happens."

There was hesitation at the other end of the call, then Lee slowly said, "I... wouldn't count on encryption as a method of keeping your secret. Quantum processors can—"

Kaem interrupted, a smile in his voice, "I'm using my own form of encryption. It's been tested against some quantum processors already. And I have some other tricks. I think the secret's secure." When she didn't say anything further—probably because she thought he was insane—he said, "Also, I needed to tell you that we've got our new stazer built. Marks seemed to think that, as our combined employee, you'd bring out some rocket parts for us to staze."

"Are you ready now?"

"Well... no. But we'll be ready Monday."

"I'll fly out Sunday and we can start testing first thing Monday."

"Um, I have classes Monday morning. Can we do it Monday afternoon?"

"You're still going to school?!" Lee asked, an astonished tone in her voice.

"Um. Yeah. I'll be the first in my family to get a degree. It's important to us."

"Not a problem. I'll look for apartments Monday morning and meet you at Staze at...?"

"One o'clock?"

"That'll be great."

After she signed off, Kaem settled down to watch the video of the lecture he was missing. That done, the three-hour trip gave him enough time left over to finalize his design for the printed version of the stazers' circuit boards and order a set of ten boards before he arrived at his childhood home in Valen.

Because trips home were long and expensive, even by bus, Kaem had only occasionally been back since leaving for UVA three-years ago. Unusually, he'd been home this past Christmas. That trip was the first time he'd begun to think of his childhood home as small. As he pulled up this time, it not only struck him as small, but dilapidated. *They haven't had the money to keep it up,* he thought.

He was ten minutes early, so it was only 2:20. He got out after checking with the Uber's AI to make sure it intended to wait for him, then headed up to the door.

The Thunder of Engines

He knocked, then opened the door. The front room was empty. "Hello?" he called out.

For a moment there was no reply, then his mother's head poked around the corner, out of the stub hall to the two bedrooms. "Kaem?" she asked, as if unable to believe the evidence of her eyes.

"Yes, Mama," he said. "I'm here to get Dad. Are you coming with us to see the doctor?"

Bana barreled around the corner. "Kaem! What the hell are you doing here?" she shouted as she ran across the room and threw her arms around him.

"I'm here to get Dad," he said, pulling his head back to look into her eyes. "Is he ready?"

"What the hell?" she said, leaning so she could look over his shoulder and out the window. "Is that an Uber?"

Kaem nodded. "It'll hold four, so you and Mom can come with us if you like."

"If we like? *Of course*, we like. I'll take any chance to get out of this hole." She leaned back and looked into his eyes. Suspiciously, she asked, "Who's paying for this?"

Suddenly, in an eye blink, all Kaem's plans to explain about the invention of stade and the foundation of his new company—they *all* changed. He remembered his thoughts about avoiding fame—and how he'd just been telling Lee he wanted to keep the stazing methods a secret. Now he suddenly realized his sister would never be able to keep the fact that *he'd* invented stade a secret. Besides, he didn't want his family to think differently of him.

Kaem heard his mouth—opened to explain about Staze—say, "I've got a job."

"Nooo!" his mother said as if in agony. "You've *got* to stay with your studies. We want you to get your degree!"

"And I will," he said, already wondering if this was a good idea. "They said I could work part-time. I've been taking more credit-hours than most students so I can take a few less next year and still graduate on time. And-and the owners of the company, they said that... that they'd pay for Dad's treatment." Having come up with this *totally* implausible lie, he smiled brightly at his family.

Bana stared at him like he'd grown horns, then exclaimed, "That's *such* bullshit! What's really going on? Employers don't even get health insurance for the employee himself if he's working part-time. And, *if* they insure the employee's family, it's the employee's spouse and kids, not his parents!"

"Um…" Kaem's mind thrashed around like a beached fish, trying to come up with a more believable lie. "It's a new company, small, but with a-a really valuable invention. It's such a… special product they think they're going to be *rolling* in money. The owner's filthy rich. A-and, he really wants me to work for the company. He wants me bad enough that… that, when I said I couldn't take the job because I was in school and my dad's sick, he said they'd let me work part-time and they'd pay Dad's doctor bills."

His mother was looking at him with a concerned expression. A look that said she couldn't believe the story she'd just heard.

But that she wanted to.

Kaem held out a hand to her, "You always told me, Mama, that someday, *somebody* would believe in me the way you do."

The Thunder of Engines

Her eyes softened and she stepped closer. Kaem gathered her in a hug.

Bana had her hands on her hips. *"That's* an *unbelievable* load of crap! What's really going on?"

Kaem looked his sister in the eyes, the eyes that had always seen through him in the past and held out his phone. He said, "Here's your phone. The company's getting me a new one."

Bana's eyes stayed doubtfully on his for another moment, then were drawn magnetically down to the phone. "Really?"

"Uh-huh," Kaem said, "Though, I've still gotta use this one until I get the new one from the company, okay?" Then his eyes went to his dad who'd just come out of the back room. Emmanuel had on a knit shirt. Instead of the trim, muscular father he'd always been, his arms looked wasted and his belly distended.

Cheeks hollow, the bones of his face prominent, neck scrawny, his dad looked… ill. Then Emmanuel smiled, "Kaem! What are you doing here?"

"I came to get you, Dad," Kaem said, heart catching in his throat as he walked over to hug his father.

His father's big belly and scrawny arms felt… disturbing.

~~~

During the drive back to Charlottesville, Kaem refined his lie, keeping to the truth whenever possible and feeding the lie to them in dribbles and pieces:

- Staze had been founded by a reclusive billionaire who worked completely behind the scenes. No one knew who he was. He communicated entirely by phone and text, often telling Kaem what to do by speaking in his earphones.

- Mr. X had based the invention of stade on his own development of ideas he'd gotten after hearing Kaem's bizarre theory of time—the same theory Kaem had told his family about before he left for college, so they were familiar with its existence, though *extremely* dubious of its truth or value.
- Mr. X had, in fact, done something completely different from the forward time-travel Kaem had envisioned with his theory. Nonetheless, X valued the insight Kaem's theory had given him. Enough so that he'd taken the patent in Kaem's name—though this was to a large degree because he didn't want his name in the public eye. He'd also given Kaem a small interest in the company.
- Kaem's job at the company was mostly a make-work gift. He supposedly worked part-time as a "technical adviser." A job that didn't really have any responsibilities. Kaem hoped that, after he graduated, he might be able to contribute something useful, but he was worried about whether he'd succeed.

From the front seat, his dad said, "But Kaem! We want you to get your degree. You shouldn't be worrying about me. I swear, *I'm* going to be fine. As I said, I'm already feeling much better and probably don't need any more treatment."

Sophia rolled her eyes, leaned forward, and opened her mouth. Kaem could tell she was about to start yelling at his dad—reminding him just how sick he was. Trying to beat down the walls of Emmanuel's denial.

The Thunder of Engines

Kaem put a hand on his mother's arm while shaking his head, and mouthing the words, "Let me talk to him."

She shook her head, rolled her eyes, and sank back in her seat, waving tiredly for Kaem to go ahead and talk to his dad.

Thinking it bizarre that his mother could both worry terribly about Emmanuel's health, yet be ready to rip his head off for denying his illness, Kaem got out the grade printout he'd brought with him and passed it forward to his dad.

"What's this?" the older man asked.

"You keep worrying about me failing out of school if I do *anything* but study. I just wanted you to see my grades. I'm hoping they'll help you stop worrying."

"Ah," his father said, his eyes going back down to the transcript. After several minutes, he said, "I'm not sure I understand. What's a good grade in these classes?"

"An A."

"I don't see anything but A's?"

"Exactly."

"But... surely..." his father began.

"Yes... *surely*," Kaem said lovingly, but also just a little impatiently. "Despite all your fears, your son *is* getting good grades."

"Let me see!" Sophia said demandingly, stretching her hand out over the seat in front of her.

His dad let the papers slip from his hands into his wife's, then turned watery eyes on Kaem. "That's very good, my son. Now, if this really is cancer, I can die with a light heart."

Kaem found his own eyes flooded. He choked out, "We're going to beat that cancer so you can stay around to see your grandchildren."

"You're getting married?!"

271 | Page

"No, no!" Kaem said, hands up in surrender. "Bana might be, but I have no plans. I'm just trying to say you're going to be alive for a long time yet!" Kaem felt Bana's eyes on him and looked over at her. She was staring. "What?"

"You've *got* to be cheating. No way my dumb brother's getting good grades in college."

Emmanuel exclaimed, "Bana!"

"I love you too Bana," Kaem said, a gentle smile on his face.

Pulling up to the hotel he'd reserved for them caused a good deal of consternation as well. The hotel wasn't particularly expensive, but they'd thought he had a friend they'd be staying with. "I can't put three of you up with a friend!"

"We can sleep on the sofa or on the floor!"

"I don't have any friends I can ask to take you!" he said, wondering briefly whether Gunnar would be willing to take them, ridiculous as that would be.

"We could sleep on the floor in your dorm room."

"No! My roommate and I don't get along. He'd report it as soon as you sat down."

Kaem's mother looked appalled, "Why don't you get along with your roommate??"

"Because he's a jerk. Remember that seven thousand dollars? He's the one that stole stuff from me."

She drew back, "He isn't in jail?"

"No Mama," Kaem said, opening the Uber's trunk and getting one of their bags.

Bana got the biggest bag and Sophia took her own. Emmanuel tried to take the big one from Bana, but she

The Thunder of Engines

pulled it away from him, "You're sick, Dad," she said. "You've got to let us help you."

Kaem checked them in while trying to convince them that Mr. X was having the company pay for the room—true enough in a way, since Kaem was Mr. X and was the majority owner of Staze—then when he had to sign, managed to restrain himself from recoiling at the total price through force of will. *I can afford it now!* he reminded himself. Then he realized he should get them a two-room suite. That'd mean he had to pay even more. His long-standing frugality had him wondering whether he should tell Bana she was sleeping on the floor in the first room. *Or,* he thought, looking at the options, *I could get this single room with two queen-sized beds they could share.* He shook his head, *I have the money and I'm damned well going to spend some of it!*

He took them out to dinner, which brought another flurry of protests. His mother had food in her suitcase and couldn't conceive of going to a restaurant when they had a long line of impending financial problems.

Leaving them in their room at the end of the evening, he felt exhausted, mostly from all the effort it'd taken to convince his parents to let him take care of them. He promised to pick them up at 12:30 the next day to take them to the doctor.

At least they hadn't argued about that. Charlottesville wasn't a big city, but it was big and frightening to them.

***

Dr. Starbach proved friendly and likable. He showed Kaem's dad pictures of the cancer cells in his marrow and compared them to images of what normal cells should look like. Though they wouldn't have recognized the lymphoma cells, the differences between them and normal cells were obvious even to laymen. Starbach explained where Emmanuel's symptoms came from and—without prompting from Kaem—how the meds he was on at present suppressed the symptoms but did nothing to stop the grinding progress of the cancer.

"So," Starbach said, "unfortunately, chemotherapy involves taking one or more poisons that kill cells. Though they're more toxic to cancer cells than to your normal cells, they are *still* going to kill some of your normal cells and that's going to make you sick. It wouldn't be so bad, except the medicines also aren't quite toxic enough to kill *all* your cancer cells. Then the cancer cells that survive will have been, in a sense chosen because they were the ones that could tolerate the chemo drugs. Thus, the surviving cells can be said to have *evolved* into a form of cancer that's resistant to chemo because a kind of survival of the fittest has selected only those cancer cells that are resistant." Starbach looked hard into Emmanuel's eyes, "Do you understand what I mean by that?"

Kaem's dad nodded. Kaem thought his dad understood the concepts since they'd talked about evolution when he was younger.

Starbach continued, "Chemo treatments will kill lots of your cancer cells at first. It'll make you sick each time but it'll be worth it because it'll set the cancer back a lot. But, usually, the cancer will come back from the evolved cells that survived. We'll do more rounds of chemo, but they'll be less effective because the remaining cancer cells will be better able to tolerate the drugs we've been using."

The Thunder of Engines

The doctor paused and Kaem's dad nodded his understanding.

"Then our choices will be to use higher doses of the chemo drugs we've been using, which will kill more of your normal cells and thus make you sicker yet, but will kill more cancer cells. Or, we'll try different chemo drugs that your cancer hasn't evolved to tolerate." Starbach looked at Kaem's dad.

Emmanuel nodded.

"Sometimes we try both things at once. Often, in hopes of preventing these problems, we *start* with more than one chemo drug because it's harder for the cancer to evolve to resist two drugs at the same time than it is to evolve to resist only one, can you see how that might be?"

Emmanuel nodded again. He said, "Like if suddenly moths are more likely to survive if their color is darker *and* if they're bigger. The chance of a moth in the next generation having both of those characteristics is much smaller than the chances it'll have one or the other."

Starbach nodded with the kind of smile you might give a particularly bright pupil. "So, chemo will make you sick, but barring particularly bad reactions it'll likely keep you alive longer. It isn't likely it'll cure you, though that does happen sometimes. Understand?"

Kaem's dad nodded, but then gave denial of his illness one more shot. "But I've been taking both the meds my doctor prescribed *and* some traditional African remedies. I've been feeling a *lot* better. What if I'm already beating it?"

Though Kaem thought Starbach must feel frustrated to get such questions, the doctor simply nodded as if it were the most normal thing in the world. "It's natural to wonder. Here's what I can tell you. As I said, the medications your doctor put you on aren't *intended* to do anything to stop the cancer. It'd be extremely unlikely that they'd accidentally do something to cure a cancer. They *are* intended to make you feel better though, so that could easily explain what you're feeling." Starbach waited for Emmanuel to nod, then continued, "Natural remedies *have* been found helpful for some cancers, but none have worked in lymphoma so far." He shrugged, "Of course, your treatment could be an exception to that rule, but there aren't any good ways to find out."

"Is there *any* way check?" Emmanuel asked, leaning forward eagerly.

"Well, unfortunately, there aren't any simple, reliable lab tests. Repeating your bone marrow biopsy," the mention of this brought a shudder to Kaem's dad, "wouldn't help because we might biopsy a different area where there were more or fewer cancer cells to begin with. Thus, it wouldn't tell us whether *all* of your marrow had more or less cancer. We could do another CT scan and compare it to the last one, trying to see whether your marrow looks better or worse, or whether there are more swollen lymph nodes inside your body. But doing another CT scan only a week or so after the last one," he shook his head, "there wouldn't have been enough time for the changes to be big enough to detect. We'd have to wait longer to let your cancer grow bigger so we could detect the change... which I wouldn't advise. Finally, we could do a physical exam to see if your lymph nodes, like the ones making lumps in your right armpit, are more or less swollen. You may be a better judge of that than I am, since I've never examined them before?"

The Thunder of Engines

Emmanuel's face had fallen, "Those lumps... I think they're bigger." He frowned, "Could that just be my body fighting the cancer?"

Starbach slowly shook his head.

Sophia opened her mouth to interject, but Kaem laid a hand on her arm and she subsided.

Emmanuel said, "Okay. I guess I need treatment. But are you saying I'll have to have chemo? I thought you were some kind of cart cell therapist?"

It took Kaem a moment to realize that his dad was pronouncing the CAR T-cell therapy "cart." Kaem felt embarrassed, but the malapropism didn't faze Starbach who'd probably heard it before.

Starbach gently explained, "I *would* suggest CAR T-cell therapy for you. The C-A-R stands for Chimeric Antigen Receptor. What happens is we'd harvest some cells from your immune system called 'T-cells.' We'd take them from your blood and send them to a lab where they'd be genetically modified to help them attach to your cancer cells. Then, one to four weeks later, you'd come back in and we'd give those T-cells back to you, all primed to find cancer cells. They're a little bit like heat-seeking missiles. Instead of seeking heat, they're looking for proteins that are on the surface of your cancer cells but not on your normal cells. They glom onto those proteins, then do their normal duty, which is to kill the cell they attach to. They kill cancer cells *without* killing any of your normal cells at all. It's like chemo, but much more specific, can you follow how that would be?"

Emmanuel nodded, "So it can't make you sick?"

"Well," Starbach said, "there's a saying in medicine that there's no treatment so benign it *can't* make you worse. This one's no exception. The biggest problem is a tendency to kill so much cancer so fast that the reaction of the immune system itself makes you sick. That used to be a big problem, but now we know more about how many T-cells to give you and we have ways of suppressing those overly-exuberant immune reactions. Nonetheless, it can still be a problem. We'd need to keep a close eye on you for a few days after you get the T-cells put back in your system."

Kaem's dad took a moment to digest this, then said, "Okay, I'd like to do it. How much does it cost?"

Apprehensive of his dad's reaction, Kaem said, "Don't worry about it Dad. Like I said, the company's going to pay for it."

"I still want to know how much it is. I'll pay as much of it as I can."

Starbach glanced back and forth from Emmanuel to Kaem, then back to Emmanuel, "I understand you're not insured?"

"No, I'm going to pay it myself."

Hesitantly, Starbach said, "With you being from out of state and without insurance, you'd have to prepay before your cells could be sent away to the lab to be modified."

Kaem said, "I'm authorized to prepay with the company's funds."

At the same time, his dad said, "We can prepay. How much is it?"

Kaem said, "Don't worry about it. Staze said they'd pay for it."

"No. I don't take charity," his dad said with a firm set to his mouth, "*How* much does it cost?"

Kaem had opened his mouth to try once again to deflect his dad, but Starbach said, "The price has come down, but it's still two hundred and fifty thousand."

The Thunder of Engines

Kaem had been expecting something more in the range of three hundred thousand so he felt relieved.

His dad, on the other hand, simply stared. "Dollars?" he asked, as if there could've been some other unit that might've been in play.

Starbach slowly nodded, "It's... *unbelievably* expensive. And, sorry to say, that's if everything goes right. There'll be even more costs if something goes wrong and you have to come into the hospital. I should point out that regular chemotherapy costs about half as much, though it rarely cures a patient. CAR T-cell therapy cures sixty to seventy percent of the patients who get it."

Trying not to look at his family, Kaem stood. "Where do I go to transfer the money?"

Sympathetically, Starbach said, "You're sure you want to do this? I'm sure you could get chemo much more cheaply back in West Virginia. It'd probably be covered by Medicaid and would make you better for quite a while."

"We want CAR T-cell therapy," Kaem said, moving toward the door and trying to will Starbach to leave the room with him. *We have to get out of here before my dad decides his life isn't worth it!* Kaem opened the door a little and repeated himself, "Where do I go to transfer the money?"

Starbach looked up at Kaem, then stood and turned toward the door.

Kaem spared a glance at his family. His parents looked thunderstruck. Bana was crying.

Kaem's dad cleared his throat and Starbach turned back toward him. Emmanuel's throat worked but he didn't say anything.

Kaem pulled the door open further and motioned Starbach toward it. Starbach finally took the hint and stepped through. Kaem pulled the door closed as quickly as he could without, he hoped, making obvious his panicked fear that his dad would say "no."

Out in the hall, Starbach immediately tried to talk to Kaem, but acquiesced to moving farther down the hall when Kaem—fearing his parents would be able to hear through the door—held a finger to his lips.

As they walked down the hall, Starbach gave Kaem a concerned look and said, "I know you've been saying that your company's agreed to pay for your dad's treatment." He shrugged, "But the clinic's financial adviser tells me the visit today was billed against your personal checking account."

"Um," Kaem wondered what to say. He settled on, "yes, the company transferred money into my account so I can pay for my dad's treatment directly. I'll, ah, have to show them receipts to justify it, of course."

Starbach looked highly dubious. "So, you're saying they've already transferred hundreds of thousands of dollars to you for you to pay for treatment of your *father*?"

Kaem nodded.

"And... Well... You can imagine we find this hard to believe. What company do you work for?"

"Staze," Kaem said. He rushed ahead, "You probably haven't heard of it. It's very new."

"You're right," Starbach said, a sad smile on his face. "I haven't heard of it. Can we pull up its website?"

I've got to set up a website! Kaem thought. He said, "The website's still being built."

"And your story's a little too good to be true. Much as I'd love to treat your dad, the medical center can't—"

The Thunder of Engines

"What if I deposit a half-million to cover my dad's treatment?"

Starbach stared at him for a moment, "I don't know if we have a way to accept prepayment..."

"Come on! I tell you we have the money but you won't believe me. I offer to pre-pay and you say you can't accept it. *Surely,* rich people have some way to get treatment!"

Starbach gazed at him for a moment as if seeing the ridiculousness of the catch-22 himself, then he asked, "Can you see how this might seem like a phishing attack if you got it online?"

"Yes. But how do you propose I *prove* I can pay?"

"I thought your company was paying? Out of the goodness of its heart, I might add."

"Yes, but they've transferred money to me, so, in a sense, I *am* rich at present. Can I show you my account balance?"

Starbach glanced at his watch and led off down the hall. "I've got patients waiting. You convince Claire, our clinic's financial adviser, you have the money. If she's convinced, my nurse'll make your dad an appointment for his apheresis. Okay?"

"Yes, sir," Kaem said, pumping Starbach's hand enthusiastically.

Starbach took him to Claire's office, explained the issue, and moved off to see his next patient.

Claire said, "If you really do have the money, you're in luck. I used to work for the plastic surgery section. They had ways of taking prepayment for their cosmetic surgeries since those weren't covered by insurance."

With immense relief, Kaem said, "Great. How much do you want me to send?"

"Two hundred and fifty thousand."

"Nothing extra in case of complications?"

She snorted, "If you can transfer a quarter of a million dollars out of your checking account today, I think you can probably cover the cost of any complications."

"Awesome." *And why couldn't I have met someone like you earlier in this whole process?*

That night, Kaem took Bana and his parents out to dinner at the Cavalier Buffalo. It was cheap and looked it, so he didn't get the complaints he would've if he'd taken them somewhere nicer.

And, they loved the food.

Chapter Nine

Saturday morning Arya called to find out what'd happened with Kaem's dad.

Kaem described the appointment and told her his dad was going to stay to have his apheresis—where they'd harvest some of his white blood cells—on Monday. Kaem's mom was taking an Uber back to Valen Saturday because she had to work at the laundromat that evening. Bana would go back with her so she could go back to work Monday morning.

"I'll go to brunch with you guys this morning," Arya said as if it were already decided.

Taken aback, Kaem asked, "Really?"

"I still think you need protection. I wanted to go with you yesterday but I didn't want to intrude on family matters. Besides, I want to meet your family."

"Um, do I get to meet your family when they come to town?"

"*Absolutely not!*" Arya said as if talking to a child begging for candy. "If I introduced my parents to a boy the questions would never stop!"

Kaem hesitated, the asked, "What if my mother asks you some questions?"

"I'll tell her I'm in business with you."

"What if she's sure there must be something romantic?"

"I'll disabuse her of the notion."

"Why can't I do the same thing when your parents visit?"

"Because my mother would be on you like a barracuda. Your attempt to disabuse her would leave you with bloody stumps."

"So, you think your mother would recognize how sexy I am, even though you don't?"

"You're *still* not funny, Kaem. Give it up."

Kaem sighed. "If you're going to meet my parents, I've got to tell you some stuff."

"What? Are they serial killers?"

In a horrified tone, Kaem said, "That was *not* funny!"

Suddenly very apologetic, Arya said, "I'm sorry! *So* sorry. I know better than to make jokes..." She paused, recognizing the sounds of Kaem stifling hysterical laughter. Sternly, she growled, "I'm gonna make you pay for that."

Getting himself in control, Kaem said, "Back to the stuff I need to tell you. Remember how I was worried about getting famous as the inventor of stade and founder of Staze? That I didn't think I'd like it?"

"Uh-huh," Arya said in a puzzled tone.

"I've decided I *do* want to be anonymous. Well, *I* won't be anonymous, the main owner of Staze, Mister X is going to be the anonymous one. I'll just be a regular schmo at the company. I'll be a guy who had an idea the real founder riffed off of to come up with stade."

"Mister X? Who the hell is Mr. X?"

"He doesn't exist. He's imaginary... Well, he's me, but no one's going to know it."

"And... how is Staze supposed to pay an *imaginary* person?!"

"Arya, this is a good thing for you too. It's how I'll become so unimportant you won't have to guard me. Everybody's going to think Mr. X invented stade. That *he's* the guy who knows how to make stazers. They can

The Thunder of Engines

try to chase him down but they won't be able to find him because he doesn't exist."

"You haven't answered the question about how I'm supposed to *pay* this imaginary person!"

"*I* don't know! That's what we have lawyers for, isn't it? Shell companies or something. Oh, and we need a website in the worst way. I'll set one up and when I do, I'll come up with an origin story for Staze that tells about Mr. X, the reclusive billionaire who got the idea for Staze after hearing Kaem Seba talk about his time theory. He took a patent out in my name and granted me a share just because I'm the one who stimulated him to have the idea. The public won't know who has how much of a share, just that some of us have something. As far as *we're* concerned, you and I'll have the same 19.5% shares, Gunnar'll have one percent, and Mr. X will have the remaining sixty percent, minus the tenth of a percent that's going to Morales for the next three years. As far as the public's concerned, you and I and Gunnar will each have one percent, Morales a tenth, and Mr. X'll have *all* the rest. That'll take the target off your back too. Oh, and X gave me a part-time job but still pays for my health insurance and he agreed to pay for my dad's medical bills."

"Come on Kaem. You'll still be in danger. Since you're the one who gave him the idea, you'd *obviously* know who he is. Someone trying to find out who X is could kidnap and torture you!"

"No, no. X *heard* me talking about my theory. He was one of a bunch of people who heard me going on about it. I wasn't talking specifically to him and I have no idea who he is."

"Kaem…" Arya said, sounding frustrated. "If you're going to lie, you need something simple. This… this's way too complex."

"It is not!" Kaem said indignantly. "Mr. X invented stade, none of us know who he is. He's the only one who knows how to staze. Simple. Oh, and I just realized, you *won't* have to pay him. Like some other CEOs, he'll take a salary of a dollar a year. His wealth will come from increases in the value of the company he owns such a big chunk of."

"What about Marks and Branzon and their people?! They've seen you in action. They aren't gonna believe you're some kind of dupe!"

"I was only doing what X told me to do. He reaches me through my earbud using a disguised voice."

"Oh, my, God! Just when I'm thinking you're getting rational, you go completely off the deep end!"

"Where are we going to brunch?" Kaem asked, as if she hadn't just questioned his sanity.

"What?!"

"You said you were going to brunch with me and my family. Now that you know the story of how stade was invented so you can carry on a conversation with them, we need to decide where we're going."

"Bistro Valentin has a nice brunch."

"Okay. See you there in half an hour. Oh, don't forget you're paying with the company's credit line. Also, be aware my family already thinks the company paid for my dad's treatment."

"I'm paying?" she asked threateningly. "You own *four times* as much of Staze as I do."

"Well, yeah, but my family doesn't know that. Of course, the high and mighty CFO with the big salary would *offer* to pay." Kaem stopped there but when she

The Thunder of Engines

didn't say anything, he decided he could *feel* her fuming right through the phone. "Keep track of it. I *will* pay you back, okay?"

"Damned right you will," she muttered. "See you at the bistro."

~~~

Bana felt as if her world was askew. The frequent rides in Ubers were something new for her. The family'd had an old car until a few years ago but sold it during a financial crisis. They'd relied on their feet and public transport ever since, only occasionally taking one of Uber's cheaper competitors when they had to. As they'd lived close to their jobs, this hadn't been much of a hardship.

She'd looked up how much it cost to take an Uber from Valen to Charlottesville and found it breathtaking.

Then there was the hotel. She knew it wasn't an especially expensive hotel, but it was nice. And its online prices were scary.

Now, despite the included breakfast, Kaem was taking them to another restaurant for 'brunch'! Her parents didn't seem to realize a breakfast came with the room or she was sure they would've gone apeshit. Bana'd considered pointing it out to them, but she'd liked eating at the Cavalier Buffalo last night. *I could get used to eating out,* she realized.

So, she was going along, though she couldn't help worrying about her brother. This Mr. X he kept going on about had already been incredibly generous. It just couldn't be possible the man would keep spending money on their family after putting up a quarter of a million dollars for their dad's treatment, could it? Even if Kaem's crazy theory *had* been behind the founding of

***287** | Page*

his new company, she didn't think it meant X *owed* Kaem anything.

No one was generous forever and Bana worried Kaem was milking that cow dry.

At the restaurant, Kaem introduced them to a very pretty Indian girl, Arya Vaii. He claimed Vaii was Staze's financial officer, but the girl was far too young. She seemed a year or two younger than Kaem—about Bana's age.

Bana watched her mother's eyes go back and forth from Kaem to Vaii several times, then realized her mother thought they were romantically involved. Sophia asked, "How long have you and Kaem known one another?"

"Since he came to school here. When he first arrived I was assigned to be his guide by the Curtis scholarship people."

"Really?!" Sophia asked with raised eyebrows. "And you're still friends?"

At first, Bana thought her mother was twitting Kaem about being hard to get along with, then she realized her mother thought that if they still knew one another it confirmed Sophia's theory that there had to be something special about their relationship.

Arya said, "Yep, still friends. We pretty much *have* to get along since we're both involved in Staze."

"And how many people work at Staze?" Sophia asked—Bana thought this was another transparent attempt to figure out how close they were.

"Not even ten," Arya said, "though we're expecting to grow rapidly in the next few months."

It turned out Arya also worked part-time for Staze, though she'd be working full time as soon as she graduated at the end of the month. Bizarrely, she *also*

The Thunder of Engines

claimed to be the company's financial officer. *As if any company would have their finances handled by a part-time employee who was still in school.*

Bana couldn't take it anymore. "So," she said dubiously, "Staze is new. It has fewer than ten employees. Two of them, you two, only work part-time. Yet," she let her suspicion tinge her voice, "it has enough money to pay for our father's medical care?"

Kaem opened his mouth to respond, but Bana stilled him with a hand on his arm, "I'd like to hear from Ms. Vaii. *She's* the financial person."

Vaii's eyes went from Bana to Kaem and back to Bana. She grinned, "From that question I might come to believe you don't trust your brother?"

Bana rolled her eyes. "He's shifty, that one."

Vaii laughed as if she found the assertion hilarious. In fact, she laughed so long and so hard she was soon wiping tears from her eyes. Bana looked at her brother and found him glaring at Vaii. Mysteriously he said, "I see you do find *some* things amusing, Ms. Vaii."

Settling down, Vaii said, "Thank you, Bana. It's good to encounter *someone* who doesn't have your brother up on a pedestal."

"Arya..." Kaem began, sounding apprehensive, but also as if issuing a warning.

Vaii glanced at Kaem, then said, "I mean, I know he gets good grades and makes the other physics students look like idiots, but seriously," she wrinkled her nose and lowered her voice, as if speaking confidentially to Bana alone, "*smart* isn't everything, is it?"

On the face of it, the words weren't funny, but something about the way Vaii had said them struck a chord with Bana. Grinning, she shook her head. "No, it surely isn't."

"In answer to your question," Vaii said, "the product..." she hesitated as if not wanting to say it, then proceeded, "Mister X, came up with after hearing Kaem's theory... People in the business world like to say selling something like that is 'like printing money.' It's already made several million dollars and it's going to make *so* much more that..." She shook her head, "It'll make so much money that putting a couple of undeserving college students on the payroll and paying for Mr. Seba's medical bills will be inconsequential. Mr. X says he's happy to do it."

Bana narrowed her eyes, "I can understand why he'd be nice to my brother since his windfall's based on Kaem's theory, but why *you*?"

Vaii shrugged, "I put up the money for the first test of Kaem's idea. That test was unsuccessful, but maybe that's how Mister X came to hear about it?"

"You don't *know*?"

Vaii shook her head. "I don't know who X is, much less what he's thinking. I'm just grateful he's taken Kaem and me on." She glanced at Kaem a little wistfully, "I don't think he had to."

~~~

On the walk back to the hotel Bana turned to Kaem. "You think I could get a job at Staze? Because, you know, they say 'it's not *what* you know, it's *who* you know.' It's occurred to me that if I know you and you seem to be in good stead with them at present, I'd probably better see if you can get me a job now, before they find out what you're really like."

Kaem didn't answer. Instead, he pulled out his phone and handed it to her. "I got my replacement yesterday, but it took me a bit to get everything switched over."

The Thunder of Engines

"Oh!" Bana said, excitement flaring. She suppressed it and looked him in the eye. "Are you trying to use this phone to distract me from the job you should be getting me?"

"No," he said, slowing a bit, then turning to look in a shop window while their parents pulled ahead a little. "I can try to get you a job. In fact, I'm pretty sure I can get you one as soon as the company expands a little. But…"

"But what?"

"But, when he's better, I'd rather get Dad a job there. I think *you* should go to college. Then you'll be able to get a job anywhere you want. You won't depend on your brother arranging jobs for you. You'll be your own woman."

"I'm not smart like you, Kaem—" she began.

He cut her off, "The *hell* you aren't. You got good grades. Maybe not as good as mine, but you *weren't even trying*. I think if someone paid your tuition," he said fiercely, "you could do anything you wanted."

She stared at him. Sarcastically, she said, "I suppose you think Mr. X is going to pay for your sister to go to college?"

"No! *I'll* pay for it." He grabbed her and pulled her close, speaking hoarsely into her ear, "I've never forgotten the little sister who knocked a bully off me in grade school. I *owe* you."

"Y-you couldn't afford college tuition!" Bana said, holding him close so he couldn't pull back and see the tears in her eyes.

"I could. I've learned how to live cheaply, going to school here while sending you guys money from my scholarship. I can *keep* living cheap… though," he snorted, "you gotta go in-state and live in the dorm. I definitely can't pay Ivy League prices.

"You're gonna tell me your part-time salary will cover that?"

"I'll stretch it. I'll still be on the Curtis scholarship and I'll keep living in the dorm. My entire salary can go to paying for your schooling."

"It'll pay *that* much?" Bana asked, still clinging to him, her voice breaking."

"Yeah," Kaem said hoarsely. Then warningly, "But *don't* you go applying to expensive schools."

Suddenly their mother's voice came from behind her. "What's the matter?!"

Oh. This has to be freaking Mom out, Bana thought, *Kaem and me hugging and crying. She probably thinks something horrible's happened!* Bana turned to her mother. "It's okay Mom," she sniffled, "Kaem says he's going to pay for me to go to college."

Sophia threw her arms around Bana, weeping. Behind her Kaem said, "You won't quit your job until you get into school though, right?"

Bana swung an arm back and managed to hit her brother, though she wasn't sure where. "Just let me be happy for a *moment*!" Then she pushed away from her mother and said, "Sorry. I shouldn't hit you. I truly am grateful. It's just that I'm so used to…" She paused, not knowing how to continue.

"You're so used to being my bratty little sister," Kaem said, "I know. But, remember what I said about grade school. I'll *always* owe you." He cleared his throat, "You and Mom stay here and be happy as long as you want. I'm gonna walk Dad back to the hotel."

***

The Thunder of Engines

Sunday, Kaem and his dad took a tour of Monticello. It was abbreviated because his dad's stamina was low. After Emmanuel took a nap, they watched a couple of movies on the hotel room's TV, going out to eat at a café between shows.

All in all, it was a very pleasant opportunity to get reacquainted with his father. His dad asked what Staze did that was going to make so much money. After swearing him to secrecy, Kaem told him about stade and its astonishing properties. To Kaem's delight, his dad immediately recognized some of the applications it might be used for, focusing mostly on how its frictionless surfaces might be used to improve machines.

~~~

Monday morning Kaem skipped classes and upset Arya by taking Emmanuel to his apheresis appointment without her protection. To prevent friction, he told his dad he didn't have classes on Monday mornings. After the apheresis, he and his dad ate an early lunch together and, after Emmanuel repeatedly said he felt fine, Kaem reluctantly put his dad in an Uber back to Valen.

Before he left, Emmanuel broke down all of Kaem's defenses by hugging him and thanking him for the chance to beat cancer.

As the Uber drove away, Kaem sat on the curb and wept. He felt like he'd been through a wringer over the last four days.

A lot of tears were shed this weekend, Kaem thought. *But enough of them were tears of joy that I've got to call it a win.*

Pulling himself together, Kaem called Arya and they took an Uber to Staze. There he opened the breadboard stazer and rearranged all the misplaced components. After testing it by stazing one of their little Mylar balloons, he bolted the lid back on and settled down to wait for Lee.

While he waited, he sat companionably next to Arya, watching his morning classes on his laptop while she studied for an exam.

They didn't even argue.

***

A banging on the door made Kaem think Lee was early. Before he could get up, the door opened and Gunnar came in with a big box—it seemed the box was what'd been banging the door while he'd struggled to open it with one hand. "Lee here yet?" He looked around, "No? Great. Let me show you the new idea I've been messing with."

Gunnar folded a sheet of the reflective Mylar around a six- by twelve-inch piece of lightweight waffle cloth, clamping the open edges of the Mylar together with a line of small binder clips. He inserted a small microwave emitter between two of the clips, then hooked it and the light guide up to the cables from Kaem's new stazer. "Arya, lie down on the table here."

She did, but when he came at her with the layers of Mylar and cloth, she sat back up. "What do you think you're doing?" she asked suspiciously.

Gunnar rolled his eyes. "Make stade." He sighed, "Stay sitting and we'll drape this on your arm." However, he couldn't get it to stay in position against her arm. With a grunt, he said, "Drape it over your thigh. With you sitting, gravity'll help hold it in place."

With Arya holding it draped over her thigh, Kaem stazed it. Once Gunnar pulled the Mylar off of it they had a piece of stade that fit the front of her thigh. It had a couple of puzzling holes in the stade that left some of the waffle cloth exposed. After a bit of thought, Kaem recognized the gaps were where Arya's fingers had been holding it against her thigh. The pressure had thinned the waffle cloth to less than a millimeter so stade hadn't formed.

Arya got it immediately. "It's custom-fitted armor! We won't be able to put it over joints, it'd block movement, but we can fit the thorax and abdomen pretty well with some sliding panels on the side to allow room for the expansion and contraction of breathing."

"It'll fit the skull too," Gunnar said. He quickly started laying out his ideas for producing a material made of a nylon material—less than a millimeter thick—that had Mylar-covered panels of waffle cloth stuck onto it. "There'd be small gaps between the waffle cloth panels. That way if you stazed it, only the waffle cloth areas would turn into stade, but they'd be held together by the nylon cloth between them."

Arya said, "It'd be awesome armor, unless the bullet went through the nylon between the stade panels."

"That wouldn't happen because we'd have another layer of the same stuff, this time with waffle cloth panels offset so the panels in the second one covered the gaps in the first one. All the layers would be molded to your body by wrapping you up with an elastic wrap, then the two layers stazed. When the Mylar was removed you'd have overlapping panels of stade held together by the two nylon cloth layers." He tilted his head, "You could even put smaller panels in areas that needed more movement. They wouldn't be as protective as the bigger panels, but it'd still be better than ordinary cloth."

Arya stared at him. "You probably don't need to custom fit most people. You could just make jackets in small, medium, large, and XL sizes, molding them to a mannequin."

Gunnar shrugged, then grinned, "*I* want one that's custom-molded. Pants too."

Arya snorted. "Men! Probably all you care about's the crotch protection, right?"

Gunnar didn't have to answer because a knock on the door announced Lee's arrival.

~~~

When Lee entered, she asked for help getting molds out of her Uber. It turned out she had two Ubers, one with its seats folded down to accommodate big boxes. There were a lot of small boxes too.

Gunnar looked at the biggest box in the Uber he was next to, asking, "Is that a mold for a cryotank?"

"Uh-huh," Lee said, working to pull out some of the smaller boxes that were blocking the removal of the big one.

She handed one of the little ones to Gunnar and he was surprised by how light it was. His eyes still on the big box he asked worriedly, "Are the molds made of glass?" If they were, a hand truck might be needed to get the big one into the building.

"Nope," Lee said, "it's aluminized acrylic. We found a company that can make acrylic molds with CAD/CAM (Computer Aided Design/Computer Aided Manufacturing). They were able to make the molds a lot thinner than some of the other people we talked to. Good tolerances too."

The Thunder of Engines

Thinner, and lighter, Gunnar thought as she handed him one of the big boxes that'd filled two-thirds of the back end of the Uber. He found it clumsy but otherwise easy to carry—though he had to set down the smaller box she'd given him earlier. He started into the building, eager to see what the mold looked like.

Inside, Lee stopped Gunnar from breaking down the boxes, since she hoped to use them to take the stade parts back to Space-Gen in California. He was very impressed by their contents. The box he'd carried held a rough-surfaced reflective cylinder intended to be the mold for the inside of the cryotank. "Why doesn't it look like a mirror?" he asked.

Lee shrugged, "The CAM (Computer Aided Manufacturing) process they used produced a slightly-rough machined surface rather than a polished surface like you'd want for a mirror. I didn't think it'd matter whether it was rough or not."

Gunnar hoped a smooth mirrored surface wasn't necessary to form stade.

At first, he was surprised the tank had square ends. He was used to tanks having rounded ends. Then he realized that such a rounded design characteristic was likely intended to improve the bursting strength of a pressure tank—it was hard to remember that worrying about strength was simply unnecessary when you were working with stade.

The mold came in two bivalved pieces that fit together to form a mold for the temporary stade. They were fitted together inside the box and held that way with tape. Because Gunnar had the mold out and was playing with it before the others finished bringing in the other boxes, they stazed that mold first. It'd been formed—per Kaem's suggestion—with attachment points for a microwave emitter head and for one of the fiberoptic laser light conduits. After undoing the tape and opening it briefly to make sure it was empty, they hooked it up and stazed it.

When they pulled off the tape and opened the mold, a perfect looking, air-density stade practically floated out. It gleamed reflectively like the mold, but the rougher mold gave it a rippled finish rather than a mirrored surface like the previous stades they'd cast. Gunnar's eyes caught on Lee staring at it with a stunned expression on her face. "What?" he asked.

"I was going to laugh at you guys because you forgot to put the liquid in... but, you don't actually *need* liquid to make stade, do you?"

Kaem said, "*We* don't need a liquid. Don't forget you work for us now. This is one of our secrets."

Pointing at the shiny cylinder, she turned wide eyes on him and said, "That's an air density stade because you stazed the *air* inside the mold, isn't it?"

Kaem said, "Are you remembering that you work for us and this is a secret?"

She nodded.

"Then, yes."

"Holy crap!" she looked over at the tables. "But, when I was here last, you poured what you called "base liquid" into the mold before you made an air-density stade, same as you did for the water density stade."

"Yeah, sorry. I just *pretended* to pour water in it."

"That *was* water?! Not some fancy..." She paused as she grasped it, looking thoughtfully at the big stade they'd just made. "Of *course* it was. That's *why* some are water-density." Her eyes turned back to Kaem, "But you said you could make stade that's lighter than hydrogen. How?!"

He shrugged, "We staze a vacuum. I should admit we haven't done it yet, but we're sure it'll work."

"Holy *mother*!" Lee said, blinking in surprise. "You don't have to have *anything* in the mold when you staze...?" Then as if speaking to herself, she said, "No, of course not. You just *said* you could staze a vacuum." She looked at Kaem again. "And you said stade isn't a material. You're doing something to a volume of space, aren't you?"

Kaem nodded.

Gunnar thought, *That didn't take her long. She's uncomfortably smart... I guess that's okay since she's on our side. Actually,* since *she's on our side, it's better than okay.*

Lee said, "And you're not going to explain it to me, are you?

Kaem shook his head. "Not yet anyway. Besides, I don't fully understand it myself."

"What?!"

"Um," Kaem said, "another guy came up with stade based on an ivory tower theory of mine. He's the one who knows how it all works. I'm just an employee like you are."

"What?! Who?!"

Gunnar was almost apoplectic at this news, but Arya quickly stepped between Gunnar and Kaem, put a finger to her lips and took Gunnar's arm. She steered him out into the anteroom. As soon as they got out there, Gunnar exploded, "What the hell is he *talking* about?"

Arya quickly ran through Kaem's desire to attribute all the intellectual property of Staze to a rich Mr. X.

At first, Gunnar thought the whole thing was insane, but he slowly came around after she reminded him of the trouble they'd had with Harris and Caron.

"...So, Kaem decided he doesn't want to live his life looking over his shoulder," Arya finished.

Gunnar could see how that could be. Then he was pissed because he hadn't been told. He settled down when Arya said Kaem had *just* decided on this insane strategy.

When Gunnar and Arya reentered the big room, Lee was starting to open the other big box, "Okay," she was saying, "we'll get out the outer molds and see if we can make a tank."

The outer mold bivalved open and they put the temporary stade inner mold, the one they'd just made, inside of it. Lee asked, "How are we going to position this thing so it stays at least a millimeter from the outer shell on all sides?"

Kaem shrugged and got a sheet of paper and some Scotch tape. They folded little bits of paper and taped them to the interior of the outer mold in several locations to keep the stade inner mold away from the walls of the outer mold.

They had to pause when Lee started worrying the bits of paper were going to weaken the stade that formed.

Kaem gently disabused her of that notion by pointing out that, other than mass, the properties of stade were always the same, no matter what it contained.

They finished the discussion with Lee raising Gunnar's eyebrows by saying, "We need to have someone make us a dispenser that puts out little one-millimeter plastic sticky-balls. This'd go faster if we could just pop a bunch of them in."

Similarly, they formed temporary stades that would hold open the channels the fuel would flow out through and inserted them in through the outflow fittings on the

The Thunder of Engines

outer mold. They closed up the outer mold and Kaem stazed the space between the temporary inner stade and the outer mold.

They opened the bivalved outer mold to expose the rippled, shiny cryotank. Lee looked up with a frown and said, "How do we dissolve the stade inner mold?"

Kaem looked at his watch, "We just wait another eighteen minutes and it'll dissolve itself."

Lee stared at him warily. Gunnar had a feeling she was suffering from "revelation-exhaustion." She said, "I know you said that some stade doesn't last as long as others, but are you saying that you can program in when it... dissolves... or fails?"

Kaem shrugged and gave another nod.

"How long will this cryotank last?" she asked, as if dreading the answer.

"About a quarter of a petasecond."

She frowned as if starting to try to figure it out, then apparently just decided to ask, "And, how long is that?"

"About eight million years."

"Holy crap! Talk about your non-biodegradable waste!"

He shrugged again, "We can break it down whenever we're done with it."

"And the breakdown products are just... air?"

"They're whatever we started with. Air in this case." He grinned, "Plus a few bits of paper and Scotch tape."

While they waited, they started stazing some of the other test molds Lee had brought with her. These included some nut and bolt combinations. These in fact would *not* stay screwed tightly, even after they stazed a set of long-handled wrenches and used them to apply extremely high torques to the stade nuts. Having expected that, the Space-Gen engineers had sent molds for stade ratcheting mechanisms that would lock the nuts in their tightened positions. This required a spring—which couldn't be made of stade—to hold the ratchet mechanism locked. Unfortunately—as expected—trial ratchet teeth smaller than one millimeter wouldn't form, so the ratchets they could make were coarse. Bolting a couple of pieces of stade together—since *nothing* had any give in it—tended to leave everything slightly loose since the ratchet just would *not* click one more tooth.

Looking disappointed, Lee contemplated the cryotank. "I was worried about this. If we want to use stade pipes to carry fuel to the engine, we're going to have to connect them with some kind of non-stade alloy-steel connectors. That'll lose us much of the advantage of the amazing strength of stade because of the old problem that the weakest link determines the strength of the chain. I'm not sure we'll be able to hold the pressures generated by your idea of combusting some fuel inside the tanks to save having to pump it. And, we'll be adding some weight."

"Or," Kaem said, "you could put a steel washer in the junction. The bolts and nuts would crush the washer until the ratchet did click tight."

"Indium," Lee said.

"Indium what?" Kaem asked.

"Indium washers would tolerate cryogenic temperatures."

"Oh," Kaem said thoughtfully. He looked up, "Or, we should also be able to do something like welding."

"What?! Welding…?" Lee stared, "Why's this the first time I'm hearing about *that* possibility?"

"Don't get all grumpy," Kaem said with a laugh. "We're *all* just figuring this out as we go. If we form

The Thunder of Engines

stade over the junction of the pipes, it'll stick the pipes together." He shrugged, "We're pretty sure anyhow."

"Does this mean we'll need to make molds to fit over the junctions?"

"No, we should be able to wrap them in Mylar."

Gunnar carefully kept his eyes from straying up to the high ceiling where what he thought of as his "holey blimp" still rested. Unlike balloons, it wouldn't gradually lose its helium and eventually come down. He'd brought a ladder on his truck that day, planning to climb up and get it down after Lee was gone.

Lee was staring at Kaem, uncomprehending.

He said, "Mylar that's aluminized on both sides. Think of it as a flexible mirror we can staze beneath. We've checked and it works."

Looking frustrated, Lee closed her eyes. "Just wrap them in Mylar," she echoed, a sarcastic tone in her voice.

"Hey!" Kaem said. "Why didn't *you* think of Mylar? Aren't you supposed to be the hot-shot engineer in this group?" He paused a moment as a shocked expression appeared on her face, then grinned, "I figured if you weren't going to stop jumping my shit for not figuring everything out already, I'd have to start jumping yours for not figuring it out yourself."

Lee studied him a moment, then cracked a smile. "You've got a point. I'd better get my ass in gear." She frowned, "Though I think it's unfair to expect much of me when you're not even telling me how it works."

Kaem grinned, "Touché. But remember I don't really know how it works either. Let's keep stazing stuff for now. Then you can take me out to dinner and I'll answer questions about what we do know."

Gunnar said, "You want me to set up a strip of Mylar for us to use to try welding things together?"

"Great idea!" Kaem said. Gunnar promptly set to work on it.

Lee opened another moderately large box and pulled out a bivalved mold for the interior of a rocket engine. It had the bulb of the chamber over the bell of the exhaust. There were horns coming up off of it that would form the interiors of the fuel and oxidizer inflow pipes coming together in a fuel injector/mixer. They stazed a temporary stade inside of it, then assembled the engine mold around it. This mold had the outer shells of the inflow pipes and injector built into it. Once a long term stade had been stazed in that mold they opened the shell and admired their gleaming new rocket engine.

They checked the cryotank and—the inner, temporary stade having vanished—it was now hollow. They had to wait another twenty minutes before the stade inside the chamber and bell of the engine disappeared to make their rocket engine functional.

They stazed fuel feed lines and parts for valves and regulators to adjust the fuel's flow.

The lines were set up to be conventionally bolted together over indium washers but they stazed an extra set. Gunnar wrapped those with his Mylar tape. Kaem stazed the space beneath the Mylar. It worked, giving them a weld, but it was incomplete, stade not having formed in places where the Mylar'd pulled tight and left a gap less than one millimeter.

Pleased to see Kaem looking daunted, Gunnar said, as if it were obvious, "This isn't a problem." He wrapped the junction again, this time with waffle cloth first, then a gentle overwrap of Mylar. They stazed it again. This

The Thunder of Engines

time it not only had a rigid junction, it had one that was airtight as well.

Kaem said, "Gunnar! Amazing idea! Way to go."

Gunnar waved off the compliment, gruffly saying, "Would've been obvious to anyone with half a brain." Secretly though, he found that getting an attaboy from the little genius felt immensely flattering.

They stazed small LOX (Liquid Oxygen) chambers that would be valve connected to the liquid hydrogen cryotank. Opening the valve, then igniting the mixture would pressurize the tank.

They stazed vanes that would go into the exhaust plume from the rocket's engine, controlling flight.

When they were done, Kaem turned to Arya and said, "You've been keeping track of the volume of stade we made for them haven't you?"

Surprise on her face she asked, "What?"

"Remember? We're charging the price of gold by volume for the stade they make while they're figuring out how to design their tanks and engines."

"*I* don't know the volume."

"Hmm," Kaem said, looking at the tank. "About five inches, or 12.5 cm in diameter by about a meter long and I'm figuring a 1.3-millimeter wall thickness. That'd be five hundred and forty-two cubic centimeters."

Gunnar thought, *The kid's amazing at math but he couldn't have just guesstimated that correctly, could he?*

Kaem continued, "Gold's worth about fifty dollars a gram, times 19.2 grams per cc would make it nine hundred sixty dollars per cc, or about $520,320 for the tank." He looked at Lee, "Did you guys figure the volume from your CAD?"

She nodded slowly, "Your estimate on the volume of the tank was pretty close. We had it at five hundred and sixty-three ccs. Plus another hundred and twenty-eight ccs for the engine."

Kaem nodded, "Call it $663,360?"

Gunnar thought, *Damn! I knew we were charging a lot for this stuff, but… wow!*

"Actually," Lee said, "the price of gold is $50.08"

Kaem waved airily. "Tell Marks we gave him a deal." He turned to Arya, "You can send Space-Gen an invoice?"

Arya nodded. "What about all the little parts we stored for them?"

"We weren't going to charge for things we were interested in, like knowing how bolts and nuts would work and whether we could make valve parts, etcetera."

Lee looked uncomfortable. "When I told them how much it was going to cost, Mr. Marks asked me to see if it'd be possible to renegotiate the prices of test objects. He points out Space-Gen's having to pay more than twenty-five percent the price of a full-sized engine for just these samples." She looked hesitant, "And, you once told me that if Space-Gen inked a deal with you that you'd charge less for test versions."

"Hah, it seems unfair to put you between us when you work for both of us."

"I told him that. He asked, 'Who better than someone with a foot in both camps?'"

"Tell him we sympathize, but we also don't want to be inundated with test objects. We'll lower the price to a hundred-dollars a cc, about a tenth the cost of gold."

"So," she asked slowly, "you're lowering the price on this stuff?" She waved at the engine and cryotank.

"No. They agreed to pay that price. I suspect they didn't figure out how much it'd cost them ahead of

The Thunder of Engines

time. Shame on them. This new deal, you can tell them *you* negotiated, is for test objects going forward." Kaem turned to Arya again, "Can you attach the new price to the invoice, specifying that it's going forward?"

"Sure."

Lee frowned, "You don't have to approve these changes with your Mr. X?"

Kaem tapped his earbud. "He's got a great AI. It listens in and tells him when he needs to give me direction." He looked at his watch. "Hey, it's dinnertime." He looked back up at Lee, "Are you flying back to LA with this stuff?"

She nodded, "Tomorrow. I'll be back to start work here later this week."

"We'll help you pack it up then."

Arya said, "I need to have her sign her contract with us before she takes off. How about if you pack up her stuff for her while I go over the contract?"

Kaem looked askance at her, "Sounds like you just want to get out of the packing."

She smiled, "I didn't get this job for being stupid."

Kaem grinned, "Did you just make a joke?"

Arya shook her head and rolled her eyes. She turned to Lee with a sigh, "How about if you and I go out to the anteroom?"

~~~

As Arya and Lee moved toward the anteroom, Kaem asked, "Lee, are you wanting your molds too, or just the stades?"

"As many of the molds as you can get back in the boxes with the stades. They're wanting to compare the sizes of the molds to the sizes of the finished stades to estimate tolerances for the future."

Gunnar and Kaem finished up their packing about the same time Lee and Arya finished going over the contract and signing it.

To Gunnar's surprise, Arya intended to go out to dinner with Kaem and Lee. *Is she jealous?* he wondered. They invited Gunnar along, but he didn't want to sit through another explanation of how stazing worked.

~~~

The dinner was pleasant. Arya took them to a restaurant called Simple Fare. Since it was a nice restaurant, Kaem hadn't ever been there before. However, he thought the food was great. *I could get used to eating in places off the University's food plan,* he decided.

Later he would look back on the evening as one of the best of his life. Out with two bright, nice-looking women. Eating some of the best food he'd ever had. Staze seeming to be on solid footing. Treatment was set up for his dad—which might not work, but Kaem had a good feeling about it. He'd worried that Arya and Lee wouldn't get along, but they acted like good friends.

He laughed at himself. *As if they could be jealous of each other over me!*

Epilogue

A few weeks had passed. Final exams were over and Arya's family had come down for her graduation. After the ceremony, she took her parents and her younger brother out for lunch at Bistro Valentin. Having placed their orders, Arya braced herself for the impending interrogation.

Her father leaned back in his chair, "We brought the SUV. Do you think we'll be able to get all your stuff in it? Or are we going to have to hire a trailer?"

"I extended the lease on my apartment. I'm going to stay here for a while." *Probably forever,* she thought, but knew better than to say it.

Her father's eyebrows went up. "How are you going to afford that?"

Arya read the subtext that her father *wasn't* going to pay for it. "I've started a business with some friends."

Her father shook his head, "Even if it's based on a great premise, it won't do well at first. Startups always lose money to begin with. This is not the—"

Arya interrupted, "It's already making money."

Looking dubious, her father asked, "Enough to live on?"

She nodded. "More than enough." Part of her wanted to tell her parents how much, but she'd always despised braggarts.

He frowned, "What kind of business is it?"

"One of our group came up with an invention. Two more have been developing it. I'm running the business end of things."

"An invention?" When Arya only nodded, he pushed, "What kind?"

"It's... a new industrial material."

Though Arya expected to be quizzed further by her father, the next question came from her mother. "What kind of people are they?"

Arya knew what her mother wanted to know—she didn't trust people who weren't of Indian descent—Arya intentionally made it hard by saying, "They're very nice."

Her mother looked frustrated by the evasion, but was interrupted by a commotion to Arya's right. Arya saw her mother's eyes go there and widen, just before she turned to see what was happening herself.

Kaem!

He dragged up a chair and sat down beside her. "Hi, Arya! Congratulations on your graduation! Is this your family?"

Arya nodded, her mind racing. *What's he doing here?! I told him what'd happen if he met my mother! I've got to get him away from us before everything goes to hell?* Arya said, "Um—"

Kaem interrupted her by leaning forward, sticking his hand out to her father. He said, "Hi Mr. Vaii. I'm a friend of Arya's from school, Kaem Seba."

Her father glanced at Arya, then stiffly shook Kaem's hand.

Kaem promptly turned to her mother, bobbing his head and saying, "Ms. Vaii. In your society, I don't believe it's proper to shake hands with a lady?"

Arya thought, *My God, he's been reading up on us!*

The Thunder of Engines

Her mother, still wide-eyed, now because she had a fear of African-American men, shook her head. She asked timidly, "How do you know Arya?"

"We're both Curtis Scholars. She helped me get oriented when I started here and we've been friends ever since. Then, this year, we worked together to start a new business."

Arya's dad gave her a sharp glance at this.

Oblivious, Kaem continued. "Your daughter's *amazing*. She knows so much about the ins and outs of business. Not just the stuff she learned in business school, but the practical stuff she learned from you guys. And she's *so* good with people. She sets me straight every time I mishandle someone. When my dad got sick and I couldn't get him a doctor's appointment, she set one up in just a few minutes! She's turned our business into a thriving concern..." He sighed as if in admiration. "I'm sure you guys aren't surprised to hear everyone around here just *loves* her." He glanced at Arya, apparently oblivious to the warning she was trying to project, "I'm *so* grateful to have met her and to be able to call her my friend." He shook his head, "You must be very proud."

"Well!" Arya's mother said.

Arya thought, *Here it comes. He's trying to butter them up and she's going to be pissed.*

Arya was not at all prepared to hear her mother say, "It's delightful to hear someone sing Arya's praises." Astonished, Arya turned to stare at the impostor inhabiting her mother's body. Her mother continued blithely, "Are you here alone, Kaem? We'd love to hear more about the new business you and Arya have started. Perhaps you'd have lunch with us?"

No! No, no, no, no! Arya thought turning to stare at Kaem and project her wishes with all her power. *Say you can't sit with us!*

Kaem smiled broadly, "I'd be delighted. Arya, is this your brother?"

Arya thought, *I should have SAID something. I ought to know by now that Kaem can't pick up on social cues!* She produced a weak smile and said, "Yes, this is my brother, Rhoall. He's just finishing his first year at the University of Maryland."

"Oh, great!" Kaem said, turning to Rhoall, "What're you going to major in?"

When the waitress came over, he slipped her a fifty-dollar tip and talked her into letting him sit at their table, though—the waitress said—it was against policy.

As Arya sat, appalled, Kaem continued charming her parents through the entire meal. Her brother liked him too.

When her father asked about the "new industrial material" their business was founded on, Kaem almost made it sound as if it were *Arya's* idea. According to Kaem, he'd had an ivory tower theory that a Mr. X had developed and Arya had turned into a practical business. When quizzed about it, he said things were still supposed to be confidential, but it was a very strong substance that should find lots of uses.

Then, at the end of the meal, though Arya didn't see him do it, he managed to pay the check. Her dad protested, but weakly, obviously impressed.

After Kaem left, her mother turned to her and said, "What a nice young man!"

What's happened to my mother? Arya wondered.

Her mother glanced after Kaem again, then astonished Arya by saying, "I was going to complain

The Thunder of Engines

about how hard it would be for us to arrange a marriage for you, with us up in Hagerstown and you down here. But, maybe you don't need our help, eh?"

When she got control of her voice, Arya jumped onto this path to freedom, "No, you're right, I decided I'd rather not have an arranged marriage. I'd rather follow the American tradition of choosing badly by myself." *Choosing Kaem?!* she wondered. *No! That'd be… crazy.*

***

With classes done, Kaem went in to Staze early in the morning. His new stazer circuit boards had come in and he wanted to install a set of components on one before anyone was around. He was getting sick and tired of opening the breadboard version's case and scrambling the electronics each time they were finished stazing for the day, then opening it again to put them back when they needed to do some stazing again. He kept wanting to just rely on the fact that no one would be able to get past the security on his laptop to command the integrated chip in the temporary stazer. Then he'd remind himself that he couldn't afford to have them learn the physical setup of the electronics, whether or not they could control the chip and actually make stade.

To his dismay, Lee was already there, working on her laptop. He couldn't very well keep up the secret of Mr. X if he built a stazer while she was watching.

I'm going to have to build this damn thing back in the dorm, he thought. Which reminded him that he needed to get an apartment now that he could afford one.

There he'd have some privacy. As he let the door close behind him, he said, "Hi, Lee. What're you working on?"

She looked up, "Oh. Hi." She smiled happily and it sent a shiver through him. "I've got video for you to watch."

Eagerly, he said, "They tested the stade rocket?"

She nodded, "Finally."

He grinned, "Wouldn't have taken this long if you were in charge out there, right?'

She grinned back, "*Damn* right it wouldn't! Here, have a look." She turned her laptop toward him, displaying the glossy surfaces of the small rocket engine with flame leaping out the back of it. The audio sounded like muted thunder.

"Why's the sound pitched so low?" Kaem asked, "When I've heard rockets that size before they've sounded… higher."

Lee'd stopped the video at his question. She shrugged, "To my understanding, *they* think it has something to do with the resonant frequency of the space between the adjacent walls. But I can't help thinking stade's so rigid that everything in the motor, feeds, valves, and tankage vibrates as one large unit that has a lower resonant frequency. Regular rockets must have lots of small surfaces flexing within them, each with its own higher-pitched resonance." Her face scrunched, "Not sure about the sound from the combustion though. It's probably producing a lot more acoustic energy than the rocket itself. If so, the resonant frequency of the space between the walls might be the best explanation for it." She shrugged, "Depends on how much of the sound comes from combustion and how much from the vibration of the motor, etcetera. Is it important?"

The Thunder of Engines

Kaem closed his eyes to ponder, then decided it probably wasn't. He'd think about it later. "I guess not," he said. "How'd the cryotank perform?" he asked.

"Oh, they're in awe. They filled it with liquid hydrogen and then just let it sit for a couple of days. Confirming what a great insulator stade is, the pressure didn't go up appreciably after the first thirty minutes. Then, though it made them extremely nervous, they tried your idea of forcing some oxygen into the tank and igniting it. That shot the pressure *way* up. The stade pressure regulator they built out of the parts we stazed for them is what's bringing the pressure down to what they wanted for the engine." She waggled a hand, "It's working pretty well, but they're hard at work designing a better regulator. But *that* rocket," she pointed at the video she'd paused, "is running off the cryotank we stazed, combusted to crazy pressures, that're being stepped down close enough to what's needed by the regulator."

She touched a key and the video continued. She said, "Here they start doing crazy things with the fuel flows to see if they can blow up our engine. First, they're running too much fuel." Kaem saw the exhaust brighten and extend, expanding outward from the nozzle, indicating that combustion was continuing even beyond the end of the nozzle. Then it started chugging. Lee said, "Here they're inducing oscillations in the combustion, something that tends to blow up motors." She looked at Kaem, "Essentially, they're doing everything they can to demolish our engine and failing. Teri tells me, everyone, on *every* design team at Space-Gen, has been reassigned. They've all been moved from whatever they *were* working on and instead they're brainstorming designs that'll take advantage of stade's properties."

"Awesome," Kaem said, then held up a finger.

His earbud had just said, "You have a call from Jerry Branzon."

He said, "I'll take it..." Resisting an impulse to say, "Hi, Jerry," instead he went with, "Hello Mr. Branzon. What can I do for you?"

Lee's eyes went wide.

Branzon said, "I hear Marks has a mole in your organization?"

"That'd probably be Ms. Lee, sir. She's an aerospace engineer who used to work for his company. At present, he's paying half her salary and we're paying the other half. She mostly works here, but goes back and forth to Space-Gen, ferrying parts out here to be stazed and taking them back there to be tested. She keeps them up to date on developments and makes suggestions as to how they might best use stade for their program."

"So, you're fully aware of her?"

"Yes, sir. She's sitting next to me."

"I'm going to need to check that agreement we signed with Space-Gen to see if this is kosher."

"Mr. Marks said his legal people checked it and said it was okay. However, he said if you got upset I should suggest you could pay for half of another engineer that'd also work for us. A good deal for everyone."

Branzon laughed. "Okay. You've got yourself another engineer. I just have to figure out who we're going to send you."

After Branzon signed off, Kaem looked around to see what Gunnar was doing. The crotchety man had come in and started working on his blimp while Kaem was watching Lee's video. He'd been working on it on and

The Thunder of Engines

off for the past weeks. Just now it was sitting on the worktable with something strapped under it that made it look more like a typical blimp with a gondola.

Gunnar picked up a device that looked like an old model airplane controller and flipped a switch. A thrumming sound came from the blimp, so Kaem got up to go get a closer look. The straps were holding the gondola to the slippery stade of the blimp. The gondola seemed to cover the area of the blimp where Kaem thought the hole had been located. It looked like the interface between the hole and the gondola was sealed by some kind of soft rubber gasket.

The blimp started wobbling, then suddenly broke free of the table and floated up into the air a few inches. The thrumming sound stopped.

"Ah," Kaem said, "That noise was a pump, right? Pumping air out of the blimp to generate a vacuum and make it lighter than air?"

Gunnar nodded. The noise started up again. Moments later the blimp started moving higher into the air. Gunnar moved one of the controllers and small propellers on either side of the gondola spun up, pushing the airship forward. Moving another controller sped one propeller and slowed the other, causing the blimp to begin describing a circle as it continued rising.

"So," Kaem said, "are you thinking a full-sized blimp could act as a heavy lifter with full control of elevation?"

Gunnar nodded. "Industry should be able to use it to move big stuff overland where there aren't any roads. Things that're too big for planes or helicopters. The military should like it too. Regular blimps are easy to shoot down, but *this* sucker's made of stade."

Kaem nodded his understanding and opened his mouth to point out that the gondola was vulnerable. Then he realized the gondola could be built out of stade as well. *Well, not the windows, but if you were going to use stade in the military, you wouldn't have windows. You'd use a crapload of cameras hooked up to high-definition screens inside. Wires passed in through long crooked tubes to prevent intrusion through them.* He hesitated a moment, wondering, *Do we even want to sell to the military? For this use maybe; the blimp doesn't seem like much of an offensive weapon... They might not even want it.*

Lee'd been watching and listening. Now she asked Gunnar, "You made this using Mylar right? Blew up a big balloon and stazed it?"

Gunnar nodded. "The first one was a temporary stade. Then we blew the balloon up a little more and stazed the space around the first one with a long-term stade. When the temporary one disappeared, we had a hollow one. Fortunately, it was off-center enough that I had an opening I could seal off with the gondola and use to pump out the interior."

Lee was looking thoughtful. She said, "I'm thinking this'd be a fast way for Staze to put up buildings." She waved around, "We should outgrow this building soon. If you buy yourself a huge Mylar blimp to make stade dirigibles, you should think about setting it up so you can have openings for doors and ventilation. Make a stade blimp, pour concrete in the bottom of it, and you've got a building."

Kaem laughed, "You might have trouble getting it approved by the building inspector but I'm pretty sure we could work that out eventually. Um, I'm a little worried about the mirror surface of Mylar stade, both

The Thunder of Engines

for blimps and for buildings. If you wind up blasting a reflection of the sun at people there're gonna be complaints. We've got to at least diffuse the reflections. I think you've got to see if they can make you Mylar with a rough surface. Something that'll produce a slightly corrugated effect on the surface of the stade like those machined molds Space-Gen used for their cryotanks. Even rougher if possible." He got a thoughtful look on his face, "If we could get *really* rough versions, rough enough so the surface could interdigitate with stuff we applied to it, that'd be even better."

"Stuff like what?"

"Epoxy coatings, asphalt," Kaem answered. "I'm afraid the one-millimeter feature limit on stade means that the interdigitations we can form will be so big that only stuff like asphalt and concrete will lock to it."

Lee said, "You want the asphalt to provide a road surface for bridges, right?" Her eyes flashed with another thought, "Bridges carried in and positioned by one of Gunnar's dirigibles." After a moment's pause, she said, "Though if they were air-density stade, one guy could carry a bridge by himself."

Kaem laughed, "On a still day. Not if there was a breeze."

Lee waved the point away as if it were insignificant. "I want to point out that the most important thing you could use a stade building for would be to give you a place to mass produce lighter than air stades. Rocket engines, cryotanks, fuel feeds, and rocket bodies being a particularly desirable set of devices we could make *very* light. Hell, the fueled rocket could weigh less than the fuel inside it."

"That's a great idea!" Kaem said, "But, I've got some other ideas for vacuum stades as well…" He frowned, "We'd have to populate the inside of your building with mechanicals that could do the stazing, since human workers couldn't be inside the vacuum, stazing things." He looked at Lee, "When you're not working on rockets, could you work on how we could do all that stuff?"

"Sure!" Lee said, sounding excited. "What kind of things did you have in mind to make out of lighter than air stade?"

"Chain for one."

Lee blinked a couple of times, then a huge smile spread across her face, "A skyhook?"

Kaem grinned and nodded, "Eventually. But don't tell your old bosses about it, okay?"

"Lord no. Can't afford to get them flustered. We'll still need them for a while."

Kaem nodded, "At least until they've launched the upper parts of the hook."

***

Kaem, his mother, and his sister were sitting with his dad in one of Dr. Starbach's exam rooms. Emmanuel had been lucky in that the lab had been able to produce his CAR T-cells quickly. He'd been reinfused with the cells only nine days after they'd been harvested. Then, though he'd had a version of the dreaded cytokine release syndrome that made some people so sick, he'd responded well to treatment and only spent two nights in the hospital.

Now they were back to find out the results of his first scan after the treatment.

To learn whether the T-cell therapy was working or not.

Though Kaem had patted his dad on the back and spoken effusively about how, "Of course, the results are going to be great," he'd had to force his smile because of the gnawing unease in his gut. *I wish this were over with,* he thought. *Bad or good, I just want to know. To have it be done with!*

A knock came on the door.

Kaem's dad gave him an uncertain look, so Kaem said, "Come in."

The door opened and a young blonde woman stepped in. "Hello, I'm Dr. Sue Snell, Dr. Starbach's fellow. He's busy with another patient and asked me to come get things started with you."

Kaem had been ready to finally get an answer. Now he was ready to chew nails.

Dr. Snell looked at them and said, "You all look anxious." She smiled, "Perhaps I should start by telling you that the results of your scan look good. *Very* good."

Kaem punched the air.

It felt like he could float out of the room.

The End

Hope you liked the book!

To find other books by the author try
Laury.Dahners.com/stories.html

Laurence E Dahners

Author's Afterword

This is a comment on the "science" in this science fiction novel. I've always been partial to science fiction that poses a "what if" question. Not everything in the story has to be scientifically plausible, but you suspend your disbelief regarding one or two things that aren't thought to be possible. Essentially you ask, "what if" something (such as faster than light travel) were possible, how might that change our world?

I think the rest of the science in a science fiction story should be as real as possible.

Therefore, in this story, the central question continues to be what if someone invented a way to stop time in a certain volume of space-time, thus creating something often called stasis in the tropes of science fiction.

Stasis is not a new idea. Niven's "slavers" used it to escape from bad situations into the future. In Vernor Vinge's *The Peace War,* people who threaten the authoritarian government are "bobbled" in stasis fields to get them out of the way. In both of these SF universes, the stasis fields are indestructible but—to the best of my recollection—they are only used to protect oneself from destruction (Niven) or also to punish offenders by sending them forward in time (Vinge) and are always spherical. Sometimes stories by other authors use stasis for the preservation of food or people but they usually ignore the presumed mechanical properties. Those stories seldom delve into other changes that would derive from an ability to stop time within a space.

The question in this series then becomes: What if these indestructible segments of space-time could be induced in non-spherical shapes? Wouldn't this provide the ultimate material for rockets, construction, and other engineering projects that would benefit from such exotic properties? What other benefits could be derived from an ability to stop time?

For those of you who are interested, the CAR T-cell therapy featured in this novel is a *real* treatment for cancer. The 2018 Nobel Prize was awarded to James Allison and Tasuko Honjo for its discovery. Though it's early days, it appears to have more potential to cure cancers than almost any other therapy. Of course, for decades we've been able to cure localized cancers by surgically removing them, and chemotherapy has been able to cure some leukemias, etc. However, this new ability to supercharge your own immune system so it attacks your cancer cells and kills them—without attacking your normal cells the way chemo does—seems to have unbounded potential.

Acknowledgments

I would like to acknowledge the editing and advice of Gail Gilman, Nora Dahners, Hamilton Elliott, Philip Lawrence, Scott McNay, Stephen Wiley, and Jim Youmans, each of whom significantly improved this story.

Laurence E Dahners

Other Books and Series

by Laurence E Dahners

Series

The Ell Donsaii series
The Vaz series
The Bonesetter series
The Blindspot series
The Proton Field series
The Hyllis family series

Single books (not in series)

The Transmuter's Daughter
Six Bits
Shy Kids Can Make Friends Too

For the most up to date information go to
Laury.Dahners.com/stories.html